It had all the makings of a massacre

All Bolan could do for them was to gather their dog tags. He knew from experience that, however macabre, they were a source of solace for loved ones back home.

Once the grim ritual was completed, he stood exhausted before the burial mound. He wasn't a man of prayer, but believed there was a higher power, and he offered the fallen soldiers a moment of silence, wishing them peace and honor in whatever world might lay beyond the one from which they were so cruelly dispatched.

Shrugging off his fatigue, Bolan stared down at the footprints that had led him to the massacre site. Tracking the prints, he soon saw signs of a trail. He began to follow it, Desert Eagle in hand, filled with savage determination.

DON PENDLETON's
MACK BOLAN®

STRIKE AND RETRIEVE

A GOLD EAGLE BOOK FROM

W✸RLDWIDE®

TORONTO • NEW YORK • LONDON
AMSTERDAM • PARIS • SYDNEY • HAMBURG
STOCKHOLM • ATHENS • TOKYO • MILAN
MADRID • WARSAW • BUDAPEST • AUCKLAND

First edition March 2003

ISBN 0-373-61489-6

Special thanks and acknowledgment to
Ron Renauld for his contribution to this work.

STRIKE AND RETRIEVE

Printed in U.S.A.

Revenge is a wild kind of justice...
—Sir Francis Bacon
1561–1626

If you prick us, do we not bleed? if you tickle us, do we not laugh? if you poison us, do we not die? if you wrong us, shall we not revenge?
—William Shakespeare
The Merchant of Venice,
Act III, sc.i, line 65

Call it what you will, but justice and revenge are the consequence of harming others. Either way, my brand is terminal.

—Mack Bolan

CHAPTER ONE

California

It was late August, the time of year when the Mojave Desert became America's closest approximation of hell on Earth. Well past midnight, the temperature was still in the hundreds as Mack Bolan, aka the Executioner, drove his rented Taurus sedan up the steep rise of State Highway 75 west of Barstow. He could barely see past the smear of insects splattered across his windshield. Over the past fifty miles he'd drained a full tank of wiper fluid trying to keep the glass clean, but the bugs kept coming.

And the bugs weren't the only things suffering. Since starting up the protracted incline four miles ago, Bolan had passed a half-dozen cars forced off the road with overheated engines. He'd shut off his air conditioner hoping to avoid the same fate, but the dash needle gauging the Taurus's engine temperature continued its slow creep into the red.

Bolan grinned ruefully as he thought back on the circumstances leading to this latest predicament. Hours ago, arriving at L.A. International Airport on the heels of his latest assignment for Stony Man Farm, he'd had the option to switch planes and fly on to Edwards Air Force Base, but he'd decided instead to rent a car, figuring a leisurely night drive through the desert would give him a chance to unwind after his recent mission. Bad move. Barely out of L.A., there'd been a forty-minute backup on the interstate caused by an overturned big rig, followed by another two delays for construction work on the highway.

And now, after plaguing him with kamikaze insects, the Mojave was ready with the coup de grâce.

As Bolan neared the top of the grade, steam began to roil up from under the hood of his Taurus, further obscuring his view of the road. Seconds later, the dash lights flashed, confirming that the engine had been crippled by the desert heat.

Bolan toggled on his emergency flashers and switched lanes, looking for a safe place to pull over. Up ahead there were two cars already parked on the shoulder—a year-old Mercedes and an older Camaro. Unlike the vehicles he'd passed earlier, neither car had its hood up. Both vehicles seemed unattended, and there was no one using the emergency call box located less than fifty yards uphill.

Strange, Bolan thought.

He drove by the cars and brought the Taurus to a stop near the call box. The receiver had been yanked free, either by vandals or a disgruntled motorist, leaving a short, useless length of cable dangling from the box. Getting out of his car, Bolan spotted the receiver, scuffed and cracked, lying in the weeds near a guardrail that separated the highway shoulder from a steep, gravelly incline. He walked past it, following the guardrail uphill for another twenty yards.

When he reached the top of the rise, Bolan stopped and glanced downhill. Roughly five miles away, he could see lights marking the outskirts of Collier Springs, the only developed area between Barstow and the air base. Bolan figured if he could put the Taurus in neutral and push it far enough, he'd be able to coast downhill to one of the service stations just outside town. There he could give the car a chance to cool down and have it looked over by a mechanic. If need be, he could leave it and arrange for other transportation to Edwards.

Waiting for Bolan at the Air Force base were two other members of the Farm's Sensitive Operations Group: mission controller Barbara Price and John "Cowboy" Kissinger, Stony Man's resident weaponsmith. Kissinger had spent the past week at Edwards helping technicians from National Avionics arm the firm's prototype ES-1 spy plane for an impromptu mission in the Far East. With some additional help from a friend stationed at the base, Kissinger and the Avionics team had managed to rig up a modified Phoenix air-to-air missile system, allowing the ES-1 to be flown out of Edwards the previous day in the belly of a Lockheed C-141 Starlifter. Once unloaded at a restricted military air base in Marjeelam, India, the ES-1—originally designed as an Unmanned Reconnaissance Air Vehicle—would be filling in as the National Security Agency's "eye in the sky" over southwestern China pending the launch of a new Odin-series satellite. The new satellite would replace the one that had finally malfunctioned after providing NSA with a steady stream of data for the past seventeen years. Over the years, Stony Man Farm had routinely tapped into NSA's satellite feeds as part of its own covert reconnaissance operations, but its interest in the URAV launch extended beyond a desire to stay on top of suspicious Chinese troop movements within the long-beleaguered province of Tibet. Because the ES-1 was being pressed into duty three months ahead of schedule, it had been deemed necessary to fasten a sled-mount cockpit beneath the fuselage and convert the plane—at least temporarily—into a manned aircraft. Once Stony Man pilot Jack Grimaldi had caught wind of the design change, he'd lobbied for the China mission, convincing Barbara Price to call in some markers at NSA—her former employer—to insure that he got the nod. The ploy had worked. In a few hours, when the ES-1 took off from Marjeelam, Grimaldi would be at the plane's controls.

As for Price, she'd flown to Edwards earlier in the day to see off Grimaldi and smooth things over with her NSA contacts and the commanding officers at the air base. Both parties had been understandably rankled by the leading role the Farm had taken in the ES-1 mission. After all, as a long-standing covert entity, Stony Man Farm had been brought into the mix unencumbered by the restraints of scrutiny and accountability that officially acknowledged agencies were subject to. NSA and the Air Force weren't even aware of the Farm's existence; all they'd been told was that Grimaldi, Price and Kissinger were special federal agents acting under direct orders from the White House. Any other information pertaining to their involvement with the mission had been designated as classified. As Price had told Bolan on the phone back in Los Angeles, she expected to have her hands full assuring the other principals in the mission that there was a good reason for them being kept in the dark as to her true affiliation and that of Grimaldi and Kissinger.

Bolan was sure she'd rise to the challenge. He'd

never met anyone as adept in the art of charmful persuasion. In fact, after nearly several weeks of separation, he was looking forward to partaking in some of those charms himself as soon as he reached Edwards, and it galled him to realize he might now miss the late-night rendezvous they'd planned at her hotel room near the air base.

Returning to the Taurus, Bolan popped the hood, then stepped back, allowing the steam to billow out of the engine compartment. As he waited, he flicked on his cell phone, planning to apprise Price of his latest delay. There was a message waiting for him. It was from Price. She'd run into delays of her own and was still out having drinks with her former NSA colleagues. Their rendezvous was still on, though. "I'll be in my room at 1:00 a.m.," her message ended provocatively, "ready to make you forget about the desert."

Bolan checked his watch and groaned. He'd be lucky to reach Edwards by one-thirty. He left a message with Price's cell service, explaining his predicament, then made another quick call to John Kissinger. The weaponsmith was in the middle of a poker game with his friend and a couple other junior officers at the air base, but he volunteered to drive out to Collier Springs to pick up Bolan.

"Thanks," Bolan said, "but let me try a service

station first and see if they can get me back on the road."

"Didn't catch all that," Kissinger said. "You're breaking up."

Bolan checked his cell. The battery was giving out. He quickly told Kissinger he'd call back on another phone once he got the Taurus downhill to Collier Springs. The phone went dead before Kissinger could reply. Bolan slipped it back in his pocket and waved away the last of the steam wafting up from the engine compartment. He flashed a penlight over the engine and quickly pinpointed the problem—a two-inch rupture in the upper radiator hose. It'd be a quick enough fix once he got the car to a service station.

After lowering the hood, Bolan went back to the front seat. He put the Taurus in neutral, then kept the front door open and stood outside the car, keeping one hand on the steering wheel as he leaned his weight into the door frame. It was oppressively hot. Sweat streamed down his face, stinging his eyes as he coaxed the Taurus slowly forward.

The car was just starting to pick up momentum when Bolan suddenly leaned inside and yanked on the parking brake, bringing the car to an abrupt stop. Glancing over his shoulder, Bolan stared back in the direction of the Mercedes and Camaro.

He thought he'd heard something near the cars.

Bolan stood alongside the Taurus, waiting for the sound to repeat itself. All he could hear, though, was the incessant buzz of insects and the intermittent whirr of traffic passing by him along the highway. He checked his watch, then glanced downhill at the lights of Collier Springs. He was in a quandary. Much as he wanted to get the Taurus to a service station so he could drive on to Edwards, his instincts were still clamoring, telling him something was wrong. He couldn't just leave, not without first checking things out.

Moving away from the Taurus, Bolan followed the guardrail back toward the other two vehicles, gravel crunching noisily under the soles of his running shoes. The Camaro was parked in front of the Mercedes, covered with grime and road dust. It had Nevada plates, and as he drew closer, Bolan saw that the front plate was far cleaner than the rest of the car and hung at a slightly lopsided angle, missing one of its mounting screws.

Stolen.

Bolan instinctively reached inside his shirt. A .44 Magnum Desert Eagle was tucked snugly in a web holster strapped beneath his left arm. In one smooth motion, he drew the gun and thumbed off the safety.

Like it or not, his rendezvous with Barbara Price would have to wait.

CHAPTER TWO

The Camaro's sunroof was cracked open several inches, but the doors were all locked. Bolan peered inside. There was an expensive-looking tooled-leather attaché case on the floor behind the driver's seat. It looked like something he'd have more likely found in the Mercedes. Bolan leaned closer to the window for a better look, then froze.

There it was again—the same sound he'd heard earlier. It was coming from somewhere behind him.

Bolan whirled the .44 held out before him, and stared into the darkness beyond the guardrail. The pitched, gravel-strewed slope led down to a stretch of desert flatland dotted with Joshua trees. Bolan was taken aback at first by the Joshuas, which looked almost human in the moonlight, their gangly limbs raised as if beseeching the heavens. Except for a faint swaying of the branches, however, there was no other sign of movement. Bolan slowly dropped to a crouch, still on the alert.

Finally he heard the sound a third time. It was a faint scratching sound off to his right, coming from the far side of the guardrail next to where the Mercedes was parked. Bolan cautiously approached the luxury car. For the first time, he noticed that the left rear tire was flat. Even more disturbing, however, was a bullet hole in the front windshield. It was on the driver's side and had clearly passed through at an angle, targeting whoever had been sitting behind the steering wheel.

Before he could get close enough to look inside the Mercedes, Bolan's attention was drawn to a faint, watery trail in the gravel on the passenger side of the vehicle. Bolan dipped a finger into the liquid and held it up to the light of a passing car.

Blood.

There was more on the guardrail. Bolan stared past it. Halfway down the slope he spotted a man in a dark suit lying on the ground, grasping weakly for a black chauffeur's cap that lay a few feet beyond his reach. The sound Bolan had heard earlier was that of the man's fingers clawing through the gravel.

Gun in hand, Bolan hurdled the railing and skidded down the slope to the chauffeur's side. The man was in his late thirties, blond hair cropped short, pale eyes filled with fear and confusion. The front of his white shirt was soaked with blood, and Bolan could hear an ominous rustling in the man's lungs. He'd been shot in the chest.

"They took him...." the chauffeur wheezed, struggling to raise his arm and to point toward the mountains rising up behind the Joshua trees. Blood gurgled up through his lips, choking his words. His arm fell limply to the ground. Bolan checked for a pulse, then ripped open the man's shirt. One look at the blood coursing from the gunshot wound and he knew there was no point in attempting CPR. The man was beyond resuscitating.

Bolan stood slowly, trying to piece together what had happened. From what he'd seen, it had all the markings of a textbook highway robbery. Ten miles back, just before the start of the incline, there'd been a rest area, an ideal place to scope out high rollers heading north on the highway to Las Vegas. Bolan figured somebody had to have poked the Mercedes's tire while its occupants were using the facilities, then followed the car away from the rest stop, waiting for it to come up lame. Usually in cases like this the victims would be so frazzled by the flat tire that the robbery would be a piece of cake, a quick hit-and-run with no one getting hurt. But here something had clearly gone wrong. From the looks of it, the robbers had to have shot the chauffeur while he was still behind the wheel, then hauled him out the passenger side and dumped him over the railing.

But what about the passenger?

Bolan glanced in the direction the driver had been pointing. He was trying to sort through the shadows cast by the Joshuas when a gunshot suddenly cracked through the night air. A slug kicked up the earth to Bolan's right and was followed by a second that struck even closer, missing him by mere inches. To compound matters, the shots seemed to be coming from separate directions.

Two shooters, Bolan thought.

When a second volley stirred the gravel at Bolan's feet, he dived to the ground and lay alongside the slain chauffeur. He fired blindly in the direction of the Joshuas, hoping to give the shooters pause while he moved to better cover. More shots quickly whizzed back in his direction, however. Several slammed into the chauffeur's body, making him twitch as if he were coming back to life.

Bolan knew he had to move, quick. Backtracking up to the highway was out of the question, though; the incline would slow him, making him an easy target. And there was no cover to his left or directly in front of him. That left only one option. Bolan took it, rolling to his right through some low brush, then scrambling on all fours toward a graffiti-tagged concrete trough that ran parallel to the highway, apparently to divert floodwaters from the road. Gunshots dogged him every inch of the way.

Once he reached the half pipe, Bolan dived to the bottom and crawled along on his belly. Bullets chipped at the concrete several yards above him, but as long as he stayed low he felt he was safe, at least for the moment.

The ditch ran straight for nearly forty yards, then led Bolan away from the highway and came to an abrupt end. He found himself staring down an eighty-foot drop to a dry gulch lined with jagged rocks and boulders. Jumping would be suicide, but he couldn't turn back, either. Judging from the angle of the gunshots ricocheting off the half pipe around him, at least one of his pursuers was closing in. One way or another, he had to get out of the ditch.

Bolan quickly holstered his Desert Eagle, then lowered himself, feet first, over the drop-off. Once he was dangling from the lip by his fingertips, he swung back and forth a few times, then let go. His momentum carried him back to the sheer face of the mountainside directly beneath the half pipe. He landed hard against the rock and immediately began to slide downward. He clawed for a handhold and finally, after an unchecked slide of nearly twenty feet, he managed to close his fingers around a protrusion the size of a doorknob. Scraped and bleeding, he clung to the facing and listened for his pursuers. After another round of gunfire, there was a lull. Bolan thought he could hear someone coming down out of the mountains toward him, but the sound was quickly drowned out by the hum of traffic up on the highway.

Bolan looked around. Off to his right, he spotted a narrow ledge jutting a few inches from the sheer rock facing. It wasn't much, and he couldn't see where it led, but his fingers were starting to ache and he didn't know how much longer he could cling to his precarious handhold. Slowly he inched sideways.

After a seeming eternity, Bolan reached the ledge. He shifted his weight to his feet, then crabbed his way to a point where the ledge widened and angled upward. He followed the rise and was soon back on level ground. He paused briefly to catch his breath, then reached for his Desert Eagle. His fingers were closing around the grip when he suddenly detected a blur of motion to his right.

Bolan instinctively lurched to one side, but he wasn't fast enough to elude his attacker. A knife blade shone briefly in the moonlight, then ripped through the fabric of Bolan's shirt and plunged into his chest.

Fortunately for Bolan, his attacker's weapon was nothing more than a cheap jackknife. The blade, less than three inches long and dull from use, deflected off Bolan's holster and grazed his ribs. He ignored the cut and struck back, clipping his attacker squarely in the chest with the butt of his Desert Eagle. The knifeman grunted and staggered back.

Bolan stayed on the offensive, lunging forward and driving his shoulder into the man's midsection. Already off balance, the man reeled to the ground, jackknife flying from his hand. Bolan loomed over him, the .44 pointed at his forehead, finger on the trigger.

Dazed, the other man waved his hands feebly in the air.

"I give up, man!" he called out. "Don't shoot!"

Bolan kept the gun trained on the man as he looked him over. He was short and wiry, wearing nothing but sandals and a grimy pair of gym shorts. His hair was unkempt, and a ragged beard hung from his chin like a bristly clump of steel wool. His skin glistened, and he smelled as if he hadn't washed in weeks. Bolan felt certain this wasn't one of the men who'd been firing at him.

"What are you doing out here?" he demanded.

"I live here!"

The man rose shakily to his feet, gesturing at the area around them, a small clearing surrounded by large boulders and a makeshift wall made of tree boughs. A bedroll was laid out on a discarded mattress, next to which were a few weathered boxes filled with clothes and other belongings. Bolan could see an old, battered skateboard, a Frisbee flying disc and a tattered, folded kite. Balanced behind the boxes atop an old tree trunk was a battery-operated police scanner.

"Man's home is his castle, right?" the man complained, rubbing his chin. "I got a right to defend myself!"

Bolan ignored the man, glimpsing past the compound's perimeter, eyes open for the gunmen.

"You're in on all that shooting, right?" the transient guessed.

"I guess you could say that," Bolan murmured. "I'm the target."

"Well, then, you owe me one, mister."

The transient pointed to his right. Bolan saw another man lying unconscious in the shadows.

"Gave him a good whack with my frying pan," the transient said, reaching for the weapon in question, a small cast-iron skillet the size of a table tennis paddle. "He wandered in here right after he took a couple shots at you. I was hiding behind that boulder over there. Guy never knew what hit him."

Bolan crouched before the gunman and turned him over, revealing the MP-5 he'd apparently fallen on after being hit. The assailant was in his early twenties, dressed in black. Blood trickled from his scalp where the transient had struck him. The man's features were Asian. Chinese, Bolan figured.

"I think there's another one of 'em still out there somewhere," the transient told Bolan.

"I know."

"Why were they shooting at you?"

"I crashed their party." Bolan quickly explained how he'd chanced upon the slain chauffeur, then asked if the transient had seen or heard anything before the shooting broke out. The man seemed hesitant to volunteer any information.

"Answer me!" Bolan demanded.

"Hey, look, I'm a dropout, okay? I don't wanna get caught up in something that's none of my business."

"This *is* your business now," Bolan told him, indicating the fallen gunman.

"I don't want any hassles."

Bolan tossed the man some bait. "If these guys have been pulling robberies like this for a while," he suggested, "there might be a reward."

"Reward?" The transient's eyes lit up. "You think so?"

Bolan shrugged. "Of course, it'd depend on how cooperative you were."

The transient thought it over, then said, "Yeah, okay. I saw something. C'mon, I'll show you...."

"Put the frying pan down first," Bolan advised him.

"Oh, yeah, right." The transient set down the

skillet, then led Bolan up a short path partially concealed by more boulders. "By the way, my name's Billy Grubb. Grubowsky, actually, but Grubb's easier to remember. Kinda fits, too, I guess, huh."

Bolan didn't answer. He'd holstered his Desert Eagle in favor of the MP-5, and he kept a vigilant eye on his surroundings as they made their way up to a vista overlooking the strip of desert flatland between the gorge and the mountains. The highway was barely visible a few hundred yards to the left. Bolan could just make out the Camaro and Mercedes on the far side of the guardrail. His Taurus parked too far uphill for him to see.

"Okay, what happened was I was just about nodding off when I got woken up by this *ka-bang* sound," the transient explained, pointing toward the Mercedes. "I figured it was just some car backfiring, so I tried to go back to sleep, only then I heard some yelling and another *ka-bang*. I crawled up here for a look-see, and these two guys were dragging some other guy down from the highway. They were talking in Chinese or something, and every couple steps they roughed this other guy up." The man's finger indicated a course down the slope from the guardrail to the hardpan, then across the sand to the first cluster of Joshua trees. "Finally, right about there, they started digging."

"Digging?" Bolan peered hard in the direction of the trees.

"Yeah," Grubb said. "They must've had shovels with 'em or something. I figured maybe they'd buried something out there and were looking to dig it up."

"Or maybe it was the other way around," Bolan suggested. "Maybe they were looking to bury something. Or someone."

"Maybe so," Grubb said. "I didn't think of that. Anyway, they weren't at it all that long before somebody showed up back near the cars."

"Me," Bolan said.

"Yeah, I guess so," the transient said. "Anyway, once all those the guns started going off, I grabbed my skillet and laid low. When Charlie Chan over there came by, I clobbered him. Next thing I knew, here you come crawling up out of the gorge like Spider-Man or something. Freaked me right out, I'm tellin' ya. I didn't cut you too bad, did I?"

"I'll live," Bolan said. He surveyed the desert and mountainside but saw no trace of the remaining gunman. "Let's go tend to your houseguest before he comes to."

"Good idea." Grubb led the way back. "I was gonna either tie him up or use duct tape. I got both."

"Let's use the tape," Bolan said.

"Coming right up."

As Grubb fished through his boxes, Bolan crouched over the fallen shooter. The man hadn't moved since the Executioner had turned him over. He thumbed the man's wrist, then his neck.

"Here we go," Grubb said, bringing the tape over.

"We won't be needing that," Bolan told him.

Grubb seemed surprised. "I killed him?"

"Looks that way."

Grubb stared at the dead man a moment, then turned back to Bolan. "That reward," he said, his voice filled with concern. "Is it one of those 'dead or alive' things? Am I still gonna be able to collect?"

"You'll have to ask somebody else about that."

Bolan frisked the dead man. There was another ammo clip for the MP-5 in one pocket. In the other, Bolan found a handful of change, a Swiss army knife and a wrinkled business card. The front of the card bore the address and phone number of an enterprise called Orient Expressions.

"Massage parlor," Grubb said, peering over Bolan's shoulder at the card. "It's in Collier Springs. Big with truckers and guys from the Air Force base."

Bolan flipped over the card. There was handwriting on the back. He held the note to the moonlight and tried to read it.

"What's it say?" Grubb asked.

"It's the make and color of the Mercedes," Bolan said. "There's some numbers and letters, too. Probably the license plate."

Bolan was telling Grubb his theory about how the Mercedes had been followed from the rest area when he was interrupted by the distant sound of a car door opening, then slamming shut. Bolan quickly stuffed the business card in his shirt pocket and sprang past Grubb, bounding back up the trail. He reached higher ground just in time to see the Camaro screech back out onto the highway, leaving the Mercedes behind.

"Must be the other guy who was shooting at you," Grubb said, bringing up the rear.

Bolan nodded. Still, he kept up his guard as he climbed down the other side of the rock heap and made his way across level ground toward the Joshua trees. Grubb kept pace alongside him.

"If there's more shooting," he told Bolan, "maybe you can let me use that gun of yours, okay?"

Bolan didn't answer. He shifted his holster to keep it from chafing his knife wound.

As they crossed the hardpan, Bolan heard the distant blare of a train whistle. He glanced over his shoulder and saw the train, several miles to the south, making its way across the desert floor like a huge black snake.

"That'll be the 12:20 out of Barstow," Grubb said. "Stops off at Collier Springs, then moves on up to Bishop and Lone Pine."

The men were halfway to the trees when Bolan heard another sound, closer, just to his right. He whipped the subgun around, but it turned out to be nothing more than a grasshopper taking wing in the hot night air. The insect buzzed past the men, then landed back on the sandy terrain and folded in its wings.

"Little bastards are tasty if you fry 'em up right," Grubb said. "Got a nice crunch to 'em, too. Like popcorn."

"I'll pass on that," Bolan said.

After a few more steps, he stopped and held his hand out, signaling Grubb to do the same. Up ahead, just beyond the nearest grouping of Joshua trees, a man lay stretched out on the ground. Beside him, two folding shovels poked up from a mound of sand piled next to the beginnings of a long, shallow trench.

"You were right," Grubb said. "They were lookin' to bury that guy."

Bolan and Grubb knelt on either side of the dead man. His lifeless eyes stared past them at the faint stars overhead. The man looked to be in his fifties, well dressed in a tailored gray suit and expensive Italian shoes. Blood seeped through an apparent bullet wound to the chest, staining the man's shirt and tie.

"Something tells me the Mercedes is his," Grubb speculated.

Bolan nodded. He took note of the man's face. It was bruised and bleeding in several spots, as if he'd been severely beaten before being killed.

"Whoa," Grubb muttered. "Bad vibes, man. I'm gonna have to move after this."

Bolan ignored Grubb. He saw that the dead man's hand was folded into a fist. Reaching over, he carefully pried the man's fingers apart. Clutched in the palm of his hand was an insignia ring. Bolan took the ring and held it up to the moonlight. Inscribed on the ring's surface was a series of small yin-yang symbols, some red and blue, the others red and black. Dead center in the ring, framed by the yin-yangs, was a swastika.

"A Nazi?" Grubb murmured. "Now I'm *really* gonna have to move."

Bolan took another look at the ring, then began to frisk the man, looking for a wallet or some other kind of identification. Before he could find anything, sirens screamed to life out on the highway. Glancing up, Bolan saw the flashing lights of two California

Highway Patrol Crown Victorias heading up the grade toward the Mercedes.

Bolan quickly weighed his options. He had papers identifying him as a special agent with the Justice Department, but he knew from experience that the ID wouldn't exempt him from being interrogated at length about the shoot-out, especially if the authorities got a look at the ordnance stockpiled in the trunk of his rental car. The greater good would be served, he figured, if he were to track down the stray shooter while the trail was still hot. And unless he was mistaken, that trail likely passed somewhere in the vicinity of the Orient Expressions massage parlor.

"What's the quickest way to Collier Springs?" he asked Grubb. "Besides taking the highway."

Grubb glanced up at the highway patrol vehicles, which had just pulled off the road behind the Mercedes, then turned to Bolan suspiciously. "You got something to hide from the cops or something?"

"Maybe you should be thinking more in terms of not having to share that reward," Bolan countered.

"It's gonna take a lot of explaining," Grubb said. "Hell, with you not around, they might blame me for this whole mess."

"Just tell them the truth and you'll be all right," Bolan assured him. "Now make it quick—how do

I get to Collier Springs without taking the highway?"

"Same way I do when I don't feel like skateboarding," Grubb said, pointing behind him. "Take the train."

CHAPTER THREE

"Almost there," Billy Grubb called over his shoulder as he led Bolan along a circuitous path that trailed down from the flatlands. The path was tightly flanked by boulders and in spots it had been nearly covered over by rockslides, as well as overgrown clumps of tumbleweed and mesquite, but Grubb seemed familiar with the maze and navigated it with ease. Bolan stayed close on his heels, scanning the terrain with his Desert Eagle at the ready.

Finally the trail leveled off and led to a clearing. The rail tracks came into view, resting on a raised bed of gravel. Less than a mile away, the train chugged across the desert floor toward the two men. A pair of diesel locomotives headed up the caravan, hauling behind them a long chain of flatbed platform cars. Bolan figured there had to be at least fifty cars in all.

"They'll slow down as they get closer," Grubb told him, waving away a cloud of gnats. "The slope here's not as steep as the highway, but it's still a chore for them to get up it, especially when they're carrying that much cargo.''

"I'll take it from here," Bolan told the transient.

Grubb ignored the hint and pointed to the tracks. "What you want to do is run parallel to the train as it's going past, then inch your way up to the tracks and grab hold of one of the cars' ladders. They're usually toward the back and hang down from the edge of the platform. And when I say hold on, I mean for dear life, 'cause no matter how much the train slows down it's still gonna feel like your arms are gettin' ripped from their sockets.''

"Got it," Bolan said patiently, humoring the transient. This wasn't the first time he'd hopped a train, and he suspected it wouldn't be the last. "You better get back and flag down the police or they're going to have problems with your story."

"Right, right," Grubb said. "I gotta say, though, part of me wants to ride along with you and see what happens. Not a lot of excitement in my life these days, if you know what I mean."

"If you get that reward, maybe you can clean yourself up and give the real world another chance," Bolan suggested.

"Yeah, maybe," Grubb said without much conviction. "Okay, you're on your own…. Say, I never got your name.''

"Probably best to keep it that way," Bolan said. He extended a hand to the transient. "I appreciate the help...not to mention the pack."

Grubb eyed the soiled knapsack slung across Bolan's shoulders. The MP-5 submachine gun was stashed inside. Bolan had paid the transient forty dollars for the pack; it would provide at least some consolation should Grubb learn, as Bolan suspected, that there was no reward linked to turning in the shooter he'd killed with his frying pan.

Bolan watched Grubb head back up the trail, then crouched low behind a clot of mesquite and turned his attention back to the approaching train. Both diesels thundered as they rolled toward him, ready to challenge the grade. Bolan waited for the engines to roll past, then slipped his gun back in his holster and broke from cover. He jogged alongside the slow-rolling flatbed cars, looking for one to board. Prospects weren't good. Most of the cars were carrying large cargo containers secured with thick steel cables, leaving little room for passengers.

Undaunted, Bolan kept pace with the caravan, all the while easing closer to the tracks. Cinders flew out beneath the fast-turning wheels, stinging him like blasts from a pellet gun. Bolan shielded his face with one hand without breaking his stride. Once he was within a few feet of a steel ladder extending from the rear of the nearest flatcar, he put on a burst of speed, then sprang forward, his arms extended. His fingers closed around the upper railing just as his right foot landed on the lower rung. The car's momentum sharply jerked him forward, but he held on and managed to pull himself up to the platform. There was a narrow space between two of the cables that secured the cargo container. Arms throbbing, Bolan wedged himself in the gap. The submachine gun in his backpack clanged loudly against the metal siding of the container as he sat. Beneath him the flatcar swayed and clattered loudly along the tracks. The hot night air rushing past him felt almost refreshing.

As the train carried him slowly uphill, Bolan unbuttoned his shirt to inspect where Grubb had knifed him. The wound had stopped bleeding and was already beginning to crust over. Bolan would have it reopened and cleaned out with disinfectant at some point, and afterward there'd no doubt be a scar, just one more of the dozens that covered his body and bore testament to a life spent mired in combat.

The soldier had lost track of the number of skirmishes he'd been through since embarking on his first vendetta, years ago, against the American Mafia. He'd targeted them after they'd brought ruin on his family, and by the time he'd exacted his vengeance, he'd come to realize that he was motivated by more than a mere thirst for revenge. He'd found his calling, and in the years since—both alone and abetted by his warrior colleagues at Stony Man Farm—Bolan had continued to battle those who preyed on the weak and innocent, be they Mafia chieftains, KGB assassins or dogma-spouting terrorists.

And now, here he was, drawn into yet another conflict. In this instance, however, he found himself in the odd position of not being sure of whom he was up against...or even if the men who'd shot at him were truly adversaries. While at first he thought he'd stumbled onto a robbery gone wrong, after glimpsing the insignia ring in the palm of the Mercedes's owner, Bolan was having second thoughts. If the swastika was sign of some sort of neo-Nazi affiliation, who was to say the gunmen Bolan had encountered weren't kindred spirits, vigilantes who had hauled some wretched excuse for humanity from his ill-gotten world of luxury and dispatched him to his Maker?

Bolan pulled out the business card taken off the man Billy Grubb had killed with a skillet. Once he reached Collier Springs and tracked down the massage parlor, Bolan figured he'd have his answers, one way or another. Once he'd cleared up matters to his satisfaction, he'd decide whether to stick around and contend with the authorities or write off the Taurus and move on to Edwards.

He suddenly remembered his promise to call John Kissinger once he'd reached a service station. He pulled out his cell phone, hoping there might be enough life in the battery to make a quick call. At some point—probably while crawling along the ditch—the flip-down mouthpiece had snapped off its hinges. He fit it back into place, but either the circuitry had been fouled or the battery had lost its entire charge. The phone refused to work. He would have to wait until he reached town to call.

As he was stuffing the cell phone back in his pocket, Bolan glanced ahead at the cargo container strapped to the flatcar directly across from him. Stenciled on the container's side was a corporate logo—PACRIM Transport. Bolan remembered seeing similar logos stamped on most of the other cargo containers. The acronym meant nothing to him, however.

He turned his attention to the surrounding countryside. By now the train had finally cleared the rise and begun the downhill run to Collier Springs. Bolan had passed through the desert city once before, more than ten years ago. Back then, times had been hard. The city's primary enterprise, Rodgers Air Force Base—a smaller adjunct to Edwards—had just been shut down as part of military downsizing, and so many businesses were failing in the wake of the closure that many had felt Collier Springs would become a ghost town by century's end. Times had changed, however, apparently for the better, because in addition to that part of the city Bolan had seen earlier from the highway, he now saw a sprawl of new bedroom communities. All of them were located in close vicinity to the old base, which, from the looks of it, had been converted into some sort of industrial park. Bright halogen beams washed the facility in a yellowish glow, and even at this late hour there were signs of activity: trucks pulling away from loading docks, workers moving between buildings and a construction crew erecting the framework for a new building. Atop one of the converted hangars was a large sign that read PACRIM Industries.

Bolan glanced back at the cargo container strapped to the platform car in front of him.

PACRIM Transport.

Bolan was pondering the connection when he became aware of a faint, eerie noise asserting itself above the clamor of the train. It sounded as if it were coming from directly behind him. Intrigued, he turned and leaned an ear closer to the metal side of the cargo container he'd been leaning against. Then he heard it again.

A voice.

Someone was inside the container, calling out to him.

Bolan listened closer, trying to tune out the rhythmic clatter of the train's wheels and focus on the voice coming from inside the cargo container. Soon he was convinced there was more than just one person calling out. He could hear moaning and sobbing, as well as the plaintive cry of a man crying out in a foreign tongue—Chinese, he thought—repeating the same refrain. Bolan knew a few words of the language and realized the man was shouting for help.

A few feet to his right, Bolan spotted a hairline gap in the siding. He shifted position and shouted through the opening. "Hello!"

There was a brief pause, then the uproar inside the container resumed. The cries blended together, urgent and persistent.

"English?" Bolan yelled through the crack. "Do you speak English?"

There was another flurry of voices, then the man closest to the opening shouted for the others to be quiet.

"We are trapped," he then cried out through the crack. "Hard to breathe."

"Help!" the others behind him shouted desperately.

"Help!" the man echoed. "Please help!"

Bolan's mind raced, trying to fathom an explanation. There was only one that made any sense:

he'd stumbled on some illegal aliens being smuggled into the States. If they were Chinese, the odds were they'd come by way of the shipyards in Long Beach or San Pedro, packed into the cargo container before it was unloaded from some sort of freighter that had brought them from their native land. If that was the case, they'd just endured at least four hours on the rails, most of it spent crossing the desert without any sort of ventilation. Bolan knew of similar operations involving the transport of Mexican illegals, but in those cases, instead of train containers, the victims had been packed like sardines into trucks by unscrupulous smugglers only interested in their fees—usually the life savings of those willing to risk life and limb for an opportunity to live and work in America.

"Help!"

Now the cries were accompanied by the faint pounding of fists against the walls of the cargo container.

"Please!" the man closest to the crack implored again. "Please help us!"

"I'll do what I can," Bolan said.

He remembered seeing a sliding door on the side of the container when he first hopped the train. Standing up, he grabbed for handholds wherever he could find them and maneuvered his way around the railcar, only to find the door padlocked. He wasn't surprised, but the sight still inflamed his rage against the smugglers.

Steadying himself as best he could, Bolan freed one hand and unholstered his Desert Eagle. The train had begun to slow again but was still hurtling along the tracks at well over forty miles per hour. Fortunately they'd reached a straightaway, and Bolan didn't have to contend with swaying as he leaned back and took aim at the lock. It took two rounds from the .44 before the tumblers gave way.

Bolan tossed the lock aside and unlatched the door, then tugged it open. Immediately a swarm of immigrants, half of them women and children, crowded around the doorway, eagerly breathing in the night air and grabbing at Bolan, all speaking at once, their faces glistening with tears and perspiration. Bolan reassured them as best he could while motioning for them to move aside.

Entering the container, he was assailed by the rank odor of sweat, urine and feces.

And death.

Lying still in the shadows just beyond those thronged around Bolan were bodies, at least a dozen of them, most of them entangled with one another. Among the dead was a young woman clutching a small child. Bolan took in the grim tableau, then stepped back toward the opening. One of the survivors tugged at his shirt.

"Thank you," the man cried out, his voice trembling with emotion. "I am Deng. You have saved us!"

Bolan recognized the voice. It was the same man who'd first called out to him. He was middle-aged, short and thin with a wisp of a beard and large brown eyes.

"Who did this to you?" Bolan asked.

The man answered indirectly, "We come for work."

"Yes, I know, but who put you in this death trap?" When Bolan saw the confused look on the other man's face, he indicated the framework of the container. "Who put you in here?"

Deng shook his head. "They tell us no names. We pay and they promise we will have work." Looking past Bolan, the man pointed and said, "There. They say we will have work there."

Bolan glanced over his shoulder. Deng was pointing at the PACRIM industrial park, now less than a hundred yards away.

The train continued to slow as it approached the railyards adjacent to the facility. Up ahead, Bolan saw work crews swarmed along the loading platform, armed with dollies and forklifts, ready to unload the night's cargo. Scattered among them were several uniformed security officers, no doubt waiting to usher the immigrants into their new life as slave

labor for PACRIM Industries. That had to be it, Bolan thought. PACRIM—short for Pacific Rim, he
figured—was probably Chinese run, smuggling in
cheap labor as a way to keep costs down and keep
its edge in the marketplace. If that was the case, the
only tragedy the firm's owners would likely see in
the railcar death toll was a short-term loss in pro-
ductivity.

Bastards, Bolan thought, once again taking in the
carnage around him. When first boarding the train,
he'd planned on bailing before it reached the railyards so he could track down the massage parlor and
get some answers about the desert killings. Now,
however, he felt yoked to the plight of the immigrants. Abandoning them was out of the question.
Unslinging his backpack, he glanced at Deng. "Do
any of you know how to use a gun?"

Deng nodded gravely. "I do."

"Here." Bolan turned over his Desert Eagle.
"Have the others move back, then we'll close the
door and..."

Bolan's voice trailed off as a gunshot echoed
across the plain and whizzed past his head. Behind
him a woman screamed. Bolan turned and saw her
clutch at her neck. Blood spurted out between her
fingers as she careened into another of the immigrants.

When a second shot dropped a young boy to Bo-

lan's right, he dropped to the floor and shouted for
the others to do the same. As he fished through his
backpack for the MP-5, Deng crouched near the
opening and aimed out at a sentry tower rising up
along the perimeter of the railyard. He squeezed off
a round, then helped Bolan slide the door until there
was only a slight opening. Gunshots continued to
ping off the door and metal siding. Bolan figured
they were after him, not the immigrants. The longer
he stayed with them, the more he would be putting
them at risk, especially once the train came to a full
stop. He had to get out before they were all trapped.

Clutching the MP-5, Bolan nudged the door back
open another few inches, then told Deng, ''I'll try
to draw their attention away. Close the door after
me.''

Without waiting for an answer, Bolan squeezed
through the opening and dropped to the ground,
tumbling on impact with the coarse gravel. He came
up firing, spraying the sentry tower. The guard
who'd first fired at the railcar dropped his rifle and
tumbled forward, to the earth. Another gunman soon
took his place, however, driving Bolan to cover behind a switching mechanism.

To Bolan's surprise, a burst of gunfire sounded
from directly behind him. Looking back, he saw that
Deng had leaped down the train, as well, and was

firing at the tower. He proved a good aim, too, quickly taking out the second sniper.

Bolan knew they were still vastly outnumbered, however. Glancing toward the loading platform, he saw the security officers leap down to the ground and began to fan out, blasting away at both him and Deng.

"Split up!" Bolan called out to the other man. He rolled clear of the switching mechanism and scrambled to his feet, dodging gunfire as he bolted toward a row of boxcars on a side track twenty yards to his right. Reaching the first car, he held off his pursuers with a burst from the MP-5, then climbed a ladder to the roof. The heightened perspective allowed him to take out a pair of guards advancing on his left. He also managed to plug another shooter who was attempting to circle behind Deng.

The Executioner's shots drew more fire his way, and he was forced to drop flat on his stomach as bullets raked the upper edge of the boxcar. He shot back whenever he had a clear target and soon he was out of ammunition.

Crawling across the roof, Bolan climbed back down to the ground, then stole his way toward one of the fallen security officers. A 9 mm Glock pistol lay in the dirt beside him. Bolan tossed aside the MP-5 in favor of the handgun, then rolled under the boxcar closest to him. Coming out on the other side, he found himself near the rear entrance of a converted hangar. A guard posted before the doorway spotted Bolan and drew a bead on him with a Kalashnikov assault rifle. The Executioner fired first, putting a 9 mm slug through the sentry's heart. The man fell to the dirt, dropping the rifle. Bolan rushed past, snatching the rifle.

There was no air-conditioning inside the hangar, which had been turned, quite literally, into a sweatshop. Bolan saw at least sixty terrified women and children, all of them dressed in rags, all of them soaked in their own perspiration, cowering near rows of benches piled high with disassembled electronic toys. Off near the walls were more rows of cheap cots where another twenty workers lay asleep, so overcome by heat and exhaustion that the firefight had failed to rouse them.

Bolan put a finger to his lips, then backtracked to the doorway, not wanting to draw the workers into harm's way. He was on his way back outside when a pair of security guards charged around one of the boxcars and fired at him. Bolan whirled to one side. A bullet tugged at the material of his shirt, just missing his rib cage. He fired back with the Kalashnikov, nailing one guard in the chest and the other in the forehead. Both men were dead by the time Bolan charged past them, making his way back toward the switching yard.

Deng was nowhere to be seen. Another handful of guards had stormed the yard, however, and Bolan found himself being fired on from all directions. He dived to the ground and crawled beneath a caboose on one of the side tracks. Bullets clanged off the rails and steel wheels he'd taken cover behind. He fired back, wounding one of the guards, but he was outnumbered and running out of ammo. It was beginning to look hopeless.

Then, above the chattering of gunfire, Bolan heard an ominous rumbling overhead. Inching forward, he peered up and saw an AH-64 Apache helicopter drifting over the railyards toward him. Bolan had no clue how the owners of PACRIM had gotten their hands on the aircraft, but he knew that the 30 mm chain gun mounted to its turret would easily rip the caboose to shreds.

The caboose, however, wasn't the chopper's target. Banking low and then pivoting to the right, the Apache turned its chain gun on a trio of security officers closing in on Bolan. Firing ten rounds a second, the gunship pummeled the gunmen off their feet, then shifted and directed its fury at yet another batch of Bolan's would-be assailants.

Emboldened by the assist from the Apache, Bolan crawled out from cover and helped turn the tide of the battle, emptying his Kalashnikov at a pair of startled guards, then rearming himself yet again with their fallen weapons.

By now highway patrol and county sheriff's officers were storming the site, as well, racing past the main gate in their squad cars, sirens blaring, rooftop lights flashing. Their arrival squelched any hopes the security force might have had of gaining the upper hand. By the time the Apache had made another pass over the railyard, the guards had either put away their weapons or thrown them down, then raised their arms in surrender.

Bolan scrambled over the side tracks, seeking out Deng. He finally spotted the man slumped near the base of a water tower, bleeding from a bullet wound to the chest.

He smiled faintly at Bolan's approach and murmured, ''We defeated them, yes?''

''For now,'' Bolan told him. ''Yes, I think we did, for now.''

''Good,'' Deng said. He was handing Bolan's gun back to him when his eyes drooped shut and his arm went limp.

Bolan took the Desert Eagle and eased the man to the ground, then slowly stood and headed toward a clearing, where the Apache was stirring up a cloud of sand as it touched down for a landing. A side door opened and one of the chopper's crew members clambered to the ground. Ducking to avoid the rotors, he vanished briefly in the sand cloud, then re-emerged, clutching a MAC-10 subgun. The man was Bolan's height and even broader shouldered, wearing jeans and a white T-shirt. He grinned as he approached Bolan.

"Sorry to crash the party," John Kissinger said with a grin, "but I figured the invitation must've got lost in the mail."

CHAPTER FOUR

"…and when you didn't call back, I had the Farm check your GPS coordinates," Kissinger said, explaining his timely arrival at the PACRIM facility.

"I'd forgotten all about that," Bolan replied. He pulled out his cell phone, marveling anew at how Stony Man's cybernetic crew had managed to embed a fully operational Global Positioning System into the base of the phone's antenna. The dime-sized computer chip came encased with its own battery and had obviously continued transmitting Bolan's position even after the phone itself had gone dead.

"Don't ask me how, but they not only knew you'd hopped the train," Kissinger went on, "but they were also able to gauge its speed and ETA at the railyards."

"I guess this is one time I'm glad Big Brother was watching," said Bolan.

"Amen to that," Kissinger said. "Anyway, by the time they got back to me, I'd already glommed a police scanner and heard about a shooting out in the desert. When they reported your car abandoned on the shoulder, I smelled trouble and rounded up the fastest set of wheels I could get my hands on.''

''Good call,'' Bolan told him.

The two men were standing just outside the perimeter fence encircling PACRIM Industrial Park. They'd just spoken with Kern County Sheriff Kit Deerson, who was now in his patrol car a few yards away verifying Bolan's and Kissinger's IDs. Along with the sheriff, it looked as if every law-enforcement officer within a hundred-mile radius had converged on the scene within the past half hour. They'd done a quick and efficient job of restoring order. Highway patrol officers had cordoned off the area and were holding back the slew of local residents drawn by the commotion, while officers from the sheriff's department had herded all PACRIM personnel into one of the warehouse buildings for questioning. INS officials and a contingent of federal agents were on their way down from Sacramento and would be arriving any minute. The Air Force pilot who'd been at the controls of the Apache, meanwhile, was off near the loading platform helping paramedics and coroner officials tend to the victims of the ill-fated smuggling operation. The last Bolan had heard, of the fifty-five men, women and children crammed into the railcar container, only seven were still alive. He could see the dead being hauled out of the cargo container in body bags. There were so many of them that a refrigerated meat truck had been pressed into duty to help transport fatalities to the county morgue in nearby Adelanto. The grim proceedings were underscored by the mournful wailing of the survivors, who stood off to one side being comforted by some of the laborers Bolan had chanced upon earlier in the converted hangar.

"I can't believe they'd let themselves get locked inside a container like that," Kissinger mused.

"I don't think they had any idea what they were getting themselves into," Bolan said. "All they knew was that jobs were waiting for them. You get people that desperate for work, they're not going to ask too many questions."

"You're probably right," Kissinger said.

Changing the subject, Bolan said, "Any word on Jack?"

Kissinger said that the last he'd heard, Jack Grimaldi and the ES-1 spy plane had reached the air base in Marjeelam on schedule. The Stony Man pilot would be starting his recon mission over China in a few hours.

Kissinger's cell phone chirped. It was Barbara Price, calling from her hotel room near the Air Force base. Bolan had already called to explain why he'd missed their rendezvous. Though disappointed, Price was more concerned about Bolan's stab wound.

"It's just a nick," Bolan assured her, gently rubbing his side. The paramedics had already cleaned the wound and dressed it. "Didn't even need stitches."

"Are you up on your tetanus shots?" Price asked.

"They gave me a booster," Bolan told her. "It hurt more than the knife did."

"Do you think there's a connection between PACRIM and those guys who were shooting at you out in the desert?" Price wondered.

"Too soon to say," Bolan said. "I plan on looking into it, though."

"Trying to avoid me, are you?" Price teased.

"Absence makes the heart grow fonder," Bolan responded. "We'll pencil in some time together once we get back to Virginia."

"If I can wait that long," Price said. "I might have to take advantage of you on the plane."

Bolan grinned. "I won't put up a fight."

Price asked about the neo-Nazi ring found on the owner of the Mercedes. Before Bolan could respond, the sheriff, a middle-aged, stocky man with gray eyes, returned from his patrol car. Bolan told Price he'd have to get back to her, then clicked off and handed the cell phone back to Kissinger.

"Okay, gentlemen," Deerson said, handing Bolan

and Kissinger their photostat IDs, "you both checked out."

Bolan hadn't anticipated any problems. His cover as special federal agent Mike Belasko—like Kissinger's, which gave his name as Alex Jordan—had been long established, and any background check on their credentials usually came back with the caveat that they were on a classified mission for the Justice Department. Deerson—like the NSA and Air Force honchos Barbara Price had had to contend with back at Edwards—was clearly less than thrilled with the lowdown he'd received after having his ID query routed to Stony Man Director Hal Brognola.

"I was also told, in so many words," he went on, "that even though this is technically my jurisdiction, I'm supposed to bend over backward accommodating you on this 'mission' of yours." There was an edge to the man's voice, and his eyes flashed with a glint of disdain.

"We don't plan to get in your way," Bolan assured him. "You've got things under control."

"We do what we can," Deerson drawled sarcastically. "Speaking of which, I ran a check on those Camaro plates you mentioned. You were right. They came off an old Subaru with a Vegas registration. I'm guessing somebody snatched the Chevy from one of the casino lots and switched plates to throw us off the scent."

"And they picked the Camaro because it'd been parked there awhile," Bolan guessed.

"Bingo," Deerson said. "This time of year, folks drive up there and don't see their cars again until it's time to come home. The owners didn't even know the Chevy was missing."

"So, the bottom line is," Bolan stated, "we can figure these people have already pulled another plate switch."

"That or they've jacked themselves another car," Kissinger ventured.

Deerson shot Bolan a sidelong glance and asked, "Incidentally, when exactly did you plan on telling me about that business card you lifted off that shooter back near Collier Gorge?"

Bolan was taken aback. He stared at the sheriff. "You talked to Grubb?"

Deerson nodded. "Yep. You gotta give that flea-bag a little credit, though. He kept mum until I told him he was out of luck as far as a reward went. That didn't sit too well with him."

"So he figured he'd throw me to the lions."

"Roar," the Sheriff deadpanned.

"You didn't charge him with anything, did you?" Bolan said.

Deerson shook his head. "We left him at his château out there in the desert but told him not to leave town. But let's get back to that business card. Grubb said it was from a massage parlor here in town.''

There seemed little point now in keeping the information to himself, so Bolan handed over the Orient Expressions business card and pointed out the writing on the back, explaining his theory as to how the Mercedes had wound up on the shoulder with a flat tire.

Deerson nodded in agreement. ''Yeah, we've had a couple robberies like that over the years. The thing is, though, in the other cases, the robbers made off with the cars and just left their victims stranded minus their cash and jewelry. Here we got two stiffs whose wallets weren't even touched, plus one of 'em was about to wind up stashed in a shallow grave. Explain that one to me.''

''The guy by the grave had an insignia ring with a swastika,'' Bolan said.

''Yeah, I know,'' Deerson said, ''but if you're thinking Nazis, don't.''

''Why not?'' Kissinger asked.

''First off, the swastika was pointing the opposite way of the ones the Nazis used,'' Deerson said. ''Secondly, there's those yin-yang symbols. Either of you guys ever hear of the Falun Gong?''

Bolan nodded. ''It's a religious sect in China.''

''That's the bunch,'' Deerson said. ''Only over there the Commies call 'em a cult and put the screws to 'em every chance they get. We've got a few followers here in Collier Springs. Mostly New Age types. You know, big on chants and all that mind-expansion shit.''

"Then it's not just a Chinese thing?" Kissinger said.

"I wish," Deerson replied. "Hell, my own damn daughter got herself sucked into a Falun group some gals started up at the community college. Buncha white girls from the suburbs, if you can believe that. Couple weeks ago I had to bust them 'cause they were picketing outside the gates here.''

"Picketing?" Bolan said. "What about?"

"Persecution of the Falun Gong back in China, what else?" Deerson said. "At the time I thought they were nuts. I mean, just because PACRIM's run by the Chinese doesn't make 'em responsible for everything that goes wrong back on the homefront, right? Of course, after what went down here tonight, who knows, maybe they had a point.''

"Any chance this guy with the ring is from around here?" Kissinger asked.

Deerson shook his head. "He's got an L.A. address on his driver's license. We're checking it out, but it'll probably be morning before we come up with anything.''

"But there's a good chance his killing has something to do with this Falun Gong sect, right?'' Kissinger said.

''Beats me,'' Deerson said.

Bolan thought back on the sequence of events on the highway and remembered something. ''There was an attaché case in the Camaro,'' he told the sheriff. ''It looked like it might've been snatched from the Mercedes.''

Deerson stared hard at Bolan. ''Anything else you're holding back on me?''

''I was going to stop by the massage parlor and see if anyone knew about the guys in the Camaro.''

''And that's the reason you hopped the train instead of sticking around to talk to us, right?'' Deerson surmised. ''You figured, hey, why let the locals cramp your style.''

''Something like that,'' Bolan answered evenly.

The two men faced off a moment, then Deerson forced a grin. ''Okay, okay, so much the chip on my shoulder,'' he said. ''You guys want a ride to this stroke joint…?''

HALFWAY INTO TOWN, Deerson fielded a call from his dispatcher. The Sheriff's office had just received a call from someone claiming to be part of the Falun Gong. They were taking responsibility for killing the occupants of the Mercedes and claimed they'd left the ring in the dead man's hand as a calling card.

"Smells fishy to me," the sheriff said once he got off the call.

"I don't buy it, either," Bolan said. "I haven't heard anything about the Gong going militant."

"And if they did, why start out on Americans?" Kissinger said. "Their beef's with the PRC back in China."

"Well, whoever made the call, they knew all the details of the killings," Deerson said. "Too bad we couldn't keep 'em on the line long enough for a trace."

"I'd guess it was the guy who drove off in the Camaro," Bolan ventured. "I think the whole Falun Gong angle is a red herring."

"As if I'm gonna turn around and haul my daughter in for questioning on this," Deerson grumbled. "I tell ya, these guys are starting to piss me off."

"With any luck," Kissinger told him, "pretty soon you'll have a chance to do something about it."

"I sure as hell hope so," Deerson said.

Five minutes later they'd reached the massage parlor. Orient Expressions operated out of a run-down two-story building located next to an equally decrepit strip mall seven miles north of the PACRIM facility. The neighborhood, dating back to the founding of Collier Springs during the early years of World War II, had never recovered from the closing of the Air Force base. Most of the mall's shop fronts were boarded up, and weeds choked the parkways, as well as the lawns of a few old farmhouses that had been converted into low-rent apartments. There was no sign that anyone had heard the shootout at the industrial park—the streets and sidewalks were deserted and only a few lights were on in the apartment houses.

"The closest thing we have to a ghetto," Deerson said as he pulled his patrol car to a stop behind the service bay of a long-abandoned gas station a block past the massage parlor. Railroad tracks ran directly behind the station.

"Normally PACRIM would be running its train through here about now," the sheriff told Bolan and Kissinger as they got out of the car. "Of course, they're going to be a little behind schedule tonight."

Kissinger watched a rat scurry past, disappearing into a dense thicket of oleander that ran parallel to the railbed. "I take it this is what they mean by the wrong side of the tracks."

"You got that right," Deerson said. He drew his service revolver and led Bolan and Kissinger in the same direction as the rat. "These bushes'll lead us right up to the back door. Just watch your step."

There was a well-worn path for the men to follow, strewn with broken bottles, litter and used condoms. Every few yards the men were able to catch a glimpse of the massage parlor through the oleander.

"What do you know about this place?" Bolan whispered.

"It's about as seedy as it looks," Deerson said. "They're licensed and all, but most guys coming here wind up with more than a massage."

"And you've never busted them?" Kissinger asked.

"Not until tonight," Deerson confessed.

"Why not?"

"Well, for starters, most of the clients are Air Force boys in from Edwards looking to get their horns clipped," Deerson said. "Hell, I was in the service and I know a man's needs. The other reason is the owners are Chinese."

"Any link to PACRIM?" Bolan said.

"Let me put it this way," Deerson said. "They opened for business a month after PACRIM leased out the air base."

"And people figured why look a gift horse in the mouth," Kissinger guessed.

Deerson nodded. "Tit for tat might be another way to put it."

Once they reached the end of the oleander, the three men came upon a gravel road that ran perpendicular to the railroad tracks. To their left, the road ran past a driveway leading to the rear parking lot of the massage parlor. Outside the dimly lit back entrance a tall, burly man the size of a sumo wrestler sat atop an old, discarded evaporative cooler. Perched on his lap was a petite, scantily dressed woman in her early twenties; compared to the guard, she looked like a ventriloquist's dummy. They were laughing together as she fondled the man's topknot. A few yards away there were three cars parked in the lot. The closest to the doorway was a year-old silver PT Cruiser with a vanity plate that read CRUZING. Parked alongside it was a dusty, open-topped military-issue jeep. At the far end of the lot, nestled between an overflowing trash Dumpster and the rear wall of the massage parlor, was the Chevy Camaro Bolan had encountered back on the highway.

"Now we're getting somewhere," Deerson whispered.

The men huddled close, but before they could discuss their next move the rear door to the massage parlor swung open. Out stepped an Air Force officer carrying a small leather attaché case. It seemed heavy in his grasp.

"That's the same case I saw in the Camaro," Bolan murmured.

The Air Force officer exchanged a few words with the doorman, then headed around the PT Cruiser to his jeep. The doorman nudged the girl off his lap and signaled for her to go inside. As he rose to his feet, the Camaro's engine thundered to life. The car lurched clear of the garbage Dumpster and screeched to a quick stop in front of the Jeep, hemming in the Air Force officer. The doorman, meanwhile, had reached to his side and pulled out a .22-caliber handgun tucked inside the waistband of his trousers. He took aim at the man in the jeep and was about to pull the trigger when Deerson fired first. A gunshot echoed through the parking lot. The doorman staggered into the PT Cruiser, bleeding from a bullet wound to the chest. As he sagged to the ground, the Air Force officer panicked and bolted from the jeep, only to be gunned down by a shot fired from inside the Camaro.

"Let's go!" Bolan hissed, bolting from cover.

Deerson and Kissinger were right behind him. As they charged toward the massage parlor, two more gunmen raced out of the back entrance. Like the doorman, they were Chinese. One was armed with a 9 mm Browning pistol, the other a sawed-off Remington 6-gauge. They traded shots with Kissinger and Deerson while Bolan beelined toward the Camaro.

The passenger inside the Chevy leaped out long enough to grab the attaché case from the fallen Air Force officer, then got back in the car as it surged forward, spitting gravel out from under its back tires.

Cutting sharply to its right, the Camaro plowed through a patch of weeds and was soon on the dirt road that led away from the massage parlor. Trying to keep up with it, Bolan veered to his right and bound onto an old stack of railroad ties stacked alongside the road. He leaped forward as the Camaro raced past, landing hard on the car's roof. The Desert Eagle fell from his grasp as he grappled for a handhold.

The Chevy's driver fishtailed down the road, trying to shake Bolan free. The Executioner managed to reach the sunroof, which was still open, giving him something to hang on to as the Chevy picked up speed. The road ramped upwards as it crossed the train tracks, sending the Camaro airborne. It came down hard on the other side. The impact failed to shake Bolan from the roof, however.

After another fifty yards, the driver turned onto a surfaced road flanked by rolling fields covered with tall grass. As the car accelerated, the gunman began to pound Bolan's fingers with the butt of his pistol. A stabbing pain ran up the soldier's arms as he struggled to keep his grip on the sunroof. Finally the gunman stopped his hammering and rose from his seat, poking his torso through the sunroof. He shifted his grip on the pistol and grinned savagely as he drew bead on Bolan's forehead.

Bolan thought fast and glanced past the shooter,

then ducked low against the roof as if the car were about to pass under a low-hanging tree branch. The shooter fell for the ruse and turned to look over his shoulder. However fleeting, the distraction gave Bolan enough time to shift his weight and lash out with his right hand, deflecting the shooter's aim just as he pulled the trigger. The shot thundered loudly past Bolan's ear.

The gunman swore, but before he could get off another shot, Bolan grabbed him tightly by the wrist and released his grip on the sunroof. Sliding backward, the soldier pulled the gunman with him, nearly yanking him up through the opening. His opponent lost his footing and toppled sideways into the driver, forcing him to lose control of the vehicle just as it was coming up on a bend in the road. The driver grappled with the steering wheel, but it was too late; the Camaro took the turn wide and veered sharply off the road.

Bolan let go of the gunman and fell away from the Chevy. The moment he hit the ground, he rolled forward, somersaulting to a stop less than two feet from a taut barbed-wire fence. The car, meanwhile, had already crashed sideways through the fence. Half-deafened by the gunshot, Bolan could barely hear the crunch of metal and shattering of glass as the Camaro cartwheeled, end-over-end, into the field.

Crawling in the grass, Bolan looked for something to arm himself with. He settled for a rock the size of a softball. Clutching it in his bloodied fingers, he rose to a crouch and slipped through the break in the fence, then followed the path the Camaro had forged through the field.

He finally reached the man who'd tried to kill him; he'd been thrown clear of the car and lay in a twisted heap, his neck snapped. His gun was nowhere to be seen. Bolan figured it had landed somewhere in the nearby grass, but he didn't intend to waste time searching for it in the dark. Instead, he continued another thirty yards into the meadow, finally reaching the Camaro, or at least what was left of it. The car had come to a rest, upside down, near the base of tall, gnarled oak tree. The roof had collapsed on the driver, pinning him behind the steering wheel. Like the other man, he was Chinese, in his late thirties, wearing cutoff Levi's jeans and a faded brown muscle shirt.

His ears still ringing, Bolan dropped the rock and crouched before the vehicle, staring past the driver into the darkened interior. The attaché case was wedged at angle between the front and rear seats. Reaching in, he worked the case free, then pulled it from the wreckage.

The attaché case was locked. Bolan grabbed the rock, slammed it against the clasps until the locks gave way, pried the lid open and stared inside. Every square inch of the case was packed with bound stacks of currency, all of them hundred-dollar bills. He had come across similar stashes several times before. He knew, without bothering to count, that he was looking at easily more than two hundred thousand dollars.

"Hold it right there!"

Even with the ringing in his ears, Bolan had no trouble hearing the shouted command. It was coming from somewhere behind him. He turned slowly and saw an Asian woman standing in the moonlight twenty yards from him, clutching a 9 mm Colt pistol. The gun was trained on him, and from the intent look in the woman's eyes and the authority in her voice, it was clear that, if need be, she would have no qualms about pulling the trigger.

CHAPTER FIVE

"Put it down," the woman demanded, gesturing at the attaché case. Behind her, two men appeared out of the darkness and flanked her. They, too, were armed.

"You heard her," the shorter gunman shouted angrily. "Put the fucking case down!"

"And move away from it!" the other man added.

Bolan quickly sized up the situation. He needed to level the playing field, quick. But how? The rock he'd used to crack open the attaché case lay on the ground a few yards away. Even if he could get to it, what was he supposed to do, bean one of the gunmen, then hope there was enough money in the valise to stop a bullet or two while he charged the others? Not likely. There had to be another way.

"Quit stalling!" the woman ordered. "Move it! Now!"

Bolan shifted the case from one hand to the other while taking a half step toward the higher grass to his right. The blades were nearly three feet high. If he were to dive into them, he thought, there was a chance they'd lose him for a second or two. It wasn't much, but it seemed like a better option than trying to take them on with the rock.

"You didn't say please," Bolan joked nonchalantly, hoping the wisecrack might throw them off guard. It didn't work. The shorter gunman fired into the dirt at Bolan's feet.

"Where do you think you're going?" he snapped.

"The woman told me to move," Bolan countered. "I'm moving."

"Listen, smartass," the gunman snarled, "this is the FBI you're talking to! Keep mouthing off, and we'll blast your sorry ass from here to Waco!"

The woman glared at the man and was about to say something, then checked herself and turned back to Bolan, who was now grinning with relief.

"FBI?" he said.

"That's right." Keeping her gun pointed at Bolan, the woman grabbed a badge clipped to her belt and held it out before her. In the dark Bolan could see only a faint, doorknob-sized glint of metal. Not that he was about dispute her credentials.

"Small world," he told her. "I'm with Justice."

"What?"

"Justice Department," Bolan said. He set down the valise and held his arms out at his sides. "Special Agent Michael Belasko. ID's in my shirt pocket.''

The woman delegated the task to the man on her right, then turned and whispered angrily to the agent who'd fired at Bolan's feet. The soldier couldn't make out the words, but he knew a reprimand when he saw one.

The agent approaching him was white, fortyish, with a Marine buzz cut, and dark brown eyes that matched the color of his ill-fitting suit.

''This better not be a trick,'' he warned Bolan.

''If it was, I'd already have your gun by now.''

The man smirked. ''Nice try,'' he said, ''but I don't goose as easily as my partner. Now, keep your hands out.''

The man pulled the ID from Bolan's pocket and inspected it in the moonlight before handing it to the woman. She looked it over, as well, then handed it back to Bolan and motioned for him to put his arms down.

''What brings you to Collier Springs, Mr. Belasko?'' she asked.

''I came here for the waters,'' Bolan responded, straight-faced.

The woman smiled faintly. ''Anybody who can recite from *Casablanca* is all right in my book.'' She took a step forward and shook Bolan's hand. ''Jen Li, senior agent, Sacramento field office.''

Bolan took in the woman. She was a few years younger than him, short and thin, with straight dark hair cropped at her shoulders. She had prominent cheekbones and large, wide-set eyes. She also had better fashion sense than either of her partners; her pantsuit seemed tailor fit, accentuating her trim, toned figure. She carried herself with the straight-forward confidence Bolan liked in a woman.

The woman quickly introduced him to the other two agents. The man with the buzz cut was named Seitzer; the one with the temper was Hunter, a small, slight man with the pinched features of someone who'd just bitten into a particularly sour lemon. He chewed at his bottom lip as he continued to glare at Bolan.

"I apologize for the short tempers," Li went on, "but we just had two months of undercover work go belly up on us, and it's not sitting very well at the moment."

"The massage parlor," Bolan guessed.

The woman nodded tersely. "We were on stakeout there when all hell broke loose," she explained. "We were headed for the parking lot when we saw you joyriding on top of the Camaro. We decided to tag along and find out what you were up to."

"Trust me, it was no joyride."

"I was joking," Li said. "The Camaro was our target vehicle."

"That doesn't surprise me."

Bolan glanced toward the road and saw a weather-beaten panel truck parked near the break in the fence. He remembered seeing the vehicle earlier, parked in the strip mall down the block from Orient Expressions.

"How about a ride back?" he asked Li. "I've got people caught up in a firefight there."

"So do we," Li responded. "Or did, I should say. They already checked in. Things are under control."

"Casualties?"

"They said something about a sheriff getting hit, but it was nothing serious."

"And the people at the massage parlor?"

"They didn't fare as well," Li reported. "Four dead and counting."

"I'd still like to get back," Bolan said.

"In a second," the woman told him. "I want to check a few things around here first."

"Fair enough."

The woman fished through her pockets for a penlight and shone its beam on the contents of the attaché case.

"A lot of cash," Bolan said.

"Sure is. I was expecting a hundred grand, tops, but there's more than that."

Bolan nodded. "I figure a quarter mill. You have any idea what it was for?"

"I wish. We've got a bug in the parlor, but all we were able to pick up was that this guy from the Air Force was ready to deal. What he was dealing, I don't know. That's why we were counting on the bust."

"Whatever it was, he was paid off, then knocked off so the guys in the Camaro could get the money back," Bolan said. "And, incidentally, it wasn't their money to begin with."

"What are you talking about?" Li asked.

As they headed toward the Camaro, Bolan quickly explained how he'd spotted the valise earlier when his car had broken down on the highway. Li listened intently, committing the details to memory.

"So, basically," she reiterated once he'd finished, "these folks committed two separate murders getting their hands on the same heap of cash."

"That's how it plays for me," Bolan said. "You have any idea who the guy in the Mercedes might have been?"

Li shook her head. "He was obviously after some kind of military secrets. And I doubt he had any ties with the Falun Gong, especially the branch here. Here they're just a handful of starry-eyed college girls."

"So I've heard," Bolan said.

Li told Seitzer and Hunter to stay with the money, then told Bolan, "Let's have a look at the car."

Bolan followed her to the Camaro. Once they reached it, Jen Li crouched over and flashed her light on the driver's face.

"Know him?" Bolan asked.

"No." Li stood. "Not the guy who was thrown clear, either. We've got a pretty good idea who they're hooked up with, though."

"I'm guessing street gang," Bolan said.

"Close," Li responded. "They're *ma jai.*"

"Little soldiers," Bolan said.

Li nodded. "That's the literal translation. 'Goon squad' might be a better word for them. They're muscle for one of the Hong Kong triads."

Bolan frowned. "We're a hundred miles from the nearest Chinatown. What are they doing out here in the middle of nowhere?"

"We're only an hour's drive from Edwards Air Force Base from here," Li reminded Bolan as they rejoined Seitzer and Hunter. "That alone upgrades this place from 'middle of nowhere.'"

"You're talking espionage," Bolan said. "I thought the triads were strictly into the vice rackets."

Li shook her head. "They've been branching out for years. We think they set up shop here so they could do some spying for Beijing."

"Out of the massage parlor?"

"I'll explain in a minute."

Li assigned Seitzer to stay behind with the Camaro and the two fallen *ma jai,* then led Bolan and Hunter back toward the panel truck. On the way, she told Bolan, "We think this gang is being financed by the MSS and PSB."

"I know the MSS," Bolan said. "Beijing's answer to the KGB, right?"

"More or less." Once they reached the truck, Li took the wheel, gesturing for Bolan to ride up front beside her. Hunter took the back, stashing the attaché case among an array of surveillance and eavesdropping equipment.

"The Ministry of State Security handles most of China's intelligence operations," Li explained. "PSB's the Public Security Bureau. They do a big business under the table smuggling people into the States. From what I've seen, it looks like they're bringing the masseuses in from Guangzhou and Shanghai."

"Is this gang connected to that PACRIM facility on the other side of town?" Bolan asked.

"We think so." She paused at a stop sign and glanced at Bolan. "Were you in on that shoot-out earlier?"

Bolan nodded. "And just so you know, they're smuggling in more than just masseuses."

As they continued down the road, Bolan told her about his ill-fated ride on the rails. At the mention of the illegal immigrants who'd died inside a locked cargo container, Li's gaze hardened and her fingers tightened around the steering wheel. She muttered a curse under her breath.

"I knew it!" she said bitterly, eyeing Hunter in the rearview mirror. "I knew we should have focused more on PACRIM!"

"PACRIM was a bird in the bush," Hunter responded. "We had a lock on the massage parlor. Besides, undocumented workers is an INS problem, not ours."

"Sixty people dead in a railcar makes it our problem, too, and I'm not just talking about crossing state lines," Li countered. "If we'd spent more time on surveillance at PACRIM, maybe we could've saved them."

"Hindsight," Hunter said.

Li slammed her fist on the steering wheel with frustration. "I knew it!" she repeated.

Bolan changed the subject. "I take it you were focused on the massage parlor because of the number of enlisted men showing up there."

The woman nodded, composing herself. "We were concerned about the pillow talk. It's happened at parlors near other bases, especially when these girls build up a clientele of regulars."

"Loose lips sink ships," Hunter called out from the back seat.

"Well, as far as what went down tonight goes," Bolan ventured, "if that officer came out of the massage parlor with the money, you've got to figure he left behind whatever he was selling. Hopefully we'll get our hands on it and start piecing this all together."

Back in the rear of the truck, Hunter lit a cigarette and blew a cloud of smoke, muttering, "I sure as hell hope so."

CHAPTER SIX

When they returned to the massage parlor, Bolan and the others saw that two backup sheriff's department squad cars had arrived on the scene along with a paramedic's van. An unmarked Buick sedan belonging to the second FBI team taking part in the stakeout was parked in the side road running past the parlor driveway. Li pulled up behind the sedan and got out to confer with her associates. Bolan, meanwhile, strode across the parking lot to the medivan. The rear doors were open and Sheriff Deerson was sitting up on one of the gurneys, grimacing as a paramedic tended to a gunshot wound in his right side.

"You missed quite a party," Deerson told Bolan. "Regular gunfight at the OK Corral."

"I had my share of thrills," Bolan replied. "How bad's that bullet wound?"

"I'll live," Deerson stated, "which is more than I can say for those sorry shits."

Bolan glanced in the direction Deerson was pointing and saw that FBI agent Hunter had joined two
deputies and another paramedic standing alongside
two of the men felled during the shoot-out. There
were three other fatalities scattered elsewhere in the
parking lot. Bolan recognized the bodies of the doorman and the slain Air Force officer, but from where
he was standing it was hard to get a make on the
other victims.

"Your buddy's fine," Deerson assured him.
"He's inside, not a scratch on him... Yeow! Easy
with those chopsticks, Betty."

The paramedic, a petite woman in her late thirties,
glanced up from the medical tweezers she had half
buried between Deerson's ribs. "Sorry, Kit," she
told him, "but the bullet's in reach and I want to
get it out so we can stop the bleeding."

"I know, I know. Just remember those are my
vitals you're poking through, not yesterday's chow
mein." Deerson looked away from Betty's handiwork and eyed Li, who'd just crossed over to join
him and Bolan. "I saw you speeding past here while
the fur was still flying."

"Sheriff, this is Jen Li," Bolan said, handling in-
troductions. "FBI."

"More Bureau people, huh?" Deerson said as he
shook the woman's hand. "Your colleagues were a

little slow on the take, but once they showed up they helped turned things around here.''

''I'm glad,'' Li said.

''I've seen that truck of yours around here a few times the past couple weeks. I take it you've been on some kind of assignment I wasn't supposed to know about, right?''

''There was a reason we couldn't bring you in,'' Li said.

''There's always a reason, isn't there?'' Deerson drawled sarcastically.

''I'll let you two sort things out,'' Bolan said.

''Before you do, you might want this back.'' Deerson winced as he reached behind him, then handed Bolan his Desert Eagle. ''My guys found it out near where you hopped the Camaro. Nice piece.''

''Thanks.'' Bolan took the gun and moved away from the van. He flashed his ID to one of the deputies guarding the bullet-riddled rear entrance to the massage parlor. The deputy stepped to one side, and Bolan passed through a beaded curtain into a drab-looking reception area that smelled of incense and cheap perfume. The woman who'd earlier been sitting on the doorman's lap was off in the corner. She puffed nervously on a cigarette as another of the deputies questioned her. When Bolan asked about

Kissinger, the deputy pointed to a hallway off to his right.

"They're all in the rec room," he said. "Last door on your right."

Bolan nodded and strode down the hall, passing half a dozen small rooms unfurnished except for lamps and mattresses set on the floor. The rec room was considerably larger, the size of a one-car garage. A middle-aged woman in a pale red pantsuit hovered near four other masseuses on the far side of a table tennis table taking up the middle of the room. The girls were all Chinese, young, in their early twenties, provocatively dressed in halters and miniskirts. Most of them had been crying and their faces were smeared with running mascara. Across the room from them, John Kissinger was talking with two men next to a row of vending machines. The men, both old enough to be the masseuses' fathers, paced anxiously as they answered questions. Bolan guessed they were customers who'd picked the wrong time to come looking for a good rubdown.

"This doesn't have to get out, does it?" one of them was asking Kissinger as Bolan joined them. "My being here?"

Kissinger nodded at Bolan, then told the man, "You'll have to take that up with the sheriff's people."

"Shit," the man grumbled, throwing up his arms

in exasperation. "That's it. I'm dead. Why don't you just shoot me dead right now and save my wife the bullets?"

"Stay put," Kissinger advised both men, as well as the women. He led Bolan back out into the hallway.

"Looks like you came through in one piece, too," he said.

"Bolan one, Camaro zero," Bolan reported.

He quickly related how he'd managed to bail from the Camaro before it crashed off the road, then he filled Kissinger in on the contents of the attaché case and the FBI's botched stakeout. Once Kissinger heard that the Bureau had planned to bust some sort of espionage transaction, he nodded slowly.

"Okay," he said, "now that makes sense."

"What's that?"

"None of the masseuses was offering any information until I mentioned the INS and green cards," he explained. "Then a couple of them starting spilling so fast it was hard to keep up with them.

"Bottom line's this—one of the girls said that Air Force guy who got shot out back was a regular customer of hers. Apparently last week he got a call on his cell phone while they were having a 'session.' He kicked her out of the room while he took the call, but she stayed near the door and eavesdropped and heard something about arrangements for some kind of swap. He mentioned money a couple times and set up a rendezvous for tonight, saying he'd bring the plans.''

''What plans?''

Kissinger shook his head. ''She says she doesn't know. But if he was selling them for as much money as was in that suitcase, you can bet they were damn important.''

''Let me guess,'' Bolan said, starting to understand what had happened. ''This girl knows the guys who bushwhacked the Mercedes.''

Kissinger nodded. ''One of them's her boyfriend. She told him what she'd heard and the next thing she knew he was off to Vegas with a couple of his buddies. They stayed the night and came back with the Camaro. He said he won it in a poker game. She didn't believe him but was afraid to say anything, 'cause apparently he's always looking for an excuse to rough her up.''

''Some boyfriend.''

''Yeah. Anyway, she says he showed up here with the attaché case, and when the Air Force guy came by he took him into one of the vacant rooms for a couple minutes.''

''And when the Air Force guy came out, he was the one with the case,'' Bolan guessed.

''Right. She claims she doesn't know what went down, but it's a safe bet this boyfriend of hers passed himself off as a middleman for the guy in the Mercedes, handled the swap, then sent the Air Force guy on his merry way.''

''Knowing he'd get clipped before he left the parking lot.''

Kissinger nodded again. ''Would've worked like a charm, too, if we hadn't come along and spoiled things.''

''And where's this boyfriend of hers now?'' Bolan asked. ''With the deputies?''

''No such luck,'' Kissinger said. ''He slipped through the cracks during all the shooting.''

''Taking the plans with him.''

''Afraid so,'' Kissinger said. ''On the bright side, this girlfriend thinks she has a pretty good idea where we might find him.''

GHOST RANCH, located two miles east of the business loop linking Collier Springs to Highway 75, was far and away the small town's most bumbling attempt to foster tourism. Twenty years ago, the three-acre site, cradled in a valley between the north and south ranges of the San Cordoba Mountains, had become the final resting place for an assortment of ramshackle clapboard buildings scavenged from old mining sites up in the nearby hills and elsewhere around the county. The idea had been to create a reasonable facsimile of an Old West ghost town that might appeal to visitors seeking a break during long trips between Los Angeles and points northward. Along with the old buildings, there had been a motel, several open-air concession stands, and a trading post offering the usual assortment of trinkets and curios.

When the ranch first opened, hired performers dressed in Old West regalia would stage simulated bank heists, as well as mock shoot-outs at high noon just outside the motel. The problem was that between Memorial Day and Labor Day—the height of the tourist season—the temperature at high noon in the desert around Collier Springs topped out at a 120 degrees.

Further, several times a week brisk winds barreling through the mountain pass would stir up the desert and pelt the site with the force of an industrial-strength sandblaster, toppling concession stands and forcing people into rickety, uninsulated buildings that were about as accommodating a refuge from the heat as a blast furnace. Living up to its name, Ghost Ranch was shut down halfway into its second season and left to vandals and the elements. Both proceeded to lay waste to most of the structures, squashing follow-up plans to rent the facility out to motion-picture companies as a film site. Now all that was left of Ghost Ranch was a collection of rubble and the skeletal cinder-block remains of the motel complex, where a crumbling, sun-faded billboard spoke of better days when the facility offered Reasonable Rates—Guaranteed Ghost-Free!

It was nearly three in the morning when the FBI's undercover panel truck turned onto the two-lane dirt road leading to the ranch. Jen Li was at the wheel again, driving slowly to minimize the amount of dust raised in the truck's wake. Bolan was back up front, as well, while John Kissinger sat in back with Agent Hunter and two sheriff's deputies, Hank Yarborough and Stan Cantrell.

Yarborough and Cantrell had just come from the PACRIM facility, where they'd helped search the cargo containers that had just been transported to the railyards from Long Beach. Apparently there'd been a second container used to smuggle undocumented workers across the Mojave. The second group had been more fortunate, if only relatively. There'd been only forty-two people herded into their container as opposed to the fifty-six Bolan had encountered, and while crossing the desert they'd somehow managed to crack open their door and create some sort of makeshift vent in the roof, providing them with a semblance of cross ventilation. Still, nineteen of the forty-two immigrants had emerged from their ordeal in body bags, deprived of the chance to so much as set foot on their would-be Promised Land.

As for the other containers, for the most part

they'd contained legitimate goods: computer game consoles, toy components like those Bolan had seen at the hangar sweatshop and a wealth of Konkemon trading cards and related paraphernalia. One hold, however, had been packed floor to roof with contraband. Yarborough had been in on the discovery and claimed there'd been nearly four million dollars' worth of heroin and—even more troubling to Bolan and the FBI agents—nineteen crates of Chinese-made AK-47s and another fourteen filled with ammunition for the assault rifles.

The latter find, at least on the surface, appeared to substantiate newfound concerns that PACRIM was operating in collusion, not only with the Young Boxers, but also Communist China's People's Liberation Army. The weapons smuggling mirrored a similar incident several years earlier in which a Chinese-run storage facility in Oakland had been busted just prior to delivering more than two thousand AK-47s into the hands of L.A. street gangs.

Cantrell and Yarborough had helped search the industrial park for other incriminating contraband, but at the time they'd been called away the best they'd been able to come up with was evidence of substandard working conditions, an OSHA violation good for little more than a judicial slap on the wrists. PACRIM officials, meanwhile, were steadfastly denying any complicity in the transportation of either the contraband or undocumented workers. A spokes-man from their law firm had even gone so far as to suggest PACRIM was being framed as part of a ra-cially motivated smear campaign by a Collier Springs–based white supremacist group.

"I didn't know whether to laugh or puke when I heard that one," Cantrell said, recalling the lawyer's hastily called press conference. "I've heard of gall, but that pretty much takes the cake."

"I don't think they're fooling anybody with that kind of talk," Li said as she drove. "And if we keep looking we're bound to turn up some more contra-band we can nail them with."

"Maybe," Yarborough responded, strapping on one of the Kevlar vests Agent Hunter was passing around. "But, who knows, maybe they ship out any drugs and weapons as soon as they're unloaded. I mean, they've got their own trucking fleet, so why not?"

"Even if that's the case," Bolan countered, "they can't dodge the alien-smuggling charges. I saw at least three dozen of them holed up in one of the hangars. Throw in their testimony with that of the people who survived that ride through the desert, and we've got PACRIM dead to rights."

"Thank God for small favors," Li responded.

"One thing I don't get," Yarborough said. "If they're bringing in that much smack and that many weapons on a regular basis, why go to all the trouble of shipping it up here from Long Beach? Why not just unload the stuff in L.A. and be done with it?''

''I'm sure they're doing that, too,'' Hunter interjected. ''But there's a market for that shit all the way up and down the coast. And I'm not talking just big cities. Sometimes supply and demand in small towns jacks up profits even higher than what they can wring out of L.A. or 'Frisco.''

''I hear that,'' Yarborough said. ''Hell, from the sounds of it, these Boxer punks are probably the same guys who've been running drugs out of the north side the past couple years.''

''We'll find out soon enough,'' Bolan said.

Li pulled off the road and eased the truck to a stop next to the abandoned motel's registration office. The men had their guns ready and were peering out the truck's windows for signs of a reception committee. The complex, however, seemed still and deserted. Once out of the truck, the group quickly split up. Cantrell and Yarborough headed for the rear of the complex, while Kissinger and Hunter started with the units closest to the road.

Li and Bolan, meanwhile, cautiously made their way toward the registration office. The windows had been long shattered and the front door was missing, allowing the hot evening breeze to moan its way through the lobby. Bolan entered first, sidestepping a clutter of fast-food wrappers, crushed beer cans and old cassette tapes warped by the desert heat. Li shone her flashlight on the floor and then the walls. The latter were covered with graffiti. A few gang signatures were mixed in with the usual profanities and crudely drawn pictures of men and women with grossly exaggerated genitalia.

"I think this is going cost them their five-star rating," Li said.

Bolan spotted something and gestured for Li to shine her light across the room.

"Looks like this place isn't ghost free after all," she said, leading Bolan to the far wall, where someone had painted a row of life-sized silhouettes with white house paint. The figures were dotted with perforations, mostly around the head and chest area. Closer inspection revealed that the holes had been created by bullets and buckshot.

"Indoor shooting range," Bolan surmised.

Li flashed her light on the floor until she came upon a scattered sprawl of spent casings. She picked one up and sniffed it. "These weren't fired all that long ago," she said.

"They probably took a little target practice getting ready for tonight."

Bolan and Li quickly surveyed the rest of the lobby. Amid the graffiti on the wall near the front window, Bolan spotted a series of smaller hand-written inscriptions. One word jumped out at him.

"Mercedes," he whispered under his breath.

Li shone her light on the handwriting. "Looks like a license plate number next to it."

Bolan recognized the number. "Belongs to the car they bushwhacked back out on the highway," he said. "It must've been called in to them here before they headed out to that rest stop."

"Makes sense," Li said.

Bolan quickly realized he was looking at the same information—make of the car and license number—he'd seen earlier on the business card taken from the gunman Billy Grubb had killed out by the highway with a frying pan. Bolan stepped back and looked out the window. He could see the panel truck, as well as the dirt road leading back to the highway.

"This must double as some sort of lookout post," he speculated. "Whoever's on duty probably has a cell phone and uses the wall for notes."

"Makes sense," Li said. She shifted the flashlight and looked back over the graffiti. Some of it was written in Chinese.

"Interesting," she murmured.

"What's it say?"

"This one says 'America will fall,'" Li said, pointing at the wall. "And this one over here could probably be best translated as 'The Dalai Lama sucks.'''

"So we've got some revolutionaries on our hands," Bolan said.

"Yeah, how about that. But, then, they're just taking their cues from the original Boxers. You know, 'Stick it to the foreign interlopers.'''

"I can see them pulling that song-and-dance on Americans," Bolan said, "but calling the Dalai Lama a foreigner is a bit of a stretch."

"They're not about to split hairs," Li told him. "If the MSS sics them on somebody, they're going to attack without asking too many questions. Hell, they turned on their own people during Tiananmen Square."

"The Boxers?" Bolan said. "They were in on that?"

Li nodded. "Not only were they in on it, but as a reward the ones who were most brutal got first crack at setting up their own turf overseas. Naturally most of them opted to come to the States. It wouldn't surprise me if some of them wound up here in Collier Springs."

"I don't know about that," Bolan said. "The guys in the Camaro looked like they were probably in diapers during Tiananmen Square."

"Like I said, they were *ma jai*," Li said. "Little soldiers. The guys who were in on Tiananmen don't need to get their hands dirty anymore. They're like generals—they call the shots, then sit back and let others do the grunt work.''

''Which means we aren't likely to find them hiding out in this hellhole,'' Bolan guessed.

''No, they've probably got million-dollar homes up in the hills somewhere around here,'' Li said. ''As a matter of fact, tonight we were hoping the Camaro would lead us to some higher-ups. Of course, with all the commotion those guys are probably long gone by now.''

''That's why your friend Hunter was so hot under the collar when you guys first caught up with me, right?'' Bolan said.

Li nodded. ''Nobody likes it when the big ones get away.''

''What can I say? If we'd known you guys were on the scene, we probably would've thrown in with you.''

''What's done is done,'' Li said. ''If we can find this guy and get our hands on whatever he bought off that Air Force officer, it'll be consolation.''

''Tell you what. If we find this guy, I'll see to it that he leads us to some higher-ups.''

''How would you do that?''

''You don't want to know,'' Bolan told her.

''Try me,'' the woman said.

Before Bolan could explain, he was interrupted by the sound of gunfire outside the building.

CHAPTER SEVEN

Agent Hunter was down.

When Bolan and Li caught up with him, behind the last of the motel units, the short man was crumpled in the sand, palm pressed to his neck, trying to staunch the flow of blood from a sniper's bullet that had nicked an artery after ripping through his trachea. One look and Bolan knew Hunter wasn't going to make it.

Kissinger was crouched behind a concrete planter several yards away, firing into the desert with his Government Model 1911-A pistol.

"Shooters on the ridge!" he called out to Bolan and Li.

As if in response to Kissinger's warning, a spray of gunfire whipped up the sand around them. Bolan dived for cover behind the planter next to Kissinger. Li, however, remained alongside her downed colleague, placing her hand over his to provide additional pressure against the bullet wound.

Hunter, his strength ebbing, weakly shook his head and was mouthing the word "go" when another bullet struck him, this time in the thigh. He twitched in pain.

"I need some help!" Li cried out.

"You can't help him!" Kissinger shouted back at her. "Get out of the line of fire!"

"I said I need some help!" the woman responded angrily.

Bolan exchanged a look with Kissinger, then rushed back to Hunter's side, grabbing him under the arms. "Keep a hand on that wound," he said. "I'll move him."

"Lemme give you a hand," Deputy Cantrell called out, rushing to join the fray. Together, he and Bolan hauled the wounded agent toward the planter. Li followed alongside, her fingers turning crimson with Hunter's blood.

"Hang in there," she shouted over the crackle of Kissinger's pistol.

Hunter couldn't hear her. He went slack in the men's grasp and when they set him down, his eyes rolled upward and his blood began to drain into the sand. Li pulled her hand away and stared at him.

"He was gone," Bolan told her. "There was nothing we could—"

"I know, I know!" She wiped her hands on her

pants, then pulled out her gun. "Let's get these bastards!"

Deputy Yarborough, meanwhile, had caught up and taken up position behind an overturned, rust-eaten vending machine ten yards from the planter. He fired up into the hills, then ducked low as return fire drummed against the old dispenser's metal shell.

"There's at least two of them," he called out. "And it's a pretty safe bet they've got scopes."

"No shit," Kissinger muttered, dropping lower as bullets danced along the top of the planter. "We're gonna need to get closer."

"Yeah, good luck with that," Cantrell said, scanning the terrain leading to the ridge. "There's nothing between us and them but sand and tumbleweeds."

Li quickly assessed the situation and said, "I'll get the truck."

"I'll come with you," Bolan told her. He turned to Kissinger and Cantrell. "You guys try to fan out. With any luck, we'll be able to keep them distracted long enough for you to close in."

"It's worth a try," Kissinger said, reloading his Colt.

Bolan and Li waited out another round from the snipers, then bolted from the planter, zigzagging past the motel units to where the truck was parked.

"Let me drive," Bolan suggested.

"I can handle it."

"They see us coming, they're going to draw a bead on the driver," Bolan said. "I've probably got a little more wheel experience."

"My truck, my call," Li retorted, taking the driver's seat.

Bolan could see arguing was pointless. He opened the passenger door but remained outside the truck and started to unfasten his bulletproof vest. "You got any rope in there?"

"I don't think so. Why?"

"I want to cover as much of the windshield as possible," Bolan said. "I know it'll cut your visibility, but it's a fair trade-off."

"Good idea." Li leaned into the back of the truck, then handed Bolan a roll of duct tape and began to take off her own vest. "You can use mine, too."

Bolan quickly laid his vest out flat across the windshield, then secured it in place with the duct tape, making sure to position one of the armpit holes at Li's eye level. Once she passed her vest to him, he repeated the procedure, covering the glass in front of the passenger seat.

"Looks like hell, but it just might work," she said wryly as Bolan rejoined her.

"We're still going to be vulnerable," Bolan told

her, "so let's not push our luck any more than we have to."

Li backed away from the registration office and circled around the nearest motel unit. Once she could see the planter, she straightened the steering wheel and pressed down on the accelerator. The truck raced forward past the other units and was soon out in the open, passing the body of the slain agent.

"I know Hunter could be a pain in the ass," Li observed, "but he was a good agent."

"I'm sure he was."

"He's got a wife and—"

Li's voice broke off as the truck came under attack. As anticipated, the snipers had gone after the driver, and most of their slugs thudded harmlessly into the vests taped across the windshield. A couple shots found their way past the Kevlar plates, however, and crashed through the glass. One buried itself in the dashboard; the other zipped past Bolan's shoulder into the rear of the truck.

"You okay?" Li said, unable to take her eyes off the desert before them. She'd begun jockeying the steering wheel back and forth, veering across the hard-packed sand.

"I'm fine," Bolan said. "Keep after them."

He glanced out the side window and spied Kissinger and Yarborough off to his right, spaced twenty yards apart in a shallow arroyo, ready to make their next move. There was no sign of Cantrell, but Bolan assumed the deputy was advancing somewhere to the left. He shifted his gaze and stared out through the makeshift peephole on his side of the windshield. Up on the ridge he spotted one of the shooters. "To your right," he told Li.

The woman changed course, keeping her foot on the accelerator. Another volley pounded the truck. The shooters had apparently wised up to the protected windshield and lowered their aim, going for the tires and engine compartment. Moments after, Bolan heard a loud pop outside the vehicle. Suddenly Li was fighting for control of the steering wheel.

"Right front tire!" she shouted, letting up on the gas as she tried to compensate for the blowout. The truck's weight and momentum were working against her, however. Veering sharply to one side, the truck went into a brief skid, then tipped onto its side. Li was thrown from her seat. She slammed into Bolan, then fell on top of him as the vehicle groaned to a stop. Both Bolan and Li were dazed, but neither had lost consciousness.

"Okay, you can drive now," Li told Bolan as they untangled themselves.

"You did fine," he told her. "Let's get out of here, though. I don't like the smell of that gas."

Li rolled free of Bolan and crawled between the front seats to the rear of the truck. Bolan yanked out his .44 and followed her. The gas fumes were getting stronger. The soldier scrambled past the woman, forced the rear doors open, then waved her out. "Hurry!"

Li tumbled out through the opening, with Bolan right behind her. Once on their feet, they broke into a run, trying to put as much distance as possible between them and the truck. Gunshots thundered around them, but they weren't coming from the snipers. Kissinger, Cantrell and Yarborough were all firing uphill as they charged the ridgeline. No shots were being returned.

"Looks like we've got them on the run," Bolan called out to the others. "Stay on them!"

He started up the rise. Li hobbled behind, favoring her right leg.

"Sprained my ankle," she called out. "Go ahead. I'll catch—"

Her voice was drowned out by a fierce explosion. Behind them, the truck had turned into a fireball, sending flaming bits of shrapnel flying in all directions. Bolan dodged one of the shards, then glanced over his shoulder. Li had thrown herself to the ground and the shrapnel had missed her. He started back to help her, but she waved him off.

"Go on," she repeated. "Don't let them get away!"

Desert Eagle in hand, Bolan rushed uphill, then dropped to the sand and crawled the last few yards to the ridgeline. One of the snipers was less than twenty feet away. He was no longer a threat, however; he lay facedown in the sand, his rifle on the ground beside him.

Bolan was approaching the downed gunman when Kissinger cleared the ridge behind him. "Looks like we nailed one of them, eh?" he called out.

Bolan turned the dead man over. Like the men in the Camaro, he was Chinese, in his twenties.

"I don't think he's the boyfriend of that masseuse," Kissinger said. "She said he was taller and had his left ear pierced."

Bolan quickly frisked the man. "No plans, either," he said.

He and Kissinger stared out at the sprawl of flatland leading away from the ridge, but in the moonlight they could see only more sand and tumbleweeds.

"Maybe he's up in the hills," Kissinger suggested, pointing to a stretch of small mountains more than a mile away.

Bolan shook his head. "He couldn't have gotten that far on foot, and I don't see any tire tracks. No, he's got to be around here somewhere."

They continued scanning the terrain until the others caught up with them. Li could barely walk and was leaning on Cantrell's arm for support. Bolan suggested she rest while he and the others checked the area for the second sniper. For once, the woman didn't protest.

The men fanned out, covering as much ground as quickly as possible, keeping their guard up for signs of other gunmen. Kissinger was the first to come upon a clue as to where they might have disappeared.

"Over here!" he called out, standing amid a thick clot of tumbleweeds.

Bolan jogged over just as Kissinger was pulling aside what, at first sight, seemed nothing more than a discarded pallet, one side of which was layered with tar paper. The skid, however, had been deliberately placed in the tumbleweeds, Bolan realized, for use as a crude covering for a gaping, manhole-sized opening in the desert floor.

"An old well," Kissinger said, directing his flashlight into the cavity. "Sucker's got rungs leading into it."

"CAME UP BLANK," Cantrell said a few minutes later as he and Yarborough returned from searching the flatland atop the ridge. "We spooked a couple coyotes, but that's about it."

"We thought we were onto something here," Kissinger said, indicating the well, "but when I flashed a light down all we saw was some trash."

"Son of a bitch," Yarborough said, peering into the hole. "I thought they'd plugged up this baby years ago."

"You know about it, then," Bolan said.

Yarborough nodded. "Goes back to the old mining days. I remember hearing how workers at the ranch would sneak up here to smoke reefer on their breaks."

"What about the rungs?" Bolan asked.

"I'm not positive," Yarborough said, "but I think the miners put 'em in after the well dried up."

"Hold on," Cantrell interjected. "The way I heard it, the well went dry because the miners tunneled into it by mistake and drained it."

Bolan looked at the deputy. "You're saying the well leads to a mine shaft?"

"If it's the one I'm thinking about, yeah," Cantrell said. "Only I thought it'd been plugged up, too."

"Well, for now let's assume it's been unplugged," Bolan said. "If any of the snipers went down there, do we have them trapped or is there another way out?"

"Hell, I don't know. I guess we'd have 'em pinned in," Cantrell said.

He turned to the other deputy. "Or do you think maybe it leads back to the main entrance?"

"Probably be a good idea to check it out." Yarborough directed Bolan's attention toward the hills in the distance. "The old base camp's up there somewhere near that butte on your right. I know for a fact they closed off the entrance a few years back after some guys hauled a gal up there for a gang bang. But, shit, if this one's come unplugged, who knows, maybe the main one's been opened back up, too."

"Why don't you two go check it out," Bolan suggested. "We'll try the well here and see what we come up with."

"Sounds like a plan."

Cantrell turned to Yarborough, whose uniform was as drenched with sweat as his face. "Up for another hike there, Hank?"

"Ready as I'll ever be." Yarborough sighed. "But when this is all over, I think we're gonna need to have a talk with the boss about combat pay."

As the deputies headed off, Bolan glanced over at Jen Li. She was back on her feet, staring past the cloud of smoke rising from the decimated panel truck. As he drew closer, Bolan saw that her eyes were actually on the motel complex. There was a concerned expression on her face.

"I'm thinking about the coyotes," she confessed. "I don't want them getting to Hunter."

"It should only take a few minutes for us to check out the well," Bolan told her. "We can head back afterward."

"Why don't you guys can go ahead and do the well. I'm going to start back."

"You're joking, right?" Bolan said, incredulous. "You can barely stand up, much less walk downhill and cross a hundred yards of desert."

"We'll see about that." Li took a few small steps, wincing whenever her injured foot touched the ground. "Okay, so it'll take a little longer than I'd like. I'm still going. I owe Hunter that much."

Bolan stared at the woman, then strode over to the fallen sniper, helping himself to the man's rifle. He handed it to her. "For the coyotes," he told her. "You can keep an eye out for them through the nightscope. A shot or two in their direction should be enough to keep them away from the body."

"It'll make a decent crutch, too," the woman said, holding the rifle by the barrel and stabbing it butt-first into the sand. She leaned into it, shifting weight off her bad ankle. Satisfied it would do the trick, she started toward the ridge. After a couple steps she glanced back at Bolan.

"Any laughing behind my back and you'll find

out what a good shot I am," she warned. She was smiling when she said it.

Bolan grinned back at her. "Won't happen," he assured her. "We'll be too far down in the well to see you."

"Watch yourself down there."

"Will do."

Bolan watched Li limp toward the ridgeline, then sauntered back to the well. Kissinger was waiting for him.

"Real trouper, that one," he said, staring at Li.

"That she is." Bolan stared down the well, then told Kissinger, "I'll go first. Keep a light on me."

"Done."

Kissinger flicked on a flashlight he'd taken from the panel truck when they'd first arrived at the motel. He shone the beam into the shaft as Bolan lowered himself down the first set of rungs. The rungs were old but still firmly anchored into the side of the well and supported Bolan's weight. He kept his Desert Eagle out, concerned at what—or who—might be waiting for him once he reached the mine shaft. The temperature dropped with each step he took down, but the air was also musty and stagnant, providing little in the way of relief from the late-evening heat. Every few steps, Bolan stopped to listen, but all he could hear was his own breathing and the sound of Kissinger following him down the rungs.

Thirty feet down, he finally came to the last rung. It was still another six feet down to the bottom of the well, however. He lowered his right leg and gently kicked forward. His toe extended past where the siding of the well should have been.

"There's a tunnel, all right," he whispered up to Kissinger. "I'm going to drop down the rest of the way."

"Gotcha covered," Kissinger whispered back.

Bolan braced himself, then pushed away and let go of the rungs. He landed hard on his feet and immediately leveled his gun at the mouth of the tunnel. Nothing. He eased back against the side of the well, giving Kissinger room to jump down and join him.

"Christ, I feel like we're the goddamn Hardy Boys or something," Kissinger said, kicking aside some of the trash.

"The Hardy Boys would've bought the farm by now," Bolan said. "Come on, let's go."

Kissinger shone his light down the tunnel, which led away from the well only a few yards before bending sharply to the right. A faint, multicolored light was barely visible around the bend.

"Looks like we're in business," Kissinger said,

switching the flashlight to his left hand and drawing his Colt.

Bolan led the way again. He stopped briefly when he reached the bend, signaling for Kissinger to kill his light. As darkness closed in around them, Bolan heard, for the first time, a faint sound coming from farther down the tunnel—a steady, mechanical drone.

"Generator," he whispered to Kissinger.

"That could mean anything," Kissinger said. "What now?"

"We've come this far," Bolan said, "let's finish it. On three..."

Kissinger moved alongside the Executioner and dropped to a crouch. Bolan did the same, holding a fist out so Kissinger could see it in the faint light spilling around the bend. He extended one finger, then the other. On three, both men lunged around the corner, guns held out before them. They found themselves staring down a long, chiseled passageway lit by an elongated strand of ornamental Christmas lights.

"Christmas lights?" Kissinger muttered. "What, we've stumbled on the North Pole?"

"No such luck." Bolan pointed at the ground, where a series of footprints could be seen in the loose dirt.

"You're right," Kissinger wisecracked. "Too large for elves."

It looked as if there was yet another bend in the tunnel twenty yards ahead. Bolan and Kissinger fell silent and slowly made their way forward. They hadn't gone far when they suddenly heard another sound—the shriek of a gate swinging open on unoiled hinges. Before the men had a chance to react, the squeaking was drowned out by a loud, insistent howl.

"Uh-oh," Kissinger murmured. "Dogs."

The barking grew louder, and moments later the tunnel was swarming with no fewer than eight snarling pit bull terriers, all of them fully mature, all of them bounding headlong, jaws champing for a chance to sink into the flesh of those who'd dared to enter their world.

CHAPTER EIGHT

Acting on reflex, Kissinger fired and took down one of the dogs. The others kept coming, undeterred.

Bolan held his fire, shouting, ''We can't get them all!''

He turned and Kissinger followed him back the way they'd come. Once they'd reached the well, they leaped upward, side by side, each grabbing for the same set of rungs and pulling themselves up. Right behind them, the pit bulls charged into the cramped space, frenzied, bounding upward, jaws snapping at the stale air just below the dangling feet of their would-be victims.

One of the rungs, unable to support the men's combined weight, began to pull away from its moorings. Bolan felt himself sinking back into the well. One of the dogs nipped at his foot, teeth glancing off the soles of his running shoes. Bolan quickly reached for the next rung and hoisted himself out of harm's way. Kissinger did the same, making sure to grab an alternate rung.

Once firmly positioned on the ladder, the men stared down into the seething darkness. All they could see were dogs' shadowy outlines, rising in and out of view in time with their continued leaping. Their barking grew more intense, amplified by the sides of the well. It soon sounded if all the hounds of hell had been unleashed on the two men simultaneously. Kissinger shone his light on the beasts, illuminating their slavering jaws and small eyes. They showed no signs of backing off from their quarry. If anything, their inability to reach the men only increased their furor.

"They aren't going anywhere," Kissinger observed, off shutting his light. "What do we do, wait them out or bail?"

Bolan looked upward. A dim circle of moonlight was visible up at the mouth of the well. Sure, they could climb back up and wait for the dogs to back off, but the soldier was concerned that any further delay would only work to the advantage of the men they were pursuing. No, like it or not, they had to stick with the game plan. And, much as Bolan had his qualms about gunning down animals, there was no way around it.

Readying his Desert Eagle, he grimly told Kissinger, "Put a light back on them."

Kissinger obliged. Bolan aimed down at the canines and pulled the trigger. A gunshot thundered off the sides of the well as one of the dogs went down, squealing. Bolan grimly continued to fire, one shot after another, filling the well with the stench of cordite. The barking dwindled, but none of the animals backed off the attack. Some continued to leap upward even after they were hit, requiring a second shot before they finally dropped. Once the Desert Eagle was spent, Bolan slipped it back in his holster and finished the job with Kissinger's pistol.

Finally the barking ceased and the dogs lay still in a grotesque, bloodied heap. The men waited a moment longer, watching for signs of movement, then finally pushed free of the rungs and dropped back down to the bottom of the well. They both landed awkwardly, trying, without much success, to avoid the fallen dogs, which layered the ground like a grisly, uneven carpet. Kissinger lost his grip on the flashlight while trying to break his fall and the lens shattered, leaving the men in darkness as they staggered clear of the carnage to the surer footing of the tunnel.

"Dammit," Kissinger cursed.

"Couldn't be helped," Bolan said. "Let's move on."

Rounding the bend, the men saw that the strung lights were no longer on. The generator had been shut off, as well, leaving the passageway deathly quiet. The men proceeded cautiously, feeling their way along the walls. Halfway to the next bend, after passing the first pit bull Kissinger had gunned down, Bolan heard an unmistakable click. He instinctively dived to the ground, tugging at Kissinger's shirtsleeve.

"Shooter!" he hissed.

Kissinger dropped alongside Bolan as a spray of submachine gun fire chattered their way, chipping away at the stone walls around them.

The shooter's gun lacked a flash suppressor. Bolan homed in on the gun's flaming barrel and returned fire, aiming a few inches above the flickering light. The other gun fell silent and clattered to the ground. Groaning, the shooter went down, as well.

Bolan and Kissinger scrambled to their feet and rushed forward. Kissinger accidentally kicked the submachine gun, then bent to pick it up. Bolan leaned over, groping in the dark until he came in contact with the shooter's body. He quickly checked for a pulse. The man was dead. Bolan frisked him and found a high-powered flashlight clipped to his belt. He took it and turned it on, directing the beam at the dead man's face. He was older than other sniper, probably in his early forties, his head shaved. He wore a pair of khaki shorts and sandals, as well as a loose, button-down shirt soaked with blood. Bolan's shot had nailed him in the upper chest, near the heart.

"Looks like Jen Li was wrong," Bolan murmured.

"What's that?" Kissinger asked.

"Back at the motel she was telling me how some of these gangsters earned their stripes during Tiananmen Square," Bolan said, "only she figured they'd all retired to the sidelines."

"Well, this guy's retired, all right. Permanently."

Bolan glanced warily past the body. "That still leaves the guy with the plans."

"With any luck, we outnumber him now," Kissinger said, clutching the man's MP-5. He gestured toward the next bend in the tunnel. "And something tells me we're closing in on him."

"I hope so."

They moved on, single file, Bolan up front lighting the way, Kissinger walking a few paces behind him. Once past the bend, the tunnel widened. Now it was more than twice the diameter of the passageway they'd just come through. There were rail tracks, too, a narrow-gauge line running down the center of the tunnel.

A thick rubberized bumper marked the end—or beginning—of the line, and as the men circled the barrier, they found themselves standing before a tall, wide archway leading from the tunnel. A retractable steel door set on rollers jutted from a slotted recess in the arch wall, and it had been left half-open. No sounds came from within.

"He's either in there or he took off down the rail line," Kissinger said. "Want to split up?"

Bolan shook his head. "Let's check the cave quick first. There's still a chance he's not alone."

"In which case we'd be walking into another trap."

Bolan shrugged. "No guts, no glory, right?"

Kissinger grinned. "You really know how to push my buttons, don't you?"

The men took up positions on either side of the opening and waited. The only sound they could hear within the cave was a faint dripping, like that of water trailing from a stalactite. Bolan held out a fist and, as before, fingered off a three count. On three, the men swept through the opening, guns leveled, Bolan holding the flashlight in his left hand.

Immediately they were assailed, not by gunmen, but by a rank, kennellike odor. Bolan shone the flashlight on a row of squalid-looking dog cells set into a hollowing carved out the rock. The gates hung open and cages were empty except for water bowls and pools of feces and urine.

"Hell, if they kept me caged like that, I'd be ready to take it out on somebody, too," Kissinger muttered.

The men moved past the cells. The cavern opened up into a large underground chamber. Bolan grabbed a pebble and sent it clattering across the ground floor. When there was no reaction from within, he motioned for Kissinger to follow him into the larger area.

"Get a load of this," Kissinger murmured, eyes following the beam from Bolan's flashlight.

Stacked along the far wall were rows of coffin-sized crates, at least forty in all, stacked two or three high. Next to the crates was the power generator they'd heard earlier, a bulky contraption the size of a minifridge. A pair of five-gallon fuel canisters was set in front of it. Thick orange electrical cords fed out from the generator, snaking along the floor in several directions. One was hooked up to a series of overhead lights suspended from metal poles that stretched across the width of the cavern, supporting a waterproof canopy that deflected the water dripping from the stalactites. Another cord trailed back past the men and out into the tunnel, no doubt linked to the Christmas lights the men had seen back in the tunnel. Two more lines reached to the other side of the cave, where a series of upright dividers had been set up to create several improvised work areas. One of the cubicles contained a desk, chairs and several filing cabinets, while another was filled with computer equipment.

"The masseuse didn't mention anything like this," Kissinger said.

"Her boyfriend probably didn't tell her about it," Bolan said.

"Speaking of her boyfriend, I've got a feeling he's flown the coop," Kissinger said. "Maybe we should check out the rail line, then double back for a look-see here."

"Hold on a sec."

Bolan aimed the flashlight to his right, past the office cubicles, revealing a steel door framed in the rock wall.

"Then again," Kissinger said, "maybe he's behind door number two."

The men moved forward. When they reached the door, Bolan turned the handle.

"Locked."

"Why am I not surprised?" Kissinger quickly sized up the lock. "I can spring it, probably, but it'd take time."

"Then let's go back to Plan B and check the rail line," Bolan said.

The men were crossing the dirt floor when they heard someone out in the tunnel. Bolan quickly took cover behind the crates. Kissinger went the other way, concealing himself next to one of the partitions. Eyes on the archway, they saw the brightening shaft of a handheld flashlight. There was murmuring out in the tunnel. Bolan couldn't make out what was being said, but there were two distinct voices. Still armed with Kissinger's Colt, he aimed at the archway, ready to fire.

"Hello?" a voice called out from the tunnel. "You guys in there?"

Bolan lowered his gun. It was Yarborough.

"Yeah, we're here," Kissinger called out, moving away from the partition. Bolan shone his light toward the ground, lighting the way for the two deputies. Both men were winded as they strode into the chamber.

"Whoa, talk about mother lodes," Yarborough said, taking in the cavern.

"Looks like you got the other shooter out there," Cantrell told Bolan and Kissinger.

"Yeah, along with his canine unit," Kissinger grumbled.

"Well, we came around through the main entrance," Cantrell reported. "Sure enough, somebody went to the trouble of opening it back up, then trying to hide their handiwork behind a heap of brush."

"Not only that," Yarborough pitched in, "but there were a couple powerized railcars at the end of the line. Nothing like the miners used, either. These were brand-new, state-of-the-art."

"There were truck tracks just outside the entrance, too," Cantrell added. "Pretty fresh, too. Could be as recent as tonight."

Bolan took in the information and looked around the cave, trying to piece everything together. "The guy we're looking for might've slipped out that way while we were busy with the dogs," he guessed.

"Afraid so," Bolan told him.

"What about that door?" Cantrell asked, pointing behind Bolan and Kissinger.

"You any good at cracking locks?" Kissinger asked him.

"Something like that? No way," Cantrell said.

Yarborough shook his head, as well. "You check the stiff out there for some keys?"

"No," Bolan confessed. "Good idea."

"I'm on it," the deputy said.

"I say we fire the generator back up and shine a little more light on the subject," Kissinger suggested.

"Go for it," Bolan told him.

Kissinger sized up the machine, then pumped the primer and yanked a pull cord. The generator bucked, then roared to life. Within seconds, the overhead lights were working at full power, washing the cavern in a yellowish glow. Bolan, meanwhile, tracked down a crowbar and used it to pry open one of the crates. Cantrell helped him pull the lid aside. Both men peered in at the contents.

"Goddamn." Cantrell whistled in awe. "Take a look at those peashooters, would you?"

Packed tightly inside the crate were four elongated tubular weapons, each one roughly the size of a baseball bat. Mounted to the tubes were triggering mechanisms and retractable sights.

"Bazookas?" Cantrell wondered.

"SAMs," Bolan corrected. "Surface-to-air missiles."

"Get out," the deputy scoffed. "You mean like those suckers they used in the Gulf?"

"More or less, only more portable," Bolan said.

Kissinger joined them and pulled one of the weapons from the crate. "HN-5," he stated. "Chinese upgrade of a Russian SA-7. Thing like this can take down a fighter jet anywhere within two thousand feet."

Cantrell eyed the other crates and did some quick math. "Must be at least a couple hundred of 'em here."

Bolan nodded. "And something tells me these are earmarked for somebody besides street gangs."

Yarborough returned from the tunnel, shaking his head. "No keys," he said.

Taking a look at the SAM Kissinger was holding, he asked, "Where the hell did you get that?"

Kissinger indicated the crates.

"Damn," Yarborough muttered. "And here we thought these punks were only dealing dope."

Cantrell was about to say something when he heard a sound behind him. The others heard it, too. It was the sound of a key fitting into a lock. All eyes turned on the large steel door on the far wall.

The doorknob was turning....

CHAPTER NINE

After turning once, the doorknob stopped and stayed in place. When it didn't rotate back, Bolan knew that whoever was on the other side was hesitating, the same way he would have if he were planning to storm into the cave. He wondered if they'd set off some sort of alarm, alerting others to their presence. Quickly he surveyed the cavern, looking for surveillance cameras. He couldn't see any.

Elsewhere in the cavern, the other men had drawn their weapons and aimed them at the door. Cantrell and Yarborough quietly took up positions behind the crates. Kissinger sidestepped toward the work spaces and crouched next to one of the filing cabinets. Bolan stayed where he was and looked back at the door. The knob was still frozen in place. He watched, waiting.

Finally, instead of flying open as Bolan had expected, the door cracked slightly open, then stopped.

The men held their fire. After another pause, there was a loud cry from the other side of the door.

"Law enforcement!"

Bolan kept his gun trained on the door. Was this a trick?

"If you're armed, put down your weapons and hold your hands out at your sides!" the disembodied voice called out. "Identify yourselves and prepare to surrender, or we'll fire tear gas in—"

"Jesus," Yarborough muttered from behind the crates. He raised his voice and shouted, "Johnson, is that you?"

There was no response at first, but then the man on the other side of the door called out, "Yarborough?"

"Yes, it's Yarborough!" the deputy said.

"Cantrell, too," his partner yelled, moving away from the crates. "C'mon, Johnson, open the damn door before somebody gets hurt!"

Bolan kept his finger on the trigger of his Desert Eagle as the door swung open. A young, blond-haired sheriff's deputy took a tentative step into the cavern. Bolan relaxed. He remembered seeing the man back at the PACRIM facility during the early moments after the firefight.

"I sure as heck didn't plan on finding you guys here," Johnson told Cantrell and Yarborough as he opened the door all the way. Behind him were two highway patrol officers brandishing riot guns.

"Feeling's mutual," Cantrell told him.

"Who the hell taught you how to storm a safe-house, Johnson?" Yarborough railed at the younger officer. "Hell, what if we'd jerked the door open on you? We'd have turned you into hamburger while you were still busy trying to talk tough!"

"I was following procedure," Johnson insisted.

"If you were following procedure, you'd have kept the damn door shut."

"I didn't think you'd be able to hear me," Johnson said. "This sucker's thicker than the vault door at Collier Savings and Loan."

"Thicker than your skull is more like it," Yarborough taunted, grinning. "But, hey, I gotta say, for once I'm glad to see your sorry face!"

The men inside the cavern lowered their weapons and stood by as the others joined them. One of the highway patrol officers had a walkie-talkie to his face and was reporting their status. Johnson and the other CHP officer, meanwhile, slowly took in the underground facility.

"Sheesh, this place looks like the freaking Bat Cave," Johnson said. "How'd you guys get here?"

"The old mines near Ghost Ranch," Cantrell told him. "What about you? Where'd you guys come from?"

"PACRIM," Johnson explained. "We were searching the buildings when we came on some guy trying to hide in a storage locker."

"We wouldn't have found him, only he crapped his johnnies," the CHP officer added. "You might say we sniffed him out. Poor guy thought we were gonna kill him on the spot."

"That's probably the way it works back where he comes from," Kissinger said.

"Anyway," Johnson went on, "this guy starts yammering how he'll tell us everything if we just won't kill him. So, hell, we called his bluff and told him he knew what we'd come looking for. Man, he took it hook, line and sinker. He goes across the room, walking kind of funny-like on account of his britches, and reaches behind the water cooler. I'm thinking maybe he's got a gun there, so I tell him to back off so I can check it out myself. Turns out there's a switch there. I take a chance and flip it and—swoosh—the wall next to it starts swinging open, and behind it there's this humungous steel door...just like the one here.

"The guy unlocks it and suddenly we're looking at this huge freight elevator. We get on it and next thing we know we're down in these damn tunnels. They've got a railcar set on some old mining tracks, and he told us to get on board and he'd take us to 'the place.'"

"And this must be the place," the CHP officer said.

"PACRIM's secret hidey-hole," Cantrell said.

"Where's the guy who brought you here?" Yarborough asked.

"There's another Chippie out watching him back by the tracks," Johnson said.

"Well, that explains why we didn't find any contraband," Cantrell said. "They must run it down here as soon as they get it off the train."

Johnson went on. "This guys says PACRIM's got this goon squad made up of gang members shipped over from China."

"Yeah, we know all about them," Kissinger called out from the computer station. "We've been trading shots with them all night."

"Make sure you keep that guy in one piece," Bolan told the CHP officers. "Sounds like he can help put a nail in PACRIM's coffin as far as their being in cahoots with Beijing."

"Especially if he knows what they planned on doing with these SAMs," Yarborough said.

"Missile launchers?" Johnson gaped at the HN-5s stored in the crates. "Man, there's enough of these babies to start a war."

"And who knows how much other stuff they've been shipping out of here," Cantrell said.

Kissinger was looking over the computer equipment when he suddenly whistled to himself and waved Bolan over. "I think I found those plans we were looking for," he said.

"What plans?" Johnson asked.

"Long story," Cantrell told him as Bolan went over to the computer station. Several of the others followed and looked over Bolan's shoulder as Kissinger showed him a few sheets of paper he'd found near the scanner.

"Looks like some kind of schematics for an airplane," Bolan said.

"It's a plane, all right," Kissinger murmured gravely. "The same one Jack's getting ready to fly over China."

"SO, AS NEAR AS we can figure, once this guy fled the massage parlor, he came here with the plans," Bolan explained to Jen Li, who'd just joined the congregation in the underground chamber. "When he heard us coming, he must have taken one of the railcars out."

"Which means the deputies just missed him," the woman said.

"Looks that way," Bolan said. "Cantrell says there were fresh wheel tracks near the mouth of the tunnel, so you've got to figure he's long gone by now."

"Maybe we should put out an APB for suspicious vehicles."

"Already been done," Bolan told her.

Li had been picked up at the motel by two other FBI agents and then driven up to the mouth of the well. She'd taped her ankle, but the climb down the well had taken its toll. She was clearly in pain just standing still. She glanced at the computer setup, where Kissinger was hard at work trying to gain use of the CPU's operating functions. From the look of frustration on his face, he was clearly having a hard time of it.

"I wonder why he was scanning the plans," Li stated.

"He probably wanted to make duplicates," Bolan suggested. "There's no copier here, so scanning must've seemed like his best shot."

Behind them, Kissinger swore and banged his fist on the desktop. "I can't figure a way to bypass the access code," he complained. "We need Aaron here. He could probably end-run this bastard with his eyes closed."

"We can probably get him flown out here," Bolan said. "It'd cost us half a day at least, though."

"I know, I know," Kissinger said. Suddenly, a thought occurred to him. "Wait! Why don't we bring in Vance."

"Vance?"

"My buddy at Edwards," Kissinger said. "He's their resident cyber-geek. He helped me on configs for the missile mounts on the ES-1. Guy's good."

"Make the call," Bolan told him.

The FBI agents Li had come with running a check on the chamber's phone system, so Kissinger made use of Deputy Johnson's cell phone to patch through a call to the air base. Bolan and Li, meanwhile, continued to sort through the night's events.

"I want to know more about the guy in the Mercedes," Bolan said, "and why he wanted to get his hands on those plans."

"I just might be able to help you out on that," said Sheriff Kit Deerson, who'd just entered the chamber by way of the PACRIM facility. He walked gingerly, the bullet wound to his side clearly still bothering him.

"I didn't expect to see you back on your feet so soon," Bolan told him.

Deerson shrugged. "Can't keep a good man down. They had me patched up and were ready to hook me up to IVs for a couple days when I got word about this damn tunnel linking PACRIM with Ghost Ranch. Damned if I was gonna sit on my can after that."

"You found out more about the owner of the Mercedes?" Li interjected.

Deerson nodded. "Guy's name is Brett Ingersoll.

He's some kind of R&D veep for an outfit called Krebbs Gillis Aerosystems.''

"Doesn't ring a bell," Li said.

"Didn't with me, either, so I made some calls. Turns out they specialize in military aircraft. They've got a bid in with the Air Force for UCRVs.''

"Sorry," Li said.

"Unmanned Combat Reconnaissance Vehicles," Deerson explained. "Spy planes.''

"Of course," Jen Li said. "Like the ES-1.''

"Exactly. Seems their prototype's running a few weeks behind schedule of the ES-1, which is why the Air Force went with that for some top secret mission they've got going on overseas. I couldn't get any more details on that on account of my being a lowly county sheriff and all.''

Li exchanged a glance with Bolan, who filled in the sheriff, telling him the bare bones about the ES-1's mission to China.

"Son of a gun," Deerson said. "So, in other words, the folks making this ES-1 lucked out big time, right? I mean, if their prototype aces this mission, they've got the inside track on landing themselves one mother of a defense contract.''

Bolan nodded. "My understanding is the Defense Department is ready to lay out a few billion dollars on a UACV program.''

"Which makes a couple hundred grand stuffed into an attaché case peanuts," Deerson said. "You want my two cents' worth, I say Ingersoll caught wind somehow that this poor Air Force shit was looking to peddle plans for the ES-1 and figured he could use 'em to speed up development of their own UACV. That way, if the ES-1 didn't pass its mission in flying colors, his people'd be ready to level the playing field and maybe even steal the bid away."

"And he might've pulled it off if the Boxers hadn't intervened," Li said.

"Now we just need to find out what their stake was in all this," Cantrell said.

"If we're saying the Boxers have ties with Beijing, you have to figure they were acting on orders from China," Bolan told him.

"I'm not liking the sound of this," Kissinger said. "Not one bit."

"I don't like it, either," Li said. "If Beijing knows about that spy plane, it opens up a whole new can of worms."

Before she could speculate further, a pager clipped to Deerson's holster beeped to life.

"Hang on a second." Deerson scanned the message, then called out to Cantrell and Yarborough, who, along with Deputy Johnson, were inventorying the crated HN-5 SAM launchers. "Either of you two got a cell that works down here? I just got a call from dispatch.''

"No dice," Cantrell called out.

"Here," said Kissinger, who'd just gotten off the phone to Edwards. He handed the cell to Deerson, then joined Bolan and the others.

"Vance says he can come out here, no problem," he reported, "but he thinks he'll have better luck if we bring everything to him so he can hook it up to his own gear."

"Let's do it, then."

Bolan asked Deerson, "Did you see the Air Force chopper on your way here?"

"Yeah. It's still over by the rail yard."

"Okay, then," Bolan said, moving over to the computer cubicle. "Let's get this stuff unhooked so we can bring it up."

Li was helping Bolan and Kissinger disconnect the computer from its monitor when Deerson got off the cell phone, shaking his head in disbelief. "I swear, this whole damn county's going to hell in a handbasket tonight," he grumbled.

"What happened now?" Bolan asked.

"We're thinking the guy who got hold of these plans fled from here in a truck, right?"

"If there was one parked out near the main entrance to the cave, yeah," Bolan said. "Why?"

"Well, CHP just tried to pull a truck over two

miles south of here, only somebody fired some kind of high explosive out the back. Caught the patrol car square and fried it, right in the middle of the highway. Took out both men inside.''

"Bastard!" Kissinger swore.

"It gets worse. A couple other CHPs gave chase, this truck wound up plowing into cars parked off on the shoulder with overheated engines. Now that they're stuck, they're holding some of the motorists hostage.''

"How many?''

"Hostages? We're not sure.''

"I meant in the truck,'' Bolan said.

Bolan turned to Kissinger and Li. "You guys go ahead and get this stuff to Edwards,'' he told them. "I'll catch up.''

"Let me guess,'' Kissinger said. "You're going after that truck.''

"Damn right.''

CHAPTER TEN

Highway 75 was closed both ways between the outskirts of Collier Springs and the rise where, hours before, Bolan's rental Taurus had first broken down. Traffic was backed up for than a mile behind the barricade the highway patrol had set up. It was downhill from the squad car that had been turned into a hulk of smoldering scrap metal by the men in the runaway truck, an unmarked eight-wheeler with a twenty-foot cargo hold. The truck itself was visible halfway up the rise, marked by a column of black smoke still tendriling skyward from the car it had rear-ended, a 1997 Hyundai.

"Snipers scoped two bodies trapped in the Hyundai," reported CHP Officer Bruce Ribot, the man in charge of the barricade.

Ribot, a twenty-year veteran with the force, was a tall, gangly man with dark hair and a pencil-thin mustache. In all his years he'd never encountered a situation of this magnitude, and it showed. There

was the faintest trembling in his voice and a trace
of fear in his pale green eyes. "They've got at least
two hostages stowed away in back of the truck.
Maybe more."

Bolan had arrived only moments before, driven
by Sheriff Deerson. On the way they'd stopped by
the impound yard, where Bolan had raided the trunk
of his rental Taurus for more ammunition for his
Desert Eagle. Deerson knew Ribot and quickly
vouched for Bolan's right to be on the scene. The
CHP officer had no problem with the arrangement.
If anything, he was grateful for the chance to spread
the burden of handling the crisis. The other officers
milling about the barricade—Bolan recognized some
of them from the aftermath of the PACRIM shoot-
out—seemed equally overwhelmed by this latest development. Having to contend with angry motorists
demanding an explanation for the roadblock wasn't
helping matters.

"We've staked out a perimeter around the truck,"
he told Bolan, "but these guys of mine aren't trained
at this sort of thing, so I've got them posted back a
few hundred yards."

"SWAT on the way?" Bolan asked.

Ribot shrugged. "We've got teams on the way
from L.A. and Sacramento, but I don't figure on
them getting here in time to be of much help."

"Any contact with the people in the truck?"

Deerson asked, rubbing his side. He'd ripped open a stitch getting into the patrol car, and his gunshot wound had begun to bleed slightly. Bolan noticed the growing red stain on his shirt and pointed to the pair of paramedics vans parked back behind the barricades.

"Go get that tended to," Bolan told the sheriff.

"It's just a slow leak," Deerson protested. "I'll take care of it later."

"We're going to need your help on this before it's over," Bolan told him, knowing it was the only way to get past his stubbornness. "Get it patched up so we can count on you."

"Yeah, all right," Deerson groused.

The sheriff turned and headed for the medical vans. One of the vehicles was just getting ready to pull away with the bodies of the officers who'd been in the downed patrol car. Bolan saw that one of the remaining paramedics was the same woman who'd first treated Deerson back at the massage parlor. One look at the sheriff, and she started to give him hell.

Bolan turned back to Ribot, repeating Deerson's query about the men in the truck.

"Yeah, we raised them on our CBs," Ribot said. "They want an armored car they can drive over to the country airport, then they want a plane ready to take them out of the country. They say they'll let the hostages go once they land."

"Where are they going?"

"They didn't say," Ribot confessed. "They just said to make sure the plane's fueled enough to cover five hundred miles."

"That leaves Mexico and Canada for getting out of the country," Bolan said. "No shots fired since they took out the patrol car?"

"Well, there was shooting both ways before they went off the road," Ribot said. "Nothing after that."

"Whoever you talked to, did he speak with an accent?"

Ribot nodded. "Asian, I think. Probably Chinese, given everything else that's gone down around here tonight."

Bolan stared past the officer at the desert surrounding the highway. He could see the CHP snipers positioned at several points offering a clear shot at the truck.

"I don't know what those maniacs are armed with," Ribot said, "but judging by what they did to that patrol car, it's gotta be something more than just guns and rifles."

Bolan glanced again at the wasted vehicle. As bad as the damage was, he knew it couldn't have been caused by an HN-5 like the ones he'd discovered back at the underground bunker. The SAM launchers, by design, could only be fired at an upward angle. He figured the Boxers had used a grenade launcher, probably some Chinese equivalent to the M-203. If, as he suspected, the truck had been hauling a load of contraband from the bunker, the odds were the gangsters had a full arsenal at their disposal. One false move, and Bolan knew there'd be a bloodbath that would dwarf anything he'd witnessed so far this night.

"You have radio contact with the riflemen?" Bolan asked Ribot.

"Most of them, yeah."

"Tell them to hold their positions," Bolan ordered, "and make sure no one starts firing unless they're forced to."

"Got it," Ribot said.

"Do you have any stun grenades?" Bolan asked.

Ribot shook his head. "We might have some tear gas, though."

"That'll have to do. Let's have a look."

As they headed for one of the patrol cars, Ribot asked, "What are you going to do?"

"I'm going to try to get as close as I can," Bolan said. "I don't see much chance of being able to take them by surprise, but we'll see what happens."

"You're going after them alone?" Ribot was incredulous.

"I'm sure they're on the lookout for activity on

our end,'' Bolan said. ''The less we give them to
see, the better off we'll be.''

''I know, but you can't take them on single-
handed. it's suicide.''

''It's our only chance, and I've been up against
worse odds.''

''If you say so.''

Ribot popped his trunk. There was riot gear for
two stored inside: helmets, shields, bulletproof vests
and a case filled with tear gas, both in cartridges and
grenades. Bolan pulled out a belt containing six of
the latter.

''How about the other stuff?'' Ribot asked.

''It'd only get in my way and make me a larger
target,'' Bolan said, strapping on the grenade belt.
''This is cumbersome enough.''

''You're sure?''

Bolan offered up a reassuring grin. ''Belasko's
first rule—travel light.''

THE CLOUDS CAME TO Bolan's aid as he left the road
and headed down a sloped embankment to the desert
floor. Trudging lazily across the night sky, the billowing clouds drew a curtain across the full moon,
dimming it. Bolan took advantage of the increased
darkness and broke into a run, taking a course parallel to the highway, which had dropped from view
to his left. Up ahead he saw one of the Ribot's

marksmen. The man whipped around his rifle but held his fire. Bolan gestured for the shooter to direct his aim back toward the truck, giving him a better idea of his proximity to his target.

By now Bolan was acclimated to the heat. He shrugged off the perspiration that streaked down his face and once again left his shirt drenched. Flying insects continued to buzz around him as he covered more ground, sidestepping stray rocks and small tufts of sagebrush. He'd covered a good two hundred yards when he spotted yet another marksman. Judging from the angle of man's pointed rifle, Bolan realized he'd almost bypassed the truck. Changing course, he started back up the hill, crouching low. After shifting his grenade belt so the hand bombs were tucked behind his back, he dropped to his stomach and snaked his way toward the vehicle. The sand chafed at his arms and swarming gnats did their best to distract him, but he remained focused.

Soon the truck was in view. It was up off to his right, less than thirty yards away. He was facing the right rear quarter panel and could barely make out the back doors. The cargo bay was enclosed, so he assumed the doors were opened slightly to allow the men inside to look out. Bolan stayed low to the ground and pondered his next move. He was still too far away to make a move. A few boulders protruded from the earth halfway between him and truck, but to reach them he would have to break cover and if anyone in the truck were to see him, he knew he'd be an easy target. Worse, such a move would be likely to trigger an attack against the hostages. He couldn't risk it.

And so he waited.

Seconds dragged by. Bolan's arms began to go numb, so he shifted position slightly. Keeping his Desert Eagle trained on the rear of the truck, he reached behind him and unsnapped the flap, securing one of the tear gas grenades. He slowly pulled the grenade free and tested its weight in his hand. When the time came, he wanted to be sure he could activate it and throw it accurately in the same motion.

Now Bolan's legs began to tingle. This time it wasn't numbness, however. A colony of ants was creeping up his legs. The sensation was unnerving—even worse than the gnats—but he steeled himself, refusing to move.

Several minutes passed, then, for the first time, Bolan heard sounds coming from inside the truck. A woman was sobbing uncontrollably. Her cries were punctuated by gruff outbursts from a man, no doubt one of the gunmen, telling her to stop. It didn't work. Her cries grew louder, then turned to a wail.

"Would you please just let us go?" she begged her captors. "We can't breathe in here!"

Bolan heard a muffled crack, then the woman fell silent. He wasn't sure if she'd been shot or struck down. Much as he wanted to come to her defense, he held his position.

Moments later, he heard angry shouting, followed by a fierce pounding. A small dimple begin to budge outward from the truck wall. Finally a narrow gash appeared. Bolan saw the blade of a fire ax wedged in the opening. The blade wriggled from side to side, then disappeared back inside the truck. Then the pounding resumed. Another bulge appeared. The captors were poking holes in the trucks, probably to let more air in. It would increase their visibility, too, he thought. Once somebody looked out through one of the openings, they'd be able to see him. It was time to move.

Scurrying on all fours, Bolan beelined for the cluster of rock ten yards away. Once he was close enough, he rolled behind the boulders and lay still. The hacking inside the truck continued, but no shots were fired his way.

So far, so good, Bolan thought to himself. He reached down and brushed away the few ants still clinging to his leg. The ground he'd gained afforded him a far better overview of the situation. Behind him, he could see the highway stretching down to the police barricades. The CHP officers were visible in silhouette, lit from behind by the flashing lights atop their patrol cars. Trailing behind them, like an orderly regiment of fireflies, were the headlights of vehicles whose drivers had decided to wait out the roadblock rather than tackle the forty-eight-mile detour suggested by the CHP. To the south, just beyond the rise where his car had broken down, Bolan saw the glow of more car lights. He could see across the road, too, and as the clouds pulled away from the moon, he spotted another of Officer Ribot's marksmen lying prone on small mound of sand 150 yards away.

As for the truck, Bolan was now almost directly behind it. Two softball-sized holes had appeared in the walls on his side of the vehicle. Someone pitched a cigarette out through one of the openings. It fell to the ground and rolled a few inches before coming to a stop in the gravel.

Idiots, Bolan thought. He could smell gas and assumed the Hyundai's fuel line had ruptured when it was rear-ended, leaving flammable puddles on the ground. Given the presumed stockpile of armament inside the truck, all it would take was one spark to trigger an explosion. Bolan crouched low behind the boulders, bracing himself.

He waited, but nothing happened; apparently the cigarette burned itself out.

There was another brief lull, then Bolan heard the rear doors of the truck creak open a few inches. He could also hear movement inside. He rose slowly and peered over the boulders.

Two women were climbing out of the truck. Once they touched ground, they reached up, lifting one child, then another from the truck. The children were young, neither of them more than a few years old. Both whimpered as the women pulled them into an embrace, then set them down, freeing their hands so they could help ease a third woman out of the truck. The third woman was limp. Bolan suspected she was the one who'd been struck earlier. Peering into the darkened interior of the truck, Bolan spotted one of the gunman. He stood near the opening, clutching an assault rifle.

"Stay put," he warned. "Try anything and we'll kill your husbands."

The women didn't respond. They lowered the third woman to the ground and huddled their children close.

Bolan wondered if the CHP had negotiated the release of the women...not that they were free. The rear doors remained partially open, and Bolan was sure that the gunman still had his rifle trained on those outside the truck. Whatever the case, the odds had shifted, however slightly. If worse came to worst and it became necessary to storm the truck, the Executioner figured he could take out the gunman nearest to the doors and give the women and children a chance to escape. It wasn't much, but at this point he would take any edge afforded him.

Several minutes passed. Bolan could hear the two mothers whispering to their children, doing their best to soothe them. When the third woman began to regain consciousness, they turned to her, quieting her when she began to cry out in pain.

"It's going to be okay," one of the mothers told her.

"No, it's not," the other woman groaned. "We're all going to die!"

"Shut up!" one of the gunmen shouted at them.

The women fell silent.

Bolan heard more activity inside the truck. Crates were being moved. Someone switched on a flashlight briefly, then there was the sound of kicking. A man let out a groan.

"Get away from those crates!" someone shouted. "Over against the wall. Both of you!"

Both of you. That meant there were only two hostages still inside the truck. But which wall? Bolan listened intently. It sounded to him as if the prisoners were shifting to his right, toward the wall nearest the road's shoulder.

Once the men had moved, the flashlight went out and it was quiet again inside the truck.

Bolan was frustrated. He knew now—as much as he was ever going to—the relative position of the hostages. If he went in firing, there was a chance he could avoid killing them by mistake. But there was still the matter of getting close enough to get a drop on the gunmen. The only way in was through the rear doors, and he was positive one of the captors was still posted there, keeping an eye on the women and children. He needed a diversion.

The soldier glanced around him. There was nothing lying on the ground but rocks and litter. He couldn't move away from the boulders, either, without risking being seen from the truck. He considered lobbing one of the tear-gas grenades past the truck. If it went off somewhere near the Hyundai or another of the stalled cars, the gunmen might be fooled—if only for a fleeting second—that someone was coming up on them from the front. But even if he backed up a few yards and flung the grenade sidearmed, he was fairly sure the motion of his arm would be detected.

No, there had to be a better way.

Bolan was wrestling with his dilemma when he heard a strange grating sound far in the distance, up near the rise. Puzzled, he looked out into the night.

Far uphill, lit by the dull glow of the streetlamp lighting the call box near where his Taurus had stalled, Bolan saw the shadowy outline of someone who'd apparently slipped past the barricades and be-gun to head down the center of the highway. Arms held out at his sides, the man crouched slightly and slalomed downhill with increasing speed as if he were competing for a gold medal in the Winter Olympics.

Finally, Bolan realized what has happening.

Billy Grubb was trying to take the hill on his skateboard.

Bolan watched Grubb zigzag down the hill, pick-ing up more speed by the second. The man had no protective gear whatsoever, and from the looks of it he was still wearing nothing but his sandals and cargo pants. He was carrying something, though.

His Frisbee flying disk.

The gunmen inside the truck were equally dis-concerted by Grubb's shenanigans, but for other rea-sons. They thought it was some sort of ploy. Gunfire erupted from inside the truck. Bolan figured they were trying to gun down the transient as he drew closer to them.

As it turned out, though, Grubb wasn't the only one they intended to take a shot at. Eyeing the rear of the truck, Bolan saw that one of the gunmen was taking aim at the women and children with his as-sault rifle. Bolan quickly drew a bead and fired first. In nearly the same breath, he thumbed the pin off the tear-gas grenade with his left hand and lobbed it.

Wounded by Bolan's gunshot, the man in the rear of the truck fired errantly, sending a burst into the dirt next to where the wounded woman lay. The grenade bounded off his shoulder and into the back of the truck, spewing its caustic gas.

Bolan, meanwhile, had already charged from behind the rocks, drawing startled cries from the women and children as he charged toward them. He put a second round through the scooter. The man pitched forward, tumbling to the ground. The hostages outside the truck screamed anew. Bolan raced past them, using the fallen gunman for a springboard as he leaped up into the truck, holding his breath, Desert Eagle still blazing.

Bolan knew there was a chance he might inadvertently set off the truck's cargo, but he continued to fire blindly, aiming shoulder high, avoiding the wall to his right. A return shot rang past his ear, then he heard a man grunt. Then, above the sound of gunfire, there was a loud thump as something struck the side of the truck with enough force to rock it slightly from side to side.

Grubb, Bolan thought fleetingly as he continued to rake the interior of the truck, choking from the tear gas, his eyes burning. Between the darkness and the foul, stinging cloud he couldn't see a thing. He tumbled over a body and crashed into one of the crates, then lashed out with his right leg. He struck something soft and heard another groan, so he followed through, torquing his body and whipping his left arm around in a karate chop. Again he came in contact with flesh. Whoever he'd struck went down under the force of the blow.

There was no further gunfire, but the deafening echo of the shots fired inside the truck made it hard for Bolan to know whether the captive husbands were still alive. He assumed they were and shouted through the tear gas, "Everybody out! Now!"

Staggering backward, Bolan rammed his shoulder into one of the rear doors, throwing it open. His momentum carried him through the opening, and he tumbled headlong from the truck. Fortunately, the gunman he'd slain earlier lay directly below him, breaking his fall.

The two captive husbands were right behind him, gagging and wretching as they clambered down to the ground. Their wives rushed toward them, hugging them and pulling them and the children away from the tear gas now spilling out of the truck.

It was over.

Bolan, his eyes stinging, fighting off a wave of nausea, slowly pulled himself to his feet and reeled clear of the truck. The first of Ribot's marksmen had arrived and stood alongside him near the rear of the truck, aiming his rifle past the opened door and shouting for those inside to throw their guns and come out with their hands up.

Bolan heard more retching inside the truck. Moments later, a young man crawled weakly forward on his knees, hands raised out at his sides. Without lowering his rifle, the marksman reached forward and grabbed the man by the collar of his shirt, unceremoniously yanking him to the ground. Bolan got a good look at him; he matched the description of the man who'd absconded from the massage parlor with the plans to the ES-1 spy plane.

By now another two riflemen had converged on the scene. One of them dragged the masseuse's boyfriend to his feet and shoved him roughly away from the hostages. Another unclipped a flashlight and shone a beam into the cargo hold. Barely visible through the dissipating cloud were two more gunmen, both dead, sprawled across a fallen stack of crates. One of the crates had burst open, revealing a cache of AK-47 assault rifles.

"Good job, partner," one of the marksmen told Bolan.

"Yeah," Bolan muttered.

Wiping tears from his eyes, Bolan moved away from the truck. Off to his right, he spotted Billy Grubb sprawled on his back in the middle of the highway. The transient was bleeding profusely, both from road rash and a savage gash he received bouncing off one of the jagged openings the gunmen had hacked in the side of the truck. Amazingly, however, he was still alive. His eyes flickered open as Bolan hovered over him.

"I kinda figured I'd find you here," he gasped weakly.

"You're something else, you know that?" Bolan told the man.

"Hey, I make that run all the time," Grubb boasted. "I crashed on purpose."

"I'm sure you did," Bolan said. "Now shut up and stay still."

Downhill, one of the paramedic vans and two squad cars had circled around the barricade and were heading uphill toward the truck. Bolan waved to get their attention, then turned back to Grubb.

"Do I get that reward this time?" the transient inquired.

"I'll pay it myself if I have to," Bolan told him. "You saved the day, you crazy fool."

"Good." Grubb smiled. "I always wanted to be a hero."

CHAPTER ELEVEN

Edwards Air Force Base

"I've got to meet this guy," John Kissinger said after hearing how Billy Grubb's daredevil run down the highway had helped resolve the hostage crisis without a loss of life among the innocent. He and Bolan were walking away from the airfield where Bolan had been dropped off only moments before.

"He's in intensive care. If he makes it, it'll be a miracle."

"Hell, from the sound of, his making it down that hill was a miracle," Kissinger said.

Bolan changed the subject. "How's your friend coming along with the computer?"

"Making progress. He's got some kind of code-breaking program hooked up to the CPU. Sucker's got more than twelve million possible code words in I forget how many languages. Hopefully it's just a matter of running down the list till he hits one, one that says, 'Open sesame.'''

"How long could that take?" Bolan asked.

"Twelve hours tops, he says." Kissinger said, "providing the word's in the hopper."

Once clear of the runway, the men strode between two barracks to the administration building. On the way, Bolan asked about Barbara Price.

"She's back at the hotel wrapping up a conference call with the chief," Kissinger explained. "Afterward she said she wants to catch a quick forty winks."

"Sounds like a good idea," said Bolan, who hadn't slept for nearly twenty-four hours.

"Given the circumstances, I think she'll go easy on you for standing her up."

Bolan grinned faintly. "That's good. I didn't get a chance to buy flowers."

Kissinger quickly filled Bolan in on the Air Force officer slain at the massage parlor after passing plans for the ES-1.

"Two-stint guy by the name of Mansfield. Worked the copier room. They're still trying to figure out how he wrangled around the security protocols. Vance knew him, said he was a malcontent, not to mention a lousy poker player."

"A couple hundred grand pays a lot of gambling debts," Bolan said.

"Ain't that the truth," Kissinger agreed. "But I don't think that's it. He wasn't going to pull another stint, so the theory is he was looking for a little severance pay to go along with his discharge."

Entering the admin building, the men passed through two security checkpoints, then took an elevator down to the base's computer room.

"Jen Li decided not to fly up," Kissinger told Bolan as they headed down the hallway. "She wanted to go to the morgue to make arrangements for Agent Hunter. While she was there, she was going to view the bodies they pulled out of those cargo containers."

"Not my idea of a fun time."

"I think she's feeling a little responsible," Kissinger said.

"Why? She didn't know anything about the smuggling operation."

"That's just it," Kissinger said. "She thinks if they'd focused more on PACRIM instead of the massage parlor, they might've come up with something."

"I heard her say that earlier."

"Hindsight's a bitch," Kissinger said. "Anyway, she wants to talk with the survivors, too."

"Trying to get a lead on the snakeheads."

Kissinger nodded. "We've put a dent in the goon squad, but whoever's calling the shots is still out there. She's got the Bureau raiding PACRIM's dock facility in Long Beach, but I'm betting they caught wind of the firefight here and moved out any evidence.''

''You're probably right.''

''She won't stop with that,'' Kissinger said. ''She says she'll take it all the way to China if she has to. Seems a little drastic, if you ask me.''

''That's how revenge works,'' Bolan said. He recalled his war with the Mob. Knocking off enforcers and low-level capos had never satisfied his hunger for vengeance. He'd held the bosses responsible for what had happened to his family, and it wasn't until their blood had been shed that he'd felt any real satisfaction.

The men passed through a final checkpoint and entered the computer room. The facility was huge, taking up the entire ground floor of the building. There were twelve separate stations visible in a central work area, and the walls were lined with another dozen private offices. Kissinger led Bolan to one with Corporal Duane Vance's name stenciled on the door. Inside the room, Vance, a short, wiry man in his thirties with red hair and skin the color of milk, glanced up briefly from his computer terminal and raised a finger, indicating he'd be with the men in a minute. Resting on a cart alongside his station was the computer and scanner taken from the underground bunker. Cables linked the two systems.

"What's the status with Jack and the ES-1?" Bolan asked as they waited.

"All systems go, as I understand it," Kissinger told him. "The feeling is we nipped things in the bud here, so the honchos decided there's no reason to scrap the mission."

"I don't know about that," Bolan said.

"C'mon," Kissinger said. "Yeah, they got the plans, but we headed 'em off at the pass before they could do anything with them."

"I hope you're right. But I'll feel better about things once we get a peek inside that computer."

"Good news on that front," Vance called out. He had a high-pitched, nasal voice that reminded Bolan of Bob Dylan. "The password was *tong zhi*. Chinese for 'comrade.'"

"Chairman Mao would be proud," Kissinger said.

"What's the lowdown on the scanner," Bolan asked.

"Not there yet," Vance said. "Won't be long, though. Take a seat."

Bolan and Kissinger grabbed a couple folding chairs behind Vance's printer and sat down.

"Vance here's a fellow MIT grad," Kissinger explained. "We met a few years back at a conference there."

"People kept thinking us for twins," Vance joked.

Bolan grinned. Kissinger had six inches and fifty pounds on Vance and was as muscle-bound and ruddy-complexioned as the corporal was frail and pale.

"Vance and I moonlighted a couple years trying to develop a smart gun," Kissinger explained, then elaborated at Bolan's puzzled look. "One that could be fired by remote control. We've still got it on the backburner, right Vance?"

"Yeah," Vance scoffed. "Filed under Bonehead Ideas."

Kissinger and Vance shared a laugh, then the corporal directed the other men's attention to his computer monitor. "Okay, enough with the shtick. Let's see what we got."

Vance had accessed the scanner's file and called up the last batch of images it had committed to memory. To no one's surprise, the screen filled, page by page, with the pilfered plans for the ES-1 Unmanned Combat Reconnaissance Vehicle.

"Did they back up any of those pages up on floppies?" Bolan wondered. "We didn't find any on the truck, but it seems like they might've tried to smuggle the plans out along with that load of assault rifles.''

"Let's see." Vance pecked at his keyboard, pulling up another screen. "Nope, looks like... Wait a second. Damn!''

"What?" Kissinger said.

Vance pointed at the screen. "Well, the good news is they didn't transfer anything onto floppies.''

"And the bad news?" Bolan queried.

"They e-mailed 'em.''

Kissinger cursed, then muttered, "Where to?''

"Where do you think?" Vance said. "Cyberspace. The plans went out to another e-mail address. You know the drill on that. They could've been picked up from anywhere between here and Tombouctou.''

"This isn't good," Bolan guessed.

"Well, it's a setback, that's for damn sure," Vance said. "But we're not whipped yet.''

"You can go to the server," Kissinger suggested.

"Right," Vance said. "They'll bark about confidentiality, but we can wave the national-security wand and they'll fall in line quick enough. Want me to get on it?''

"Absolutely," Bolan said.

He turned to Kissinger. "Meanwhile, we need to get word to that base Jack's flying out of.''

"You're thinking sabotage?" Kissinger guessed.

"Damn right I am," Bolan said. "Maybe Ingersoll just wanted those plans for his firms R&D, but if we're saying there's a link between the Boxers and Beijing, it's a whole different ball game."

"Shit, you're right," Vance said. "Hell, when you lay it out that way, it sounds like the Chinese know they've got a spy plane coming their way."

Kissinger jumped to the bottom line. "Which means Jack's gonna be flying into a trap."

COMMANDER KYLE Peterson bit the tip off his cigar and spit it into the trash, then planted the stogie between his lips and resumed pacing the administration building's communications center, two stories up from the computer room.

"C'mon, c'mon, dammit!" he growled. The cell phone pressed to his face was dwarfed by his large, meaty hands.

The commander was waiting to be put on the line with authorities at the Indian military air base in Marjeelam. He'd been on hold for only twenty seconds, but the man had no patience for delays, especially in times of crisis. Even though he was perhaps getting ahead of himself, he found himself barking what had become his mantra during the nine years he'd manned the helm at Edwards Air Force Base.

''Don't you know there's a war going on?'' he yelled into the receiver.

Bolan and Kissinger stood a few yards away, watching the commander wear down the carpet. Elsewhere in the large, brightly lit chamber, other junior officers moved about with a sense of urgency. Bolan wondered if they were actually performing tasks or just feeding off the old man's nervous energy and eager to look as if they were at least trying to help out the situation...the situation being that a top-secret mission overseas was now in apparent jeopardy because someone within the ranks at Edwards had gone turncoat. Peterson had made no excuses and assumed full responsibility for the breach in security, but the men around him knew that in the coming days and weeks, heads would roll as the commander started to look for answers as to how a goddamn copy clerk could have been allowed to sully the base's reputation.

Finally Peterson was on the line with someone in charge in Marjeelam. The news wasn't good.

''When?'' the commander bellowed. He waited for an answer, then snapped, ''What's with that? Takeoff wasn't scheduled for another thirty minutes!'' Once he got his answer, Peterson placed a thumb over the mouthpiece and quickly told Bolan and Kissinger, ''Bird's already flown. Nearly an hour ago. Some crap about jumping on a break in the weather.''

"They can radio for him to turn back," Bolan suggested.

"Oh, really?" Peterson said, his voice thick with sarcasm. "Why the hell didn't I think of that?" He turned his anger back on the cell phone, telling the unseen party on the other line, "Get that flyboy on the horn and tell him to boomerang his ass back to your base, pronto!... What do you mean, will I translate that? I thought you spoke English! I said radio for the pilot to turn back. Abort mission. Is that clear enough for you?... Yes, I'll hold. I'll be fucking delighted to hold! I like nothing better in this life than to be put on fucking hold!"

Another length of cigar fell victim to Peterson's grinding jaws. He spit it out, then snapped what was left in two and threw it across the room.

"A copy clerk!" He resumed pacing, fuming to no one in particular. "All this because a goddamn clerk helps himself to some plans. We have surveillance cameras in there, right? We double-check page counts on every sheet of paper that goes in and out of those machines, right? Everybody's searched coming in and out of that room to make sure everything's on the up-and-up, right? Then what the hell happened? Tell me that, would you? What happened!"

The other officers cringed at the outburst. The one who had the misfortune of feel Peterson's gaze fall on him at the end of his diatribe offered up meekly, "We're looking into it, sir. There'll be a full-scale investigation."

"Wonderful," Peterson scoffed. "And when it's over, you'll probably make copies, and we'll be right back where we started!"

Kissinger wandered to the coffee machine to get out of the line of fire. Bolan already had a cup. He turned his back on the commander and stared out through a wide, tinted window that took up most of the entire east wall. Outside, the mountainous horizon was tinged with a predawn gray. It was only four-thirty. The sun wouldn't be rising for at least another hour. Bolan couldn't believe this was still part of the same night that had begun with his Taurus stalling back on the highway near Collier Springs. Even with the surge of adrenaline racing through him at the discovery that Grimaldi's life might be on the line, fatigue had finally begun to weigh on him. He shrugged it off and took another sip of coffee.

"Okay, I feel better now," Peterson said, falling alongside Bolan to take in the view. As an appeasement offering, somebody had just handed the commander a headset phone, allowing him free use of both hands. And not a moment too soon. Bolan saw that Peterson had pressed the cell phone so tightly to his face that he still bore its imprint on his right cheek.

"I think we've still got reason to be optimistic," Peterson said, already starting to unwrap another cigar. Bolan watched the man go through the ritual with an eerie sense of déjà vu. Back at the Farm, Hal Brognola routinely went through the same motions, using cigars as a prop the same way some people busied their hands with worry beads. "The plane was already out of here before the plans changed hands," he reasoned, "and it's been under constant watch ever since. Even if these shitheads got their e-mail through to somebody overseas, there's no window of opportunity time-wise for them to have done anything."

Bolan said nothing. He didn't want to set off the commander again by mentioning that if there could be lapses in security here at Edwards, the same could be true in Marjeelam.

"Yeah, I'm here," Peterson said, speaking into headset. "Let's have it...."

Bolan watched the other man's face as he received the news. Peterson's face reddened and his jaws clamped down so tight on his cigar it severed, sending the longer half tumbling to the carpet. He didn't seem to notice. His eyes, large, baleful orbs the color of slate, flashed, first with anger, then grim resignation. For the moment, at least, he was unable to respond with his usual vitriol.

"Do what you can," he muttered. "We'll stay in touch."

Kissinger joined the men, stirring his coffee. "What's the word," he asked.

Peterson eyed both men and shook his head. "They've lost radio contact with the pilot," he reported. "Not only that, the plane's dropped off radar."

CHAPTER TWELVE

Two hours later, the sun was up and had already burned off the ragged morning cloud cover. Returning to the Air Force administration building after a brief, fitful nap and a much welcomed shower, Bolan, wearing a change of clothes from the tote bag he'd retrieved from the Taurus, touched a finger to the tinted windows of the command post and could feel the blazing heat radiate off the glass. He'd overheard one of the junior officers say that this day would be even hotter than the previous. Bolan was glad to be inside.

Kissinger would be joining him soon; he was off in the mess having breakfast with Duane Vance. Bolan had begged off, making do with coffee and a nutrition bar purchased from one of the barracks vending machines. The bar tasted like hardtack covered with yogurt frosting. He forced down half and tossed the rest in the trash.

He was waiting for a briefing on the situation

overseas. That would come shortly, once Commander Peterson had finished conferring with aides and some federal agents in his office downstairs. The commander had left explicit instructions not to be disturbed, and Bolan, in no mood to witness another of the man's tirades, had decided against barging in on the meeting. He assumed the Feds Peterson was meeting with included the CIA and NSA.

A bank of monitors lined the south wall of the command center. Most dealt with Air Force matters: recent directives passed down from Washington, flight status of aerial squadrons and topographical maps showing the position of overseas air bases relative to various global hot spots. From the looks of it, Bolan's colleagues from Phoenix Force and Able Team still had their hands full with their current mission. He wasn't surprised. As with his unexpected foray in Collier Springs, he knew that Stony Man missions had a way of running into complications.

One of the monitors was tuned in to CNN. It was the top of the hour, so Bolan ventured over to see the headline news. He expected the downing of the ES-1 to be the top story. To his amazement, however, the anchorman led off with news of a pending fight on Capitol Hill over the President's latest proposed tax bill. Two stories into the newscast there was a brief piece on the incidents at Collier Springs.

Conspicuously absent in the story, however, was any mention of the slain Air Force officer or the fact that he was suspected of espionage involving plans for the ES-1. The words *spy plane* never came up, and there was no indication that anyone at CNN knew that the ES-1 had gone over China during the night.

Press blackout, Bolan thought.

Moments later, Peterson strode into the room, followed by two women. One was Jen Li. She, too, had had a chance to change and looked reasonably rested. If her ankle was still bothering her, she didn't show it. Spotting Bolan, she offered a nod and slight smile.

The other woman was Barbara Price. Tall and trim with honey-blond hair that reached down to her shoulders, Stony Man's mission controller wore jeans and a pale green sleeveless sweater. Bolan was surprised to see her. They traded faint smiles.

"I got here an hour ago," she told him. "You were still asleep and we decided you'd earned some shut-eye. I hope you don't mind."

"Not a problem," Bolan said. "Good to see you."

"Same here," Price replied.

"I'll let the ladies fill you in," Peterson told Bolan. "I've got a few other fires to tend to."

The commander corralled a few of his junior officers into a huddle near the monitors. Alone with the women, Bolan mentioned what he'd seen—or, more correctly, what he hadn't seen—on the morning news.

"Yes," Jen Li confirmed, "we're keeping the media out of the loop."

"That won't last long," Bolan said. "Aren't the Chinese tooting their horn for having brought the plane down yet?"

"As a matter of fact, no," Li said. "There's been no word from them. No bragging, no rhetoric, not even an acknowledgment that they know anything about the plane."

"That's not like them," Bolan said. "Last time this happened, they couldn't turn out the propaganda fast enough."

"I know," the FBI woman recalled. "We're at a loss, to be honest."

"And there's been no contact with Jack?"

"Zip," Price said. "NSA's going to shift orbit with one of their other satellites and try to get a read on the area where we lost Jack on the radar. That's going to take time, though."

"If they can shift satellites, why didn't they just do that in the first place instead of going with an unproved prototype," Bolan wanted to know.

"Because it means robbing from Peter to pay Paul," Price explained. "The satellite they're moving's been eyeballing Afghanistan for movement by pro-Taliban rebels. Now we'll lose our bird's-eye on that and have to rely on field agents."

"What else do we have?" Bolan said.

"The Bureau slapped an injunction on the server that fielded the e-mail sent out from the bunker." Jen Li reported. "Turns out the address it was sent to belongs to some firm called Dragonard Imports, based out of Shenzhen."

"That's near Hong Kong, right?" Bolan asked.

Li nodded. "The thing is, though, the ground address is a post-office box, so we're guessing it's a fictitious business. And it doesn't even mean that we're looking for someone in Shenzhen. Whoever owns the account could've accessed the plans from anywhere within range of the server."

"There's a name with the account, though, isn't there?" Bolan said. "I mean, besides Dragonard. A person."

"Chin Yeung," Li told him. "That's a common surname. Tracking him down'd be like looking for John Smiths in New York City."

"And the odds are that's an alias, anyway," Price said.

"I'm sure it is," Bolan replied. "So we're saying it's not much of a lead."

"I'll take looking for needles in a haystack," Li said.

"Right now I'm more concerned about looking for Jack," Bolan said.

He turned to Price. "How soon can you get me overseas?"

Price smiled wanly. "I knew you'd ask that. Peterson's arranging for a pair of B-1s to fly out of here to Marjeelam in two hours. He said he'll short-crew both planes so we can send a team over. You can rendezvous at the base Jack flew out of and decide your next move."

"I'm sure Cowboy wants in," Bolan said.

"So do I," Li announced. Before he could protest, she went on, "I've field training and you're going to need someone who speaks the languages over there, right?"

"Yes, but—"

"Besides," Li went on, repeating the rationale Kissinger had told Bolan about earlier, "after seeing what happened to people stuffed into those cargo containers, I want a piece of whoever sent them to their deaths. So I'm going with you."

"Is that a problem?" Price asked.

Bolan shook his head. "Let's do it."

"I just need to make a few arrangements with Sacramento," Li said. She excused herself, leaving Bolan and Price with a moment alone.

"Sorry we couldn't hook up last night," Bolan said.

"You had your hands full. Watching Li stride out of the command center, she teased, "I might've known you'd take up with another woman first chance you got."

Bolan grinned. "It wasn't exactly dinner by candlelight."

"That offer still stands," Price told him. "Once you're back, though, I'm going to pick you up at the airport so you don't go off another scenic drive somewhere."

"I like that idea," Bolan said.

"One more thing," Price added, steering the conversation back to business. "Hal's already been in touch with the President and Joint Chiefs. They can't afford to stand by while you're airborne, so they're sending a Ranger squad across the border to start searching for Jack."

"If they can get job done, that's fine by me," Bolan said.

Price checked her watch. "Well, we've got an hour before you're on that plane," she said. "I'm starved. Is there any chance you'd be up for buying a girl a decent breakfast?"

CHAPTER THIRTEEN

Marjeelam, India

Marjeelam Indian Royal Airfield, located fourteen miles north of the small town whose name it shared, was laid out along an east-west axis on a fallow plain at the foot of the Himalayas. The mountains, tall and imposing, boasting some of the world's highest peaks, cradled the air base, shielding it from sun, wind and, more often than not, brutal summer monsoons that would otherwise have posed visibility problems for the constant stream of combat aircraft making use of this, India's closest military installation to the Chinese border. It was this strategic location that had made Marjeelam the most logical site for the launch of the ES-1 spy plane.

Now, with the unexplained downing of the ES-1 forcing a likely confrontation between the United States and China, logic similarly dictated that Marjeelam should be not only the base of operations in the search for the plane and its missing pilot, but also a primary staging area for any military force the U.S. might feel compelled to bring to bear against the Chinese.

India, which initially had been more than happy to accommodate the launch of the ES-1 as a means to curb China's designs on Tibet—which, as many domino theorists in New Delhi feared, might open the door to further military incursions—had balked at the idea of an increased U.S. presence at the base. Some officials feared, perhaps rightly, that in the event of an all-out conflagration, China would lash out first, not at the U.S., but rather its closer adversary on the Asian subcontinent. Washington had called in some markers and put pressures on the Indian government, however, and air force personnel at Marjeelam were now making arrangements to accommodate an influx of tactical U.S. warplanes and airmen.

Conversely, U.S. Air Force Commander Kyle Peterson had never intended to dispatch two B-1 Lancers to Marjeelam for the sole purpose of speed-shuttling a trio of high-ranking civilians across the Pacific. Even before the high-tech bombers had cleared the runway at Edwards, Peterson had secured assurances that, upon landing, the B-1s would undergo maintenance and refueling so that they could remain at MIRA on a standby basis for possible use in the crisis. Three systems officers—two defensive, one offensive—were en route from a U.S. carrier in the Bay of Bengal to take up the crew positions that had been temporarily vacated to make room on board the Lancers for Bolan, Kissinger and FBI Agent Jen Li.

As for the crisis, it was slowly escalating.

Ten hours had passed and the Chinese still had yet to come forward with any knowledge that a spy plane had broached its airspace, much less released information as to the plane's whereabouts or the fate of its pilot. The few accusations that had been directed its way through diplomatic channels had been soundly rebuffed and met by counteraccusations that the U.S. was fabricating the entire incident, just as it was misrepresenting routine military exercises within Tibet as a harbinger of an impending takeover. The United States was up to its usual bullying, as one Beijing official put it.

In the absence of hard facts, rumors were rampant as to what had happened. Most prevalent was the notion that China, still stinging from criticism over its handling of the 2001 incident where one of its fighter jets had forced down a larger U.S. EP-5 spy plane after tailing it too closely during a recon mission over the South China Sea, was this time merely playing it more closely to the vest. According to this theory, the Chinese had once again brought down a spy plane, only this time it had been deliberate, with the plane quickly hauled off to a secret location where it could be inspected at leisure.

As for pilot Jack Grimaldi, in this scenario skeptics feared that his fate was sealed, that—be it through execution after trial in a kangaroo court or due to so-called unfortunate circumstances related to his forced landing—his life would be forfeited as payback for the death of the Chinese fighter pilot lost at sea during the earlier incident. Others felt the Chinese had blasted the ES-1 to smithereens with antiaircraft fire and elected to sweep the incident under the rug in the naive belief that the U.S. would do the same rather than own up to the ill-fated mission. And, out on the fringe, there were the usual gadflies and delusionaries who either saw the work of extraterrestrials or felt that perhaps the ES-1's pilot had defected to China or, even more improbably, flown into the Himalaya's answer to the Bermuda Triangle.

John Kissinger had another theory.

Prior to flying out from Edwards, Kissinger had been interviewed at length by investigators from Air Force Internal Affairs, who, under orders from Commander Peterson, were questioning everyone who'd come in contact with the ES-1 while it was at the base. He'd been cleared of suspicion, but throughout the flight he'd been troubled and uncharacteristically quiet. Now, as he and Bolan disembarked and strode away from the first of the B-1s to land at Marjeelam, he voiced his concerns.

"I keep thinking back," he told Bolan, "and wondering if maybe it had something to do with the weapons system."

"What are you talking about?" Bolan asked. Like Kissinger, he spoke low so as to not be overheard by the pair of uniformed Indian MPs escorting them from the runway.

"The missile pod Vance and I helped rig up," Kissinger explained. "I know we had the plane take a few test runs over the desert afterward to make sure its aerodynamics hadn't been compromised, but maybe there was some glitch that just didn't catch," Kissinger said. "You know, an accident waiting to happen."

"Don't even go there," Bolan told the weaponsmith. "Look, even if we're talking malfunction, that plane was fast-tracked and rushed out the door so fast it could've been any component, not just the weapons. Hell, it wasn't even built with a pilot in mind. You told me yourself that cockpit they strapped under it was practically held together with spit and baling wire."

"I was just bullshitting," Kissinger said. "I don't think the cockpit was really a problem. If anything, I think it made for a better plane. If you ask me, this whole UCRV program smacks of kids out playing in their backyard with model airplanes.''

''I'm sure there's more to it than that,'' Bolan said.

They cleared the tarmac and stood before one of the hangars, watching the second bomber come in. An enlisted man from the Indian air force base drove by in a military jeep, pausing long enough to tell the men that a field chief from the intelligence bureau was waiting for them at the hangar where the ES-1 had been kept prior to launch. Bolan told the man they'd be there once the rest of their party had arrived.

''Whatever the case,'' Bolan went on as the jeep pulled away, ''there's no sense beating yourself up over this, Cowboy. Let's find the plane and get Jack back, then we can worry about sorting things out.''

''Yeah, you're right,'' Kissinger said. He didn't sound convinced, however.

Jen Li had asked to fly separately from Bolan and Kissinger so that she could sleep and then have some legroom to do stretching exercises with her sore ankle. The regimen had to have worked, because she got off the plane and crossed over to the men without so much as a hitch to her stride.

''It wasn't exactly business class, but I can't complain,'' she said when asked about her flight. ''I'm amazed how fast we got here.''

"Mach 1 at thirty thousand feet eats up the miles," Kissinger told her.

"Any news yet?"

"No," Bolan said, "but we're supposed to meet with an IB chief. Maybe he'll have something."

Walking a few paces ahead of their escorts, the three of them followed their shadows toward the hangars. The sun shone on their backs, but it didn't pack the wallop it had back in the California high desert. Bolan figured the temperature was only in the mideighties, made even more tolerable by a faint mountain breeze.

It was even cooler inside the hangar, which hummed with the drone of air conditioners. A maintenance crew was circling one of two fighter jets in the service bays. Off in a far corner, two men in suits were hunched over a workbench, each sifting through folders thick with computer printouts. One of them noticed Bolan and the others approaching and signaled to his partner. When the second man turned around, his face lit up.

"Belasko!" he called out, stepping away from the bench and smiling warmly as he extended a hand toward Bolan. "What a surprise!"

"Nhajsib Wal," Bolan said, shaking the other man's hand. "I wasn't expecting you."

"I've been promoted," the Indian said. "Thanks in no small part to you."

Wal was a compact man with dark skin, jet-black hair and youthful features. He turned to Kissinger and shook his hand, as well. "You are Cowboy, if I remember correctly."

Kissinger nodded. "Good to see you again."

Bolan introduced the agent to Li, explaining that he, Kissinger and Nhajsib Wal had collaborated on a mission several months earlier, helping to thwart Kashmir separatists from assassinating India's prime minister, as well as America's President while the latter was in Bangkok as part of a peacekeeping mission on the subcontinent. Even more recently, Wal had briefly abetted a successful effort by Able Team and Phoenix Force to put down a nuclear threat in neighboring Myanmar.

While his partner resumed poring over his computer printouts, Wal exchanged a few more pleasantries with Bolan, then got down to the matter at hand.

"I'm sorry, but the plane is still missing," he reported. "I've been told that we may have some sat-intel to look at in a few hours, but until then I suspect we'll still be in the dark."

"The Rangers?" Kissinger asked.

"The last I heard, they'd crossed the border undetected and expected to be in the vicinity where we lost contact with the plane sometime tomorrow morning," Wal reported. "They bypassed the Himalayas, but they still have some treacherous terrain to negotiate, and there is also the matter of border patrols.''

''I'm sure they can take care of themselves,'' Bolan said.

''I'm sure you're right.''

''Have we heard from the Chinese yet?'' Li asked.

''Regarding the plane? No, not yet,'' Wal replied. ''They have made some veiled threats, however. They claim you Americans are looking for an excuse to increase your military presence in the area and try to meddle in their affairs.''

''Now, there's a spin on the truth for you,'' Kissinger muttered.

Wal nodded. ''It has been good grist for their speech writers. I understand there has been a communiqué from Beijing calling the U.S. 'warmongering interventionists.'''

''Which is probably the same way the Tibetans are looking at Beijing right about now,'' Bolan observed.

''True,'' Wal said. ''From the intel I've had a chance to look at, they've mobilized more troops for these war games inside Tibet than at any time since the height of the Korean War.''

Wal had already received a few sketchy details about how plans for the ES-1 had been smuggled out of Edwards Air Force Base and transmitted to unknown parties via the Internet. He had a few questions, and Bolan answered them as best he could while stressing that some of the specifics would need to remain classified. Wal didn't take offense, claiming that in the few months since his promotion he'd learned just how protective intelligence agencies could be when it came to sharing information.

"Which isn't to say you won't have our fullest cooperation," he added quickly. Indicating the paperwork he and his partner had been sorting through, he went on to explain, "We're in the process of going over background checks on all personnel who could have possibly had access to the ES-1 while it was hangared here."

"I know that drill," Kissinger interjected.

"We have also made arrangements to have a small squad of Gurkhas cross the border and assist the Rangers," Wal said. "As you know, they are our elite in these sorts of matters."

"We'll take all the help we can get."

Bolan knew the Nepalese warriors were the stuff of legend, with a celebrated history dating back to eighteenth-century skirmishes with the Mongols. More recently, their facts of valor and incredible endurance on the battlefield had made them the pride of both the English and Indian military. More than a hundred thousand Gurkhas were presently enlisted in the Indian army, and, from the sounds of it, the cream of that crop would now have yet another chance to feather their reputation.

"They'll be at your disposal after the Dalai Lama's visit this afternoon."

Bolan frowned. "The Dalai Lama? What's he doing visiting here?"

"Not here," Wal told him. "Down in the village. Outside of Dharmasala, Marjeelam has the highest number of Tibetan exiles in all of northern India. We are also as close as he can get to Tibet without crossing the border. He will be addressing a rally calling for a return to full autonomy in his country."

"After all these years, I'm sure he has that speech down pat," Kissinger observed ruefully.

"Regrettably, yes," Wal conceded. "There is the hope, however, that he can form some sort of alliance, in only in spirit, with others in China similarly disaffected. Falun Gong, the Taiwanese, student dissidents. Together perhaps they can make a difference."

"It might at least help split the Beijing's focus," Bolan said.

Wal was about to ask Bolan how the Americans wanted to proceed when his partner, an older man whose hair was a white as Wal's was black, stepped away from the bench.

"Excuse me," he interrupted. "But I think I may have found something."

The man handed Wal two pieces of paper. Wal skimmed the information, then nodded and glanced at Bolan. "This man Ingersoll, the one who was killed before he could get his hands on the plans for the spy plane...the firm he worked for was called Krebbs Gillis Aerosystems, correct?"

"That's the outfit, yes," Bolan said. "Why?"

"It may only be coincidence, of course," Wal said, referring to the printout, "but this company has a branch here in India. In Mysore. It seems that one of the maintenance workers here at the base was employed by them before joining the service."

"How recently?" Bolan wondered.

"A year and a half ago," Wal responded.

"Was he with R&D?" Kissinger asked, beginning to see the connection.

"Let's see...." Wal again scanned the documents his partner had given him. "Yes, research and development. That was Ingersoll's field?"

"Sure was," Kissinger said. "And being a VP, you can bet he did his share of globe-trotting to other facilities."

"Meaning there's a chance he knew the worker here," Bolan interjected.

"Which also means he could have made arrangements for the guy here to receive a copy of the plans and then tinker with the plane so it would go down," Kissinger said. "What better way to up the odds of them landing that defense contract?"

Li, who'd been listening quietly to the exchange, spoke up. "The only problem with that theory is that Ingersoll was killed before he got his hands on the plans. Remember, he's not the one who sent out that e-mail. One of the Boxers sent it out from PACRIM's bunker."

"Damn, you're right." Kissinger groaned with disappointment. "Hell, I thought we were onto something there."

"We still might be," Wal said, referring to the readout. "We have passport documentation on this worker, too. He's visited China five...no, six different times over the past three years. Twice while on furlough with the military."

"Hong Kong?" Bolan asked.

"Yes, as a matter of fact," Wal confirmed. "Does PACRIM have offices there?"

"I don't know about that," Bolan confessed, "but those plans were e-mailed to an account with a Hong Kong address."

"Let's not forget that the Boxers come from one of the triads operating out of Hong Kong, too," Li reminded Bolan.

"Wait," Kissinger said. "Are we suggesting that

we have a maintenance worker here who has ties with both Krebbs Gillis *and* Beijing?''

"I know it's a reach," Bolan stated, "but it fits if you think about it. If Beijing knew what the plans were for even before the Boxer got hold of them, it stands to reason they had a game plan in mind when they had them intercepted.''

"So, if the ES-1 was sabotaged like we're thinking," Kissinger said, "China's behind it, not Krebbs Gillis.''

"There's one way to find out.''

Bolan turned to Wal. "Let's track down this maintenance worker and have a little talk with him.''

CHAPTER FOURTEEN

Airman Third Class Dilip Chozin, as it turned out, was off the base.

"Just our luck," Kissinger groused as he left the barracks with Bolan, Jen Li and Nhajsib Wal. They'd been told that Chozin had been assigned to part of a crew sent to Marjeelam to unload a shipment of military provisions arriving by rail from New Delhi. The crew had left the base less than half an hour earlier in a four-truck convoy.

Their search of the barracks hadn't been a complete loss, however. Inside Chozin's locker they'd found a laptop equipped with a wireless modem. Lacking a password, they were unable to log on, but the computer's mere presence was incriminating.

"He'd have had no problems accessing the e-mail with the plans," Bolan said. "He's our man."

"Now we just need to get our hands on him," Wal said.

He attempted radio contact with the lieutenant in

charge of the convoy, but the reception was poor and the IB agent didn't want to risk having his message garbled.

"They must still be in the mountains," Wal concluded. "I should have better luck once they reach the valley."

"In case that doesn't work, is there a way we can get to town ahead of them?" Bolan asked.

"I could see if there is a helicopter available," Wal suggested. "That, or we could take my car. There is a back road that is too treacherous for trucks. I have a Mercedes, however." The agent offered a sly smile. "In America, I think you call it a 'perk.'"

"Let's take the car," Bolan said.

"I was hoping you'd say that." Wal instructed his partner to keep trying to reach the convoy by radio, then led the others from the hangar. His Mercedes turned out to be a twenty-five-year-old 450 SL. A layer of road dust covered the exterior, but inside the car was clean and meticulously maintained. Wal was clearly as proud of the vehicle as if it had just come off the production line. Bolan rode up front with the Indian while Kissinger and Jen Li took the back seat.

Less than a mile past the air base, the plain gave way to a rocky slope riddled with crags and ravines. As Wal had forewarned the others, the road was a winding dirt strip no more than a lane and a half wide that carved a grueling path down the incline. Rock slides were apparently common, as they came across two road crews tediously clearing the way.

"They're mostly caused by mountain yaks," Wal explained, pointing out a group of the large, oxlike beasts treading along an unseen path high up in the hills to their left. "They will dislodge a few rocks, and by the time the rocks reach the road, they have brought along a small army with them."

Aside from the workers, there was no sign of human presence in the mountains for several miles. Then, off to the right, Bolan spotted a terraced area planted with rows of soybean. Laborers were out in the small field, stooped over their crops.

"Agricultural settlement," Wal explained. "The mountains are dotted with them."

"Must be wash day," Kissinger said, indicating strips of fabric strung out along a long length of rope near a pair of small farmhouses.

"I think they're prayer flags," Li said.

"Yes," Wal concurred. "The villagers' way of offering worship to Buddha."

As they rounded the bend, Bolan stared out the windshield and saw they were approaching the valley Wal had spoken about earlier. Marjeelam was visible at the far end of the valley, with the land in between mostly parceled off into more farm plots.

There were also several modest stupas, small, spired structures surrounded walking areas around which, as Wal explained, worshipers could recite chants or spin prayer wheels spaced at regular intervals.

Kissinger asked Wal about a procession men in reddish-maroon robes—more than a dozen of them—trailing away from one of the stupas.

"Monks," Wal replied, "walking to Marjeelam for the Dalai Lama's speech."

"They've got a ways to go," Bolan said. "It looks like a good ten miles to town at least."

"I'm sure villagers will stop to give them a—"

Wal's voice suddenly trailed off. The sound of gunfire carried across the valley. He rolled down his window and listened.

"I think it's coming from the other road," he said, motioning to the glove compartment. "Could you hand me my cell phone, please?"

Wal brought the Mercedes to a stop in the middle of the road and quickly dialed his partner back at the air base. The men exchanged a few words, then Wal turned to Bolan.

"He got through to the lieutenant and gave word for Chozin to be detained once they reached town," he explained. "Something must have gone wrong."

"I'm guessing the lieutenant missed the part about waiting until they got to town," Kissinger said.

The gunfire continued a few moments longer, then tapered off. Wal shifted back into gear and eased down on the accelerator, urging the Mercedes down the dirt road. Soon his cell phone rang back to life, however, forcing him again to stop.

It was his partner. The news wasn't good.

"It appears you were right," Wal said, eyeing Kissinger in the rearview mirror. "Apparently the lieutenant stopped the convoy and confronted Chozin on the spot."

"Idiot," Kissinger muttered. "And Chozin made a run for it, right?"

Wal nodded. "The convoy had two motorcycles escorting it. I don't know the details, but Chozin must have somehow commandeered one of them and, as you say, he made a run for it. Unfortunately the motorcycles were dirt bikes. He had no problem leaving the road when they started firing at him. A soldier on the other bike crashed trying to overtake him."

"He got away, then," Bolan said.

Wal nodded miserably. "Into one of the ravines."

Staring out the window at the craggy terrain that surrounded the valley, Li murmured, "Maybe we should have taken the helicopter after all."

TWO MILES DOWNHILL from where Nhajsib Wal had taken the call about Chozin's escape—the zigzag course of the road actually made it twice the distance by car—the Indian turned his Mercedes onto a crossroad.

"This leads over to the truck route," he told the others. "If Chozin comes back up to the road, we might cross paths with him."

"That would be karma, right," Kissinger said, "for him to jump right back on the hook like that?"

"I suppose that's one way of looking at it," Wal agreed.

They hadn't gone far before they came upon evidence that the renegade airman had indeed used the road. Off on the shoulder, a woman knelt by the side of the road, keening and wailing as she stared at the lifeless body of a man lying in the dirt before her. Surrounding her, attempting futilely to offer consolation, was a handful of monks ranging in age from a young boy who couldn't have been more than ten to an elder in his late seventies. All the men were dressed in their traditional robes except for one, who stood out conspicuously amid the others, wearing only sandals and a white dhoti.

Wal pulled off the road twenty yards from the congregation, flashing his IB identification and announcing himself the moment he got out of the car. The others followed him to the body. The victim was a man in his fifties, roughly the same age as the woman.

"What happened?" Wal asked gently.

Before any of the monks could speak, the woman looked up at Wal and spoke hurriedly, her voice breaking several times. She was speaking in a Tibetan dialect, and the IB agent had trouble following her.

"Please speak slowly so that I can understand you," he beseeched her.

"She says a madman jumped in front of their tractor and attacked her husband as they were driving the monks to Marjeelam," Li said. When Bolan glanced at her with surprise, she reminded him, "I told you back in the States that I spoke the languages around here. I meant it."

While Li tried to calm the woman and learn more details, one of the monks caught Kissinger's attention and pointed insistently to a spot in the brush twenty yards from the road. Kissinger jogged down the embankment for a closer look.

"Here's the dirt bike," he called up to the others. He quickly inspected the motorcycle, then strode back up to the road.

"Bullet creased the gas tank," he told Wal and Bolan. "He took one, too, from the looks of it. Seat's smeared with blood."

"He must've needled on empty," Bolan said, "then ditched the bike in favor of this guy's tractor."

"If that's the case, we might have a chance of catching up with him," Kissinger reasoned.

Li put a sympathetic hand on the woman's shoulder, then rejoined the men, telling them, "She also says he forced one of the monks to give him his robe. He put it on right over his uniform, which apparently had blood on it."

Bolan glanced back down the way they'd come. "If we assume he stayed on the road, there was only one way he could have turned at the crossroad without us seeing him." He turned to Wal. "How many monks are we talking about in Marjeelam?"

Wal shook his head. "Hard to say. Two thousand perhaps. But with the Dalai Lama coming, there are likely to be more. Tens of thousands, in fact. You'll see. The closer we get to town, the more it will look like a river of red is running through it."

"Then I suggest we turn the Mercedes around and put the pedal to the metal," Bolan said. "We need to get to him while he's still on the road."

JEN LI ELECTED to stay behind with the monks and woman. Before the others left, however, she talked briefly with the woman and then passed along a description of the tractor.

Once back in the Mercedes, the men turned and headed back toward the road that had brought them

Marjeelam. No one spoke for a ways, then Wal broke the silence.

"We have troops stationed at the outskirts of town," he recalled. "Perhaps we should forewarn them of what's happened."

"And risk another miscommunication?" Bolan said. "I'd rather not. If it looks like we can't catch up with him, that's another matter."

Wal nodded his assent. When they reached the crossroads, they turned right and were soon traveling along the valley floor. Farms were more abundant, packed adjacent to one another, creating a patchwork of varied crops: barley, soybeans, wheat and, flanking a watershed fed by a crystalline mountain spring, paddies. There were also several small hamlets consisting of no more than a few homes abutting a common area set aside for loading harvests for delivery into town. And, too, there were more *gompas,* meditation centers marked by more gilded stupas like the one the men had passed earlier. Most of the shrines were set far off the road, on small hillocks, but several, larger facilities lay within easy access of motorists and were flanked by dirt parking lots.

"For the tourists," Wal explained.

"Not to mention the occasional errant airman," Kissinger said, pointing to a parking lot two hundred yards down the road.

Bolan spotted the tractor. It stood out conspicuously among the other vehicles, mostly small sedans and station wagons. There was no sign of Chozin, however.

"He's not there to pray," Wal said.

When a late-model Fiat pulled out of a parking spot next to the tractor and raised a trail of dust racing for the driveway, Bolan drew his Desert Eagle and said, "I think he just upgraded to something faster. Step on it."

Wal gave the Mercedes more gas and sped forward, trying to intercept the Fiat before it left the parking lot.

"Let's take him alive if we can," Bolan said.

Despite the burst of speed, Wal was unable to cut off the Fiat. The smaller car screeched from the driveway without stopping and cut sharply to the left, heading for Marjeelam. It's driver was paying no more attention to the posted speed limit than Wal. Within seconds it was racing along the two-lane road at seventy miles per hour and showing no signs of slowing. The Mercedes had the superior power plant, however, and Wal quickly began to close in.

"It's gotta be him, all right," Kissinger said. Like Bolan, he had his gun out.

"You're probably going to have to force it off the road," Bolan warned Wal.

"I know," the Indian said, clearly displeased with the idea of using his prized possession as a four-wheeled battering ram.

The initial eighty-yard gap between the vehicles was quickly halved. As Wal continued to close in, a gunman suddenly leaned out of the left rear passenger window of the Fiat and drew a bead on the Mercedes with an Uzi submachine gun.

"Looks like Chozin's got some company with him," Kissinger said.

"Maybe he didn't steal that car after all," Bolan surmised. "Cut it, Nhajsib!"

Wal was already on it. There was no oncoming traffic, so he abruptly veered left, crossing the median. Bullets caromed off the Mercedes's right front quarter panel, missing those inside. Wal reflexively tapped the brakes, then revved the engine again, fishtailing after the other car.

Bolan and Kissinger, meanwhile, leaned out their windows and returned fire, doing little more than cosmetic damage to the Fiat. By now they could see that there were four occupants inside the other car. Only one of them was wearing robes. Bolan fired off another burst, missing the man with the Uzi and scarring the Fiat's rooftops. As the Mercedes inched closer, he finally got a good look at the shooter's features.

"Chinese," he said.

As the chase continued, with both sides wasting ammunition trying to strike their swerving targets, the cars found themselves coming up on a slow-moving pickup truck filled with villagers bound to Marjeelam. There were so many of them that they overflowed the cargo bed, with some passengers standing precariously out on the back bumper, clinging to those more securely positioned on the other side of the tailgate.

"This could get ugly," Kissinger murmured, forced to hold his fire.

The Fiat continued veering from lane to lane until it was within a few yards of the pickup. Then, at the last possible second, the driver sped past, grazing the toes of several passengers whose legs were dangling outside the truck's bed.

The Mercedes was right behind, but as he committed to the passing lane, Wal saw, to his horror, that the lane up ahead was already taken. Pinned in by the pickup truck, racing along at more than eighty-five miles per hour, the Mercedes found itself on a collision course with an oncoming Suburban.

CHAPTER FIFTEEN

Nhajsib Wal had only one option. Removing his foot from the brake, he jerked the steering wheel hard to his left. The driver of the Suburban, fortunately, had had no time to react and sped past, still in the middle of the lane, the SUV snagged the Mercedes's right rear bumper with just enough force to rip it free of the car's frame without throwing it into a tailspin. The bumper danced spastically on the asphalt as the Mercedes swept off the road, bounding roughly along the gravel shoulder. It took all his doing, but Wal kept the vehicle under control and after another thirty yards, he was able to ease back onto the tarmac. Another car was coming his way, but he had time to get to the right lane.

"Nice piece of driving, Bullitt," Kissinger called out.

"It was all instinct," Wal confessed. "I barely know what I did."

"What you did is save our bacon," Bolan told him.

The men in the Fiat had taken advantage of the situation and pulled away, but now that they were getting near to Marjeelam, traffic was picking up in both lanes. In fact, less than a half mile down the road, cars were beginning to flash their brake lights, forced by the congestion to slow. A high-speed chase was no longer an option.

Rather than become tied up in the traffic jam, the Fiat's driver turned off onto a side road and headed westward. As it was making the turn, a second man leaned out another window, echoing the Uzi blasts being fired by his cohort. The Mercedes took hits in the grillwork and hood. A ricochet smashed through the windshield and lodged in the headrest where Bolan was sitting. He was spared only because he'd hunched over to reloading his Desert Eagle.

"Hang on!" Wal said.

He took the Mercedes off the road once again and forged a diagonal course across an untended field. The ground was hard and even, allowing Wal to keep up his speed. Once again, the Mercedes began closing in on the Fiat. Wal didn't bother with any evasive maneuvers. Jaws clenched, fingers tight around the steering wheel, he used the front hood ornament as if it were a rifle scope, keeping it centered on the seam between the front and rear doors of the other vehicle.

Bolan and Kissinger, meanwhile, continued to fire at the gunmen in the Fiat. One shot found its mark, taking out the gunman leaning out the front window. The man dropped his Uzi and slumped halfway out the vehicle. When the Fiat hit a bump in the road, the man's weight shifted and he toppled from the vehicle, rolling a few times across the asphalt before coming to a rest.

By now less than twenty yards separated the vehicles.

"Go ahead and take them out," Bolan told Wal.

The IB agent didn't need to be told. With a last burst of speed, he rammed the passenger side of the Fiat, broadsiding it at a forty-five-degree angle.

The Fiat lurched wildly and spun out of control, crossing lanes and plowing, rear end first, into the shallow waters of a paddy. The Mercedes, meanwhile, came to a grinding halt in the middle of the road. Bolan, thrown sharply forward during the impact, was momentarily dazed. When he came to, his left arm was numb from striking the dashboard, but he was in far better shape than the others. Wal was groaning in pain, his legs pinned beneath the collapsed steering wheel, which had also taken a toll on his rib cage, making it difficult for him to breathe. Kissinger was out cold in the back seat, blood streaming from a gash across his forehead.

Wal grimaced and told Bolan weakly, "Go. Get them."

Bolan threw open his door and staggered out onto the road. His legs felt like jelly, and he leaned against the front quarter panel for support as he slowly circled the vehicle. He saw that the Fiat's driver was still behind the wheel, but he wasn't moving. The other gunman had climbed out, apparently unharmed, and was standing knee deep in the mud-colored water of the paddy. Livid, he returned Bolan's gaze and raised his Uzi. The Executioner had the drop on him, however, and pumped three shots his way, striking him twice in the chest. The man reeled forward, landing face-first in the water.

That left Chozin.

Bolan willed his legs to cooperate and pushed away from the Mercedes, heading down the faint slope that led to the paddies. He heard a car door swing open and saw Chozin stumble away from the Fiat, his stolen monk's robes trailing through the mud. Gun drawn, he made his way toward a trio of older women who'd been tending to the rice. The women cried out but were too horror-stricken to move.

Bolan was in a quandary. Much as he wanted to take the airman alive, he couldn't let Chozin reach the women and jeopardize their safety. His left arm, though tingling, had come back to life, and he used it to steady his aim as he raised his .44 into target acquisition. He aimed low, avoiding a killshot, and punched a round into Chozin's lower back area.

With a scream of pain, the airman dropped to his knees, grabbing at the wound. The women, seeing that he was armed and—more importantly, that he wasn't Tibetan and therefore only masquerading as a monk—overcame their fear and, as a group, slogged through the mashy soup toward him. When Chozin raised his gun at them, one of the women took a swipe at him with her rake. The airman screamed again as the gun flew from his hand, sinking into the mud. The other two women began striking him with their tools, as well, peppering him with welts. Bolan finally caught up with them and pulled them away.

"Leave him to me," he told them.

The women backed off.

Bolan grabbed the man by the scruff of his robes and jerked him sharply about. Chozin's face was contorted in pain.

"I'm dying," he gasped.

"I don't think so," Bolan said, "but by the time I'm finished with you, you'll wish you had."

Bolan stared hard at Chozin, gauging his reaction.

He was looking for a trace of fear, and he finally saw it in the man's eyes.

Good, Bolan thought. He knew from years of experience that if a man could be made to feel fear, when it came time for interrogation, he could also be made to talk.

ONCE HE'D MANAGED to wriggle free of the wreckage of his prized Mercedes, Nhajsib Wal, wincing with every step, waded through the paddies toward Bolan and Chozin.

"Your friend is conscious," he told Bolan. "I told him to stay put and wait for the medics. They are attending to some members of the truck convoy but will be here shortly."

"You should probably be taking it easy yourself," Bolan told the IB agent.

"I only have a few cracked ribs and a bruised knee," Wal guessed. "I have work to do."

"What about me?" Chozin implored. "I'm dying!"

Bolan leveled his Desert Eagle at the airman's face. "I don't want to hear it."

Chozin fell silent, glowering at his apprehenders. With help from the field workers, Bolan had pulled off Chozin's robes to get a better look at his gunshot wounds. Though his uniform was soaked with blood, neither of the airman's wounds appeared serious. Fleeing the convoy, he'd been struck just below the right shoulder, and Bolan's contribution had been a bullet through the flesh slightly above the left hip. Both wounds were through-and-throughs, shedding a lot of blood. No vital organs had been hit. Once the bleeding was stopped—a task one of the women was grudgingly performing with mud packs—he could forego hospitalization, at least for the time being.

"Let's get him out of this field before the gawkers start flocking," Bolan suggested.

He pointed to a nearby two-wheeled wooden cart yoked to a domesticated water buffalo. The cart was filled with tools and burlap bags. At Wal's beckoning, the other two women brought the car and rearranged the load to make room for Chozin. Bolan had to holster his gun while helping the airman up, but Chozin, unable to put any weight on his left leg without writhing in agony, was clearly not about to attempt another escape. With Wal's assistance, they transferred him to the cart. The woman treating him held the mud packs in place until Chozin was situated, then gruffly showed him how to apply the right amount of pressure to staunch the bleeding. The airman had to contort himself to hold both packs in place and he began to complain about mistreatment.

"This is not allowed!" he complained. "I still have my rights."

The man's protests were ignored. Wal asked the field workers for permission to use of one of their storage sheds, located fifty yards from the road at the edge of the paddies. The women were more than happy to oblige. One led the way, tugging the water buffalo's reins to coax it through the mud, while the others trod along either side of the cart, one armed with a rake, the other a hoe, both glaring at Chozin as if looking for an excuse to resume beating him. Bolan and Wal walked slowly behind, conserving their strength.

"I spoke to the lieutenant by phone," Wal explained. "Chozin killed one soldier and wounded another making his escape. He feels responsible."

"He should," Bolan said. "Even if he heard the instructions wrong, he should have been smart enough to wait until they'd reached town to make his move."

"What's done is done." Wal coughed. "The important thing is that we have Chozin back in custody, alive."

The Indian coughed again, this time louder. Bolan didn't like the sound of it. When he saw Wal dab a handkerchief to his lips, he reached out, holding the Indian's wrist so he could get a better look at the cloth. It was spotted with blood.

"One of those cracked ribs must've scraped your lungs," he said.

"I'm fine," Wal insisted.

"I think you should go back and wait for the ambulance," Bolan suggested.

"I'm fine," Wal repeated, this time more forcefully. "I can take care of myself."

Bolan knew Wal had made up his mind. He let the matter drop.

Once they reached the shed, a small structure made of hammered planks, Bolan and Wal helped Chozin from the cart and took him inside. They cleared away some equipment and laid out a thin mattress of burlap bags, then told their prisoner to lie down, positioning mud packs underneath him so that his weight would hold them in place, leaving Chozin with just the two exit wounds to tend to. Wal sent the women off, then closed the door. Light shone through gaps in the walls. Bolan laid some of the burlap over Chozin's ankles, then tipped over a workbench, easing its weight onto the airman's feet, pinning his legs to the ground. Then he loomed over Chozin.

"Let's talk," Bolan said.

"I want to go to a hospital," Chozin groaned.

"That's not what we want to talk about," Wal told him. Another cough rattled up from his chest. He deliberately looked away from Bolan, and he went for his handkerchief again as he told the airman, ''We want to talk about your work on the spy plane.''

When Chozin hesitated, Bolan lowered the boom. ''We know you're in collusion with both the Chinese and your former employers at Krebbs Gillis. We know the plans for the ES-1 were sent to you by the Internet. We checked your locker back at the barracks and found your computer. Once we bypass your access code, I'm sure we'll find that you downloaded those plans in time to tinker with the plane before its launch. We have you dead to rights.''

Chozin was unfamiliar with the term. Wal provided a rough translation, then told him, ''We have you for espionage, resisting arrest and murder. Being taken to the hospital should be the last of your worries right now.''

The airman was stunned. He remained silent a moment, then said, ''My life is over. Why should I talk?''

Bolan was in no mood to play cat and mouse. He wanted this finished. He drew his Desert Eagle and, without hesitation, fired three quick shots. The first two thumped into the earth on either side of Chozin's head, leaving a ringing in his ears. The third shot ripped through the fabric of the man's pant, grazing his inner thigh three inches from his testicles. Bolan then crouched before Chozin and quickly jerked one of the mud packs from his grasp, pressing it against the man's face so that he couldn't breathe. When Chozin tried to struggle, Wal reached down and pinned his arms to his sides. The prisoner's face turned red, and the fear came back into his eyes.

Bolan waited a moment longer, then pulled the mud pack free and placed it back over the man's shoulder wound. He stood and calmly began to reload his pistol. Chozin spit mud from his bruised lips. He'd changed his mind about not talking.

"It's true," he confessed. "Everything you said."

"I want to hear it from you," Bolan demanded.

And so Dilip Chozin laid it out for them.

Yes, he'd known Brett Ingersoll. Yes, the men had met on several occasions while Ingersoll was visiting the Krebbs Gillis in Mysore, where Chozin was part of the R&D team specializing in navigational and communications systems for unmanned planes. They'd kept in touch even after Chozin had left the firm to go into the service, meeting another time only two weeks previously, when Ingersoll had first brought up how Krebbs Gillis was falling behind in the race with National Avionics for a defense contract involving UCRVs. Ingersoll had said there might be an opportunity over the following few weeks for Chozin to help his former employers get back on track. Ingersoll had couched his proposal carefully, specifically avoiding any message of the words *espionage* or *sabotage,* but the airman knew what he'd be getting himself into and had at first said he had no interest in getting involved.

"But Ingersoll knew you had your price," Bolan interrupted.

Chozin nodded miserably. "When we got into money, he wrote down an offer on paper. I was relieved, because it was so little money, I knew I could easily walk away. But I was angry, too. Insulted that he would have me risk so much for so little, so I took his piece of paper and added three zeros on the end. I was—how you say?—playing hardball."

"And he came back with a counteroffer," Wal said. The Indian's coughing had subsided, at least for the moment.

Chozin nodded. "He crossed off one of the zeros and said he could meet me halfway on the second if it turned out the assignment turned out to be more difficult than he anticipated. I was shocked."

"You changed your mind," Bolan said.

"Yes, I changed my mind. At the time, I had no idea how I was supposed to help him out while stationed here in Marjeelam, but three days later he contacted me again and talked about an American spy satellite going out of commission over China. He said the U.S. was planning to use the Avionics plane to take its place until a replacement could be put into orbit."

"Your assignment was to sabotage the plane before it took off," Bolan guessed.

Chozin nodded. "The way he explained it, the ES-1 used many components similar to the one we had been developing, with the navigation and communications. What Ingersoll wanted was for the ES-1 to fail without anyone suspecting it had been tampered with. He said he would prefer it if the pilot didn't have to die."

"A man with principles," Wal remarked ruefully.

"I suggested fixing things so that the pilot would lose radio contact at the same time his navigational systems went down. He would still be able to fly the plane, but only for a short time. And if he could find a safe place to land, he would be fine."

"A big if," Bolan said, "especially when you've got a man flying over the Himalayas."

"A good pilot would be able to handle it," Chozin insisted.

"The pilot on that plane was one of the best around," Bolan said.

"Then I suspect he is fine."

"Except for the fact that you dropped him right into the laps of the Chinese."

Chozin was silent a moment, then decided to avoid answering. He backtracked to his story. "I told Ingersoll that no matter how similar the ES-1 might be to the Krebbs Gillis plane, there would be significant differences that could prevent me from doing what I suggested.''

"You said you needed to see the spec sheets,'' Bolan stated.

"Yes, the schematics. If I could have the plans to refer to, I could make whatever adjustments were necessary.''

"All right, I think we're clear on all that,'' Bolan said. "But we both know the plans wound up being sent to you by the Chinese, not Ingersoll.''

"I had no part in his being killed,'' Chozin claimed. "We'll see about that,'' Bolan said.

Outside the shed, the men heard the bleat of an approaching siren. Chozin appealed to Bolan and Wal. "That is the ambulance. I've told you what I know. Can I please be seen by the medic? I'm hurting.''

"We're not through yet,'' Bolan told him. "You still haven't explained how the Chinese fit into this, not to mention the fact that three of them conveniently showed up in that parking lot with a getaway car after you bolted the convoy.''

"I will tell you after I'm treated with something besides mud packs,'' Chozin bartered.

Bolan pointed the gun back at him. "At this point, we really don't need you to piece things together. But if you save us a little extra legwork, then we can change the conversation to your medical benefits. Not before.''

"We'll help you to keep it brief,'' Wal interjected. "We know you've been to China several times, and we're sure that at some point you must have fallen into the wrong crowd.''

"My sister-in-law is Chinese,'' he explained. "I went there the first time with her and my brother to visit her family in Hong Kong. Their neighborhood, it is heavy with gangs. They are involved in the usual things, and in a moment of weakness I—''

"We don't need to get into your personal problems,'' Bolan interrupted. "You fell in with a gang that wound up having ties with a firm called PACRIM. They call themselves Boxers. Yes or no.''

Chozin nodded again. "Yes.''

"And at some point after you cut your deal with Ingersoll,'' Bolan theorized, "you decided that with a little double-dealing you might be able to tack those extra zeros back onto your take from all this.''

"Yes,'' Chozin repeated. "I made a separate deal with the Chinese. Only the way it was supposed to work was that I'd pass along the plans after Ingersoll sent them to me. I had no idea they would get into the middle of things and kill him first.''

"They killed him so they could pay you off with his money,'' Bolan said. "They wound up getting the plans for free.''

"Not only that," Wal added, "but unless you bungled your sabotage and destroyed the ES-1, you've given them the plane, as well, in the bargain."

"They played you for a chump," Bolan said. "A sucker."

"What do you think of yourself now?" Wal asked.

Chozin clearly hadn't considered the idea that he'd been used. He was silent a moment, his features hardening despite the pain he was in.

"The men in the Fiat," he said bitterly. "They were supposed to meet me at the rail station in Marjeelam to pay me off."

"To silence you is more like it," Bolan surmised.

Angry tears began to well in the airman's eyes. He freed his hand from one of the mud packs and reached for his pocket. Bolan stopped him, grabbing his wrist.

"I was just going to show my cell phone," Chozin explained, his voice breaking. "I called them once I'd escaped from the convoy and told them what had happened. They arranged to pick me up."

"And I'm sure they were thrilled about it, too," Bolan said. "It would have been a lot easier for them to get rid of you out here in the country. Fewer witnesses and plenty of places to dump your body where nobody would find it until the animals picked you clean down to the bones.''

Chozin began to sob. ''And to think that I trusted them,'' he moaned.

''They were gangsters, Dilip,'' Wal said. ''What did you expect?''

''They'll pay,'' Chozin promised bitterly. ''I will make them pay!''

''It's a little late for that,'' Bolan said. ''They're all dead.''

Chozin looked up at the men and smiled sickly. ''Not all of them. They did not come to Marjeelam alone.''

''What do you mean?'' Wal asked.

''I will make you a deal,'' Chozin said. ''Get me to a hospital and promise me that I will be given some consideration when charges are brought against me.''

''In exchange for what?'' Bolan said.

Chozin smiled again. ''In exchange, I will tell about the plans these 'gangsters' have to assassinate the Dalai Lama while he is here in Marjeelam.''

CHAPTER SIXTEEN

Chozin, understandably, knew few specifics about the plan. The gangsters who'd picked him up in the Fiat had merely bragged to him that they had brought along a few other men, including two sharp-shooters to—as the airmen put it—"put a few holes in the holy man." That was it. No time, no location.

"Security will be tightest during the rally," Bolan thought out loud once the men were back up on the road. "If they're smart, they'll try to take him out before or after, probably while he's in transport."

"I agree," Wal said. He was standing alongside his Mercedes, sadly watching a driver hook the car to his tow truck for hauling it to a salvage yard in Marjeelam. The IB agent's coughing fits had re-sumed, and his handkerchief had turned crimson from the blood coming up from his lungs. Reluc-tantly he had agreed it would be best for him to accompany Chozin and Kissinger to the hospital. The other two men were already inside one of the two ambulances on the scene; Chozin gladly, Kissinger less so. The wound to the Stony Man armorer's forehead would need stitches, and in response to Bolan's urging, he'd conceded that X rays were in order to make sure he hadn't suffered a concussion.

Jen Li, who'd arrived with the medics, was grateful to a chance to fill the void.

"I've been beginning to feel like a Sister of Mercy," she told Bolan as they took the back seat of a nondescript Buick driven by Wal's partner. The man, whose name was Hanji, had driven down from the air base after reporting Dilip Chozin's escape from the convoy. At Wal's suggestion, he'd put a call through to the Gurkha soldiers who'd been assigned to complement the security detail for the Dalai Lama's visit. The Gurkhas, like most commando forces, were an insular group, not inclined to bring outsiders into their ranks. Despite the gravity of the situation, this was to be no exception. Hanji had expected as much; all he wanted was for the squad to meet the Americans to make sure that, in a worst-case scenario, Bolan and Li wouldn't find themselves accidentally gunned down by friendly fire. Or vice versa.

They took the truck route into Marjeelam. It was longer but far less congested. Within twenty minutes they had reached the train station, located a mile outside town. The convoy was there, already unloading supplies from a freight train that had been routed away from the terminal, which teemed with thousands of exiled Tibetans arriving for the Dalai Lama's visit.

"How's he getting here?" Bolan asked Hanji after they passed through a security checkpoint. "Not train, I hope."

The older officer shook his head. "A military helicopter is bringing him in from Dharmasala."

Li turned to Bolan. "Did Chozin mention anything about these snipers having SAMs at their disposal?"

"No," Bolan said, "but I was thinking the same thing."

"The military has men stationed on the ground all along the air route," Hanji told them. He'd been directed to take a service road leading to the railyard, allowing them to circumvent the throngs spilling from the terminal. "They're also sending along another three helicopters as decoys."

"Still, that's a lot of area to cover," Bolan said.

"Perhaps," Hanji said, "but there is no safer way."

"When's he due here?" Li asked.

Hanji checked the dashboard clock. "Not for another hour."

"What are they doing for aerial recon?" Bolan wanted to know.

"Two light planes and one helicopter," Hanji replied. "The planes will make passes from separate directions while the helicopter zigzags."

"What kind of chopper?"

"That I don't know. In cases like this, we usually use a Colwyss."

Bolan was familiar with the craft; he'd flown in one during his earlier mission in India. Modeled after the old Bell Model 47, the Colwyss was highly maneuverable but unarmed.

"Let's go ahead and meet with the Gurkhas," Bolan said, "then I want to see about hitching a ride on that bird."

WHEN EXILED TIBETANS had first come to settle in Marjeelam, there was nothing to the area but a small, long abandoned British prisoner-of-war camp overrun with jungle foliage. Their first lodging had been in thirteen Spartan barracks encircling an asphalt courtyard surrounded by barbed wire. During the hot summer months, the asphalt would absorb the sun's blistering rays, making the courtyard unusable while at the same time throwing off so much heat that the barracks were turned into caldrons. After only a few weeks of these unbearable conditions, the settlers had fled from the compound, hacking a new clearing out of the adjacent jungle, an enterprise that carried its own travail in the form of malaria outbreaks and attacks by marauding bull elephants. The Tibetans persevered, and over the next thirty years Marjeelam slowly grew and evolved into the small city of ten thousand that made it now one of the larger concentrations of Tibetan exiles in all of India. The old prisoner-of-war camp, meanwhile, was once again left to the elephants. There would be times when the town's elders would take their progeny on hikes out to the forlorn outpost, located less than a half mile from town, so that they could better understand and appreciate the sacrifices that Marjeelam's founding fathers had endured on their behalf.

For the past few days, the old camp had come back to life, serving as command post and staging area for those providing security during the Dalai Lama's much anticipated visit. A deployment of military troops had set up camp in the old barracks, running fans powered by gasoline generators to stave off the heat. The courtyard, fragmented by kudzu vines and overgrown by lilting jungle grasses, had thankfully surrendered its reputation as an inadvertent solar panel, and troops with machetes had chopped away a clearly large enough to serve as a helipad for two helicopters, a Colwyss-8H and as a fully armed British-made Lynx gunship.

Both aircraft were still on the pad when IB agent Hanji pulled up to the site in his old Buick. As Bolan and Li quickly learned, however, the Gurkhas—who'd been content to camp out in the surrounding jungle rather than indulge themselves in the relative comfort of the barracks—had dispersed within minutes of hearing about the plot on the Dalai Lama's life.

"They are scattered, gone off into the mountains," said General Yuli Avari, acting commander of the security detail. "You will not find them unless they wish to be found." He quickly added, for Bolan's and Li's benefit, "I did pass along word, however, that two Americans were joining the effort, one of them a woman."

"Not a very thorough description," Li stated. "One look at me and they'll see one of the Chinese they're on the lookout for."

Avari, a middle-aged, balding man with a graying beard and ample midsection, could only shrug. "I could only tell them what I knew. I may be in charge here, but, as I'm sure you have heard, the Gurkhas march to their own drummer. They had no desire to wait for your arrival."

"Then I guess we'll just have to take our chances," Li said.

"And, under the circumstances, perhaps we'd be better off in one of the choppers," Bolan suggested tactfully, suspecting that the general wouldn't take kindly to having yet another group of outsiders usurping his authority.

He was right.

"The helicopters will be going up shortly," Avari said. "I have already assigned men to both aircraft." There was a ring of finality in his voice.

Bolan wasn't about to take no for an answer.

"How many sharpshooters will be aboard the Colwyss?" he asked.

"The Colwyss is strictly for reconnaissance," the general replied.

"Suppose it sights the Chinese and they turn an HN-5 on it?" Bolan said. "I'm assuming the Lynx will be elsewhere and not able to lend a hand."

"That could be problematic," Avari conceded. "What are you suggesting?"

They were standing near a barracks serving as a makeshift arms depot. Bolan had already spotted an opened crate stocked with Mannlicher sniper rifles.

"May I?" he said, picking up one of the rifles, as well as a box of shells. When the general nodded, smiling with bemusement, Bolan loaded the weapon with quick precision, then aimed it across the courtyard. More than a hundred yards away, a rust-eaten weather vane spun lazily atop one of the far bunkers. When Bolan pulled the trigger, there was a dull clang. Struck squarely, the vane stopped a moment, then resumed spinning, now slightly off kilter.

The general turned to Bolan, the smile gone from his face. "What about the woman?"

Bolan was about to argue her case when Li reached for the rifle.

"May I?" she said.

Bolan handed her the Mannlicher. Without hesitation, she hoisted it to her shoulder and took aim at the same target. The weather vane gave off a second clang and fell from its mooring, sliding down the roof to the ground. Li calmly handed the weapon back to Bolan.

Avari regarded the Americans, straight faced, then said, "Let me see about getting you some parachutes."

As the general headed off, Li turned to Bolan.

"I *told* you I was field trained."

THE COLWYSS-8H LIFTED off slowly, fanning the untrimmed grass growing through the fractured courtyard, and drifted lazily toward town as it gained altitude. As Nhajsib Wal had predicted, the preponderance of maroon-robed monks making their way down the narrows streets made it seem as if indeed a reddish river were wending its way through Marjeelam.

"Let's just hope it doesn't turn into a river of

blood,'' Bolan said, taking in the procession from the chopper's rear cabin. Jen Li sat behind him. Like Bolan, she had one of the Mannlicher rifles straddled across her lap. Up front, a reconnaissance officer peered down through high-powered binoculars while the pilot banked the helicopter slightly, shifted course southward.

The rally was to be held in a rolling pasture just beyond the city limits. The meadow was flanked on one side by the same wide stream Bolan and Li had seen earlier. Rising on the other side were mountains lush with vegetation. The small stage from which the Dalai Lama would address his followers faced the mountains.

''They should have set the stage at the other end of the field,'' Li murmured. ''The Dalai Lama will have the sun in his eyes.''

''So will the security teams on the ground,'' Bolan said, sharing Li's concern. ''And any snipers in the hills won't have to worry about the sun reflecting off their rifle scopes.''

Bolan called up front, suggesting that Avari be apprised of the situation in hopes the stage could be moved.

''We already thought of that,'' the pilot called back, raising his voice to be heard above the drone of the rotors. ''But the Dalai Lama insisted we keep the stage where it is. He wants to face the mountains because Tibet lies just on the other side. He wants it to appear as if he is appealing directly to his homeland and those who oppress it.''

''Big price to pay for a little symbolism,'' Bolan commented.

''Great men are willing to take such risks,'' the pilot said. He was Indian, but had clearly been moved by what he'd witnessed the past few days in Marjeelam. ''This could well be a telling moment for these people, not to mention their homeland.''

''I'm sure you're right. Let's just hope it's in the way they want.''

The reconnaissance officer spoke up for the first time. ''It's a can't-lose proposition for them,'' he said sardonically. ''If all goes well, maybe the Dalai's words will inspire enough people to turn the tide in China. If it doesn't, the result could be even more dramatic.''

''You mean if he's shot,'' Li stated.

The recon man shrugged. ''Everyone loves a martyr, yes? If the Dalai Lama were to be assassinated, he would probably mobilize even more people in death than he did in life.''

Neither Bolan nor Li responded. They both knew there was more than a kernel of truth to what the man had said. Bolan even wondered fleetingly if the Dalai Lama, once forewarned of the assassination plot, would only be more determined to carry out his address, not so much out of defiance, as in the knowledge, like the reconnaissance officer had suggested, that his voice would resonate even louder through the land once it was silenced by enemy gunfire.

"The Tibetans have their own small militia encircling the pasture," the pilot told Bolan. "You can be sure they've sent plenty of their men up into the mountains as a precaution."

"Let's hope so," Bolan said.

Off to the right of the Colwyss, the soldier spotted one of the surveillance planes. It was passing over the field on a southward course, sticking to the far side of the river, where the land was flat, dotted with a few agricultural settlements and endless tracts of jungle. The Colwyss was heading in the same direction, but staking out a course closer to the mountains. Soon they were flying over a series of small lakes fed by other mountain streams. In several places, waterfalls showered gracefully over the rocks, some dropping hundreds of feet into glimmering pools. The sun reflected off the mist given off by one of the cascades.

"Look," said Li. "A rainbow."

"That is a good omen," the pilot said.

"Yes, but for whom?" Bolan wondered.

Before takeoff, Bolan had requested extra binoculars for both him and Li. He raised his and began to scan the surrounding countryside. He spotted a small procession of villagers plodding downhill through the high mountain brush. Fifty yards behind them, another string of prayer flags fluttered brightly in the breeze. Other than that and the gentle swaying of tree limbs, all was still and calm.

Then, as they passed an area where a mountain flank extended deep into the valley, Bolan noticed movement up near one of the higher peaks. It appeared at first as if a thicket of brush had dislodged itself from the rocks and begun to tumble downhill. Training his field glasses on the object, however, he saw instead that it was a man with leafy twigs attached to his camou fatigues. The man carried a rifle. One of the Gurkhas, he thought. Still, he continued to watch the man, waiting to get a better look at his features. Finally, after the man had proceeded a good twenty yards down the mountain, he paused and glanced up at the helicopter. The man's face, streaked with greasepaint, was hard to discern. He was armed with more than the rifle, however, and when Bolan got a better look at the tubelike weapon slung across his shoulder, he knew he wasn't dealing with one of the Nepalese foot soldiers.

Bolan lowered his binoculars and shouted to the pilot, "Sniper at two o'clock, and he's packing a launcher!"

CHAPTER SEVENTEEN

"He's probably not alone," Bolan said, sliding open the window beside him. A blast of wind roared into the Colwyss, amplified by the increased sound of the rotors. Li gauged Bolan's trajectory and trained her binoculars on the same area. The chopper, meanwhile, closed in.

"I don't see anyone else," Li said.

"Keep looking," Bolan told her.

He brought the Mannlicher to his shoulder and told the pilot, "A little closer, then hold it steady."

"Done," the pilot responded. Beside him, the reconnaissance officer peered down through his field glasses, as well.

"I see a second man fifty yards to the left," he called out. "Next to the waterfall."

Bolan locked on the first target. The man on the ground raised his missile launcher, tracking the chopper's approach. Bolan squeezed the trigger. The Mannlicher bucked against his shoulder. The sniper went down, but he wasn't out. Scrabbling on all fours, he scrambled into the brush, disappearing behind an escarpment jutting from the mountainside. Bolan cursed and put his eyes back to the rifle's scope, raking the crosshairs across the rock line, hoping for a second chance.

Li, meanwhile, had shifted position, kneeling on her seat and leaning forward alongside Bolan, taking aim through the same window.

"Freeze it!" she told the pilot.

As the pilot cut the throttle and hovered in place, Li fired.

The second gunman sagged visibly, dropping his rifle. He pitched sideways and toppled into the water. The current carried him to the brink of the waterfall, where he snagged briefly on the rocks, then plummeted into the pool below.

"Nice work," the recon officer told her.

Bolan was still focused on the escarpment. Soon he saw the launch tube of an HN-5's launch tube slide into view between two rocks. The shooter was fully concealed except for his forehead. Bolan knew better than to think he could hit such a small target.

"Pull away!" he told the pilot. "Now!"

The pilot had just begun to bank the Colwyss when Bolan saw a puff of smoke issue from the SAM launcher. A high-explosive fragmentation warhead raced toward the chopper at 500 meters per second. Bolan knew the missile's infrared homing system was locked on to the chopper's heat signature and would seek it out no matter how deftly it maneuvered. He tossed his gun to the floor and bucked his shoulder against the door, rolling it open.

"Out!" he shouted. "Everyone out! Now!"

Bolan threw himself from the chopper, grabbing for his rip cord. As close as they were to the ground, he doubted the parachute would deploy in time, but it was his only chance.

The chute sprang from its pack and immediately began to unfurl. Staring up through the untangling strings, Bolan saw Li twenty yards off to his right, spread-eagled in the air while a silken, mushroom-like canopy bloomed out of her back. He couldn't see the two crewmen, however, and a second later the Colwyss-8H turned into a fireball, trailing smoke as it began to drop from the sky.

Bolan's chute finally snapped open, jerking him briefly upward. He was less than fifty yards from impact, however, still plunging earthward at a pace that would surely prove fatal unless he could use something to blunt his fall. Bolan glanced down, then yanked his shroud lines sharply to the right, shifting his course toward the nearest lake.

The placid water rushed up to greet him, and a sharp pain rushed through his legs as he crashed into its embrace. The lake was shallow, but the water had slowed his momentum and when he touched bottom, he was able to cushion his landing and spring back upward toward the surface, swimming clear of the collapsing tangle of chute lines.

Once he broke the surface, Bolan filled his lungs, then quickly unhitched his parachute and headed for the nearest embankment. Looking for Li.

The woman had missed the lake and crashed through a high canopy of treetops. Her chute had snagged on the upper branches, leaving her dangling ten feet off the ground. By the time Bolan reached the bank, she'd slipped out of the harness and dropped into the foliage.

The soldier was halfway to her when he spotted the man responsible for bringing down the helicopter. Limping down a mountain trail, he'd ditched the missile launcher, intent on finishing off the survivors with his rifle.

Bolan wasn't about to give him the chance. Dropping to a crouch, he raised his Desert Eagle and fired. Struck in the chest, the would-be assassin stopped in his tracks. Before the sniper could bring his rifle into play, Bolan fired twice more. A killshot to the head dropped the man in the middle of the trail. The big American jogged forward to inspect the body. The man was Chinese, the same age as most of the Boxers Bolan and Li had contended with back in California.

"That was close," the woman said, joining Bolan as he was frisking the dead man. "I don't think the others made it, though."

Bolan shook his head. Behind them, through the treetops, smoke trailed up from the other side of the mountain where the chopper had fallen.

"We're not out of this yet," he told Li. "There might still be more of them."

"I hope not." She looked around. "What do we do now?"

Bolan handed her the dead man's rifle, a 7.62 mm Dragunov, then helped himself to a Walther P-99 pistol tucked in the assassin's holster. "We do what we can down here," he told the woman. "We can follow this trail back up to the mountains. We'll have better vantage points, and we can signal to one of the other choppers when they swing past."

"That could be a problem," Li said. When Bolan eyed her questioningly, she thrust her out right leg. She'd worn high-rise desert boots to further reinforce her taped ankle, but the fall from the trees had taken its toll. The woman's foot had already swollen so much that it seemed ready to burst the shoe from her foot.

"I can barely put one foot in front of the other," she confessed. "Sorry."

"No need to apologize," Bolan told her. He

pointed to a fallen tree lying beside the trail. "Go ahead and take your weight off it."

The three steps it took Li to reach the tree were excruciating. As she sat on the trunk, she let out a long sigh.

"This sucks," she said.

Bolan helped her swing her leg up onto the trunk, then quickly untied her shoe. She groaned as he pulled it free. The tape around her ankle was bloodied and, with her ankle swollen as it was, it was cutting off the circulation to her foot. Her toes had begun to turn blue.

"The glass slipper doesn't fit," she said, forcing a smile. "I guess this means I'm not Cinderella."

"I'm no Prince Charming," Bolan replied, "so I guess that makes us even."

He peeled away the tape. The blood was coming from a small break in the skin just above the ankle. He doubled up the tape and was pressing it against the wound when they heard a droning sound in the sky. When the sound grew louder, both Bolan and Li glanced skyward through the treetops. One of the Lynx helicopters was headed their way.

"I'll hold this," Li said, taking the bandage, "while you see if you can get their attention."

Bolan broke into a run, trying to get clear of the tree cover. The Lynx was flying low, less then fifty yards above the trees, but it showed no signs of slowing.

"Down here!" Bolan shouted, waving his arms. He was still obscured from those overhead, however, and by the time he'd reached a clearing, the chopper had flown past him. Soon it had disappeared from view behind the mountain ridge. Bolan considered trying to scale the mountain, but the rise was too steep and there was no path through the overgrowth. It seemed pointless to backtrack to the other trail. To get to the other side he would have to climb all the way up and circle the ridge. It would take too long, and he was wary of leaving Li by herself. Cursing, he went back to where he'd left her.

"They followed the smoke from the Colwyss," he told her. "They're on the other side of the mountain."

"If we wait, maybe they'll come back."

"We don't have much choice, I guess." Bolan glanced at her ankle. "We need to get the swelling down on that."

"The lake," Li suggested. "Scoop mud into some grass and I can use it for a poultice."

"Back to mud packs again," Bolan said. "I'll see what I can do."

He jogged back to the lake, stopping along the way to yank free a few tufts of jungle grass. Crouched before the embankment, he was digging his hands into the wet, loamy soil when he heard a familiar droning in the sky. It wasn't the Lynx, however. Glancing southward, Bolan saw a scattered formation of four other helicopters headed his way, flying high over the valley floor.

The Dalai Lama was on his way to Marjeelam.

Bolan rose to his feet and moved along the edge of the lake, waving to get the attention of those in the helicopter. Soon the chopper he'd seen earlier lofted back into view. But instead of doubling back toward him, it hovered above the valley, waiting for the other choppers to catch up.

"Over here!" Bolan shouted. He kept waving, but the aerial procession drifted past without any of the choppers breaking formation to head his way. Finally he lowered his arms and watched as the Lynx fell in with the other aircraft and led the way to Marjeelam. His only consolation was that there was no further sound of gunfire from the mountains, no other whoosh of surface-to-air missiles. It appeared the Dalai Lama would reach his destination unscathed.

Frustrated, Bolan returned to the embankment. Once he'd slathered enough mud onto the tufts of grass, he cradled the crude pack in his hands and started back toward the trail.

Suddenly he stopped.

Up ahead, three men surrounded Li, each brandishing a Galil assault rifle, each dressed in camou fatigues nearly identical to those of the man lying dead on the trail in front of them.

Bolan heard a twig snap to his right and found himself staring at a fourth gunman who'd materialized out of the dense overgrowth. Armed, for the moment, with nothing more than two fistfuls of mud, there was little Bolan could do but watch as the gunman stepped out onto the trail. His Galil was aimed at Bolan's chest, and his finger was on the trigger.

CHAPTER EIGHTEEN

The man standing before Bolan sized him up, then turned and shouted out to his colleagues. The Executioner could understand only one of the words that was said: *Americans.*

Bolan relaxed; it was the Gurkhas.

At first glance, they bore little resemblance to the American notion of an ideal soldier. The men were all short and wiry, built more like racehorse jockeys than warriors. But their dark eyes shone with a fearless confidence and, to a man, they exuded a hard-earned air of near invincibility, the look of men who, like Bolan and other members of the Stony Man Farm commando teams, routinely stared into the jaws of death without blinking. They'd traded their traditional garb for fatigues to better blend in with the surrounding jungle.

Jen Li knew the men's language and spoke to them quickly, telling them what had happened. In return, one of the men filled her in on their contribution to the mission. When Bolan and the fourth commando joined them, Li explained, "They surprised two more of the Chinese a mile from here. Killed them both with crossbows before they could get off a shot."

"My kind of guys," Bolan said.

"They're pretty sure this area is secure now," Li stated. "They want to head back up to the hills to make sure, though."

"Ask them if they have a vehicle we can use to get you back to town," Bolan suggested.

When Li passed along the request, the men laughed and pointed at their feet.

"I think *those* are their vehicles," Li said.

One of the men spoke briefly to the woman, who told Bolan, "He says there are a few stragglers still down on the road. We should be able to hitch a ride."

The Gurkhas turned, left the path and ventured into he foliage. Within seconds they had disappeared from view. It was as if they had never been there.

"They tend not to be sociable," Li said.

"So I notice."

"I see you have my poultice," the woman observed, staring at the clump of mud Bolan was still carrying.

He nodded and knelt before the fallen tree, pressing the pack to her ankle. The swelling had already gone down some, but walking on it was still out of the question. There were vines snaking along the ground at the base of the tree. Bolan tugged at one of them, snapping it free and stripping its leaves so he could use it to tie the poultice in place around Li's ankle.

"This is getting to feel like Tarzan and Jane," the woman commented.

Bolan grinned as he knotted the vine. "All we need is a pet chimp we can send for help."

Li laughed. Once Bolan finished with the knots, he sat on the ground and leaned his back against the tree trunk. He was exhausted.

"We can head out in a minute," he said.

There was a lull in their conversation, then Li tapped Bolan on the shoulder. "Tell me something about this pilot friend of yours."

"He and I go way back. I met him years ago when he was a pilot for the Mob. It's a long story, but basically I won him over to our side and we've been friends ever since."

"How long is that?" Li asked.

Bolan shook his head. "You don't want to know."

"Fair enough. I take it he's a good pilot."

"The best," Bolan said. "If anybody could have landed that plane after the way Chozin sabotaged it, it's him."

"Something tells me that landing the plane was only the first of his problems."

"He's been in rougher scrapes than this and walked away," Bolan told her. "He'll pull through."

"Maybe he already has," Li suggested. "Maybe we'll have some good news when we get back to the air base."

"That would be nice." Bolan rose to his feet. "Speaking of which, when's the last time you had a piggyback ride?"

Li stared at Bolan with disbelief. "You can't be serious."

"Do you have a better idea?"

"No, but—"

"Then I say we give it a shot," Bolan said. "You can sling the rifles over your shoulder so they're not digging into my back."

"And if we encounter anyone, what am I supposed to do, fire at them like I'm riding an elephant on safari?"

"Seeing the way you shoot, you just might be able to pull it off," Bolan told her. "Now, come on, let's do it."

"This is crazy," Li said, carefully standing on the log, then slipping her arms around Bolan's neck and clasping her legs around his trunk. He crouched forward, balancing her weight on his lower back and grabbing her legs, then clenched his fingers together, strengthening his hold on her legs.

The first few steps were the most difficult, but once they fell into a rhythm they began to cover ground more easily. Bolan followed the trail around the lake, then headed down toward the road. It was a good mile away, a barely visible ribbon of asphalt threading along the valley floor.

"I have a confession to make," Li said after they were halfway there. Her voice was soft in Bolan's ear. "I was a little disappointed when I met your lady friend."

"Barbara?"

"I was sort of hoping you were unattached," Li said. "I know it sounds cliché, but there aren't a lot of good men out there."

Bolan didn't know how to respond to that, so he remained silent. He carried Li through a last stretch of overgrown trail, then they found themselves walking alongside an open field.

"I'm sorry," Li said. "I didn't mean to make you feel uncomfortable."

"I'm flattered, actually," Bolan called back to her.

"Perhaps under other circumstances..." Li let the implication ride.

"Perhaps," Bolan admitted.

As they drew close to the road, they saw an old

man riding an ox-drawn cart toward town. The cart was filled with unbaled hay. Loose straws fell to the road every time the cart passed over a bump. The man hadn't noticed them and would soon pass by if they couldn't get close enough to catch his attention.

"Gidda," Li teased Bolan, patting Bolan on the shoulder.

Bolan picked up his pace, joking back, "Just don't get any ideas about strapping on a feed sack once we get near that hay."

Li laughed and called out over his shoulder in Tibetan. The old man glanced over his shoulder, puzzled by the sight of two Americans. Li asked him to wait. He tugged on his reins, stopping his cart in the middle of the road.

Once they'd reached him, Bolan let go of Li's legs and helped her down to the ground. She quickly explained to the man who they were and asked the man for a ride to Marjeelam. The man thought it over, then motioned to the cart behind him.

"What a sweetie," Li said. "He says he knows he's going to miss the rally, so he'll go ahead and take us all the way to the command post."

"Thank you!" Bolan called up to the man. The man smiled and nodded.

Li used the cart for support and hopped around to the back on her one good leg. Bolan helped her up, then joined her amid the straw. The man up front whistled to the oxen and slapped his reins. The cart began to move, wooden wheels creaking as they rolled across the asphalt.

"What do you know," Li said, picking up a handful of straw. "We wound up having a roll in the hay after all."

As IT TURNED OUT, there was a series of preliminary speeches given at the rally, and the Dalai Lama had just been introduced when the old man brought his oxcart to a stop at the perimeter of the security command post. The ovation given the holy man carried away from the meadow like a roll of thunder, echoing loudly throughout the valley. Hearing the din, the old man got down from his cart and dropped to his knees, staring wistfully in the direction of town, tears in his eyes. Bolan and Li tried to thank him for his help, but the man was oblivious to them.

"Devotion is an awesome thing," Li said, watching the man.

Bolan nodded, but he'd turned his gaze from their benefactor. He was watching a gathering of uniformed officers, including General Avari, huddled beneath a canvas tarp stretched taut between four weathered posts to create a canopy. He left Li at the man's side—she, too, was enthralled by what was taking place across the valley—and went to investigate.

The men were standing before a pair of small, battery-operated television sets, watching a live feed of the Dalai Lama's opening remarks. Avari noticed Bolan and his eyes widened with shock. He excused himself from the others and strode over.

"I was told you had perished in the Colwyss," he said.

"The rumors of my demise are greatly exaggerated," Bolan said.

Avari smiled wanly. "Mark Twain, yes?"

Bolan nodded, then explained what had happened, passing along the report from the Gurkhas that others in the assassination plot had been taken out of the picture, as well. Avari was elated.

"I know we will still have to be on our guard, but this is good news," he said, "excepting, of course, the loss of two good men."

"Has there been any news regarding the downed spy plane?" Bolan asked.

"Yes and no," Avari replied. "Your secretary of state has come forward and announced that the plane is missing. He insists it was flying well outside China's borders when it went down, which, as I understand it, is a slight stretch of the truth."

"It's semantics," Bolan said. "It was flying in Tibetan airspace. China might claim sovereignty, but they'll get a hell of an argument on that one."

"That is what is surprising to me," the general

said. "No matter which side of the border the plane was threading, we are all assuming it came down on Chinese soil, yes?"

"Yes."

"This is much different from the EP-5 incident." Avari went on. "In that case, the plane was far out into international waters when it was struck. The Chinese argued their own definition of territorial airspace, but I think even they knew their argument was flimsy at best. They were just posturing."

"They're good at that."

"Exactly, and here they have a far stronger case, but even now, with the incident out in the open, they have yet to come forward and say they know anything of the plane's whereabouts."

"That won't last long," Bolan told the general. "I think they're just biding their time. Things are in their favor, and they want to make sure they handle it right this time. I also think they like the idea of seeing us squirm."

Avari grinned. "You have a point. No offense, but they aren't the only ones in this world like to see the mighty Americans brought off their high horse once in a while."

Bolan let the remark pass and inquired about the status of the team of U.S. Rangers that had been deployed to search for Grimaldi.

"I've heard nothing one way or the other," the

general told him. "You're aware that the Gurkhas have offered to help once they've finished their assignment here."

Bolan nodded, then said, "If I could, General, I'd like to ask a couple favors."

"I suppose we owe you that much. Within reason, of course."

Bolan exchanged a few words with Avari. Afterward, the general led him to the canopy. When Bolan left a few moments later, he was carrying one of the portable television sets. He set it on a supply crate set in the shade of an acacia tree several yards from the oxcart and turned up the volume. Jen Li and the old man were a few yards away. At the sound of the Dalai Lama's voice, they both turned.

From the look on the man's face, Bolan guessed he had never seen a television before. Rising slowly to his feet, the driver carefully approached the set, his eyes filled with wonder. The Dalai Lama's bespectacled face filled the screen, and his words came forth from the small speakers as if he were standing directly before the old man, addressing him directly. Again the man sank to his knees, and tears resumed their slow cascade down his ruddy cheeks. With considerable difficulty, he tore his gaze from the screen and turned to Bolan, uttering the only English he knew.

"Thank you," he murmured. "Thank you."

Bolan offered the man a slight bow, then turned to Li, telling her. "The general's calling over one of the helicopters so we can airlift you to the hospital. It should be here any minute."

Li nodded, then glanced briefly back at the old man. She, too, had been moved to tears, but for another reason.

"You are such a thoughtful man, Michael Belasko," she told Bolan.

"He did us a favor," Bolan replied modestly. "This was only payback."

"Baloney. I tell you, I'm envying your friend Barbara more and more all the time."

CHAPTER NINETEEN

"No concussion," John Kissinger said as he led Bolan from his hospital room. "These rocks in my head save me every time."

A bandage covered the stitches on the weaponsmith's forehead, but he seemed otherwise recovered from the collision with the Fiat. Bolan walked alongside him down the hallway of the hospital, which was really no more than a large clinic. The corridor was lined with Tibetans seeking treatment, mostly for minor injuries sustained when the crowd had been funneled through the entrance to the field where the Dalai Lama was making his appearance. The holy man's address was being broadcast over the intercom, and there was a reverential calm in the hallway as those waiting to see a doctor stared intently at the speakers mounted on the walls.

Toward the end of the hall, an armed soldier stood outside the room where Dilip Chozin was recuperating from his bullet wounds. Bolan told Kissinger that General Avari would arrange for a court-martial upon Chozin's release from the hospital, with the understanding that his tip-off on the assassination plot would be taken into consideration.

"No matter how easy they go on him, he'll wind up behind bars till his hair turns gray," Kissinger stated.

"I'm sure he'll take that over a firing squad," Bolan said.

Next door to Chozin, Jen Li had been put into the same room as Nhajsib Wal. Bolan and Kissinger found them both hooked up to IVs. Li's foot, red from iodine and swaddled with ice packs, was elevated on several pillows. She'd been given painkillers and had dozed off watching the Dalai Lama on a small TV anchored to the ceiling. As for Wal, his ribs were taped beneath his hospital robe. He was on his cell phone, but when Bolan and Kissinger approached his bed, he quickly finished the call, then greeted them a nod.

"I understand Chozin was telling the truth about assassins in Marjeelam," he told Bolan.

"He sure was."

"I also understand you were shot out of the air by a missile launcher."

"All in a day's work," Bolan replied. He changed the subject. "How are you doing?"

"Collapsed lung," Wal said, touching his side.

"They pumped it back up like a basketball. I'll be as good as new in a few weeks."

"Glad to hear it," Bolan said.

"That was my associate on the phone," Wal said. "The Chinese have finally made a statement on the spy plane. Their minister of defense says they have sent troops to search for the plane and promised that no harm would come to the pilot. Provided, of course, that he was able to land safely."

"A shrewd call on their part," Kissinger said. "Leaves them with plenty of options."

"I think they're just stalling," Bolan said, repeating the same theory he'd shared with General Avari. "They already know that any military action in Tibet is going to draw fire from all sides, and they don't want to stir things up on another front any more than they have to."

"On the bright side, it buys us more time to try to find the plane ourselves," Wal said. "Not to mention the pilot, of course."

"What are they saying about the Dalai Lama's speech?" Kissinger wanted to said.

Wal indicated the television broadcast while saying, "Once he's finished speaking, I am sure they will consult with their spin doctors and come up with an appropriately innocuous response. As for the assassins who might have silenced him without your help, I will lay you money that the Beijing dismisses them as freelance hoodlums with no ties to the government.''

"I'm sure they'll sing that same song when it comes answering questions about what went down in Collier Springs," Kissinger said.

"No doubt," Wal said. "All along they have insisted that PACRIM is an autonomous business. And as for the Boxers, they'll say they're just more hoodlums pursuing their own agenda.''

"Well, they can peddle that crap all they want," Kissinger said. "It's only going to come back and bite them on the ass.''

Bolan asked Wal the same question he'd asked Avari. "What's happening with the Rangers?"

"I wish I knew," the intelligence bureau agent responded. "My understanding is that twice in a row they've failed to report back as scheduled.''

Bolan couldn't believe it. "The Rangers are missing, now, too?''

"I'm sure there is an explanation.''

"Maybe," Bolan said impatiently, "but I don't want to stand around waiting for it.''

He turned to Kissinger and told him, "We're going in.''

JEN LI WAS still asleep when Bolan and Kissinger were informed that one of the Lynx choppers was ready to fly them to the air base. Bolan left behind a note apologizing for having to leave her behind. He knew she'd understand. No matter how well her ankle responded to treatment, it wouldn't be able to withstand the rigors of the mission that lay ahead.

Once back at the base, Bolan stopped by the communications center and arranged for a secure line to Stony Man's Virginia headquarters. Something had been troubling him since earlier in the day, when Chozin had pulled the cell phone from his pocket while explaining how he'd been able to contact the men in the Fiat.

"Why haven't you been able to get a GPS off Jack's cell?" he asked Aaron Kurtzman once he had the Farm's cybernetic wizard on the line. "Hell, if you could pinpoint me when I hopped a train back in Collier Springs, it seems you'd be able to pick up a signal from him, no problem."

Kurtzman was quick to respond. "There's a simple explanation," he said. "Two, in fact. For starters, the satellite they would have had to rely on for coordinates was the same one that had gone out of commission, prompting Jack's mission in the first place."

"Okay, I got that," Bolan said. "What's the second reason."

"Secondly," Kurtzman told him, "and more to the point, Grimaldi had left his cell phone behind."

"Why the hell did he do that?" Bolan wondered.

"For the same reason those pretty stewardesses tell everybody in first class to shut off their laptops and Palm Pilots before takeoff," Kurtzman explained, trying to keep it in layman's terms. "So they don't screw up instrument readings in the cockpit."

"Well, then why didn't he just shut the thing off but keep it with him so he could use it if he had to?" Bolan asked.

"He *couldn't* shut it off," Kurtzman responded. "Not completely. Remember, the GPS ship runs off its own chip and sends off a constant signal even when the phone's down. That's how we were able to track you even after your cell stopped working in California. Grimaldi wasn't about to assemble the thing and yank out the chip. There seemed no point."

"What about the plane?" Bolan said. "I'm sure it had some kind of black box, right?"

"Yes," Kurtzman confirmed, "but that bastard airman booby-trapped it along with the rest of the communications systems."

"I thought those boxes were stand-alones."

"They are, but they're just boxes, Striker. Any mechanic worth his salt can crack them open."

"How about some good news for a change," Bolan said. "Give me something we can use before we head in."

There was a brief delay on the line, then Kurtzman told him, "That satellite we're shuffling over from Afghanistan should be positioned in another few hours. It'll only be able to cover half the ground as the other one, but fortunately that half includes Jack's likely drop zone. If there aren't any kinks, we'll start getting sat photos by morning, your time. If there's something to report, we'll pass it along. Just make sure you and Cowboy pack your cells so we can keep tabs on you."

"Will do," Bolan said. On that same topic, he asked what the consensus was at the Farm as to why the Ranger force had gone incommunicado.

"Your guess is as good as ours," Kurtzman responded. "Could be as simple as equipment malfunction or a problem with reception."

"Or they could all be down," Bolan said.

"That's definitely a possibility," Kurtzman said. "I don't need to tell you that once you cross the border into China, you'll be in the lion's den. Whoever they've got patrolling the area is going to have home-court advantage over you."

"I like a good challenge," Bolan responded.

"Well, you're in for one. Good luck, Striker."

Once off the phone, Bolan left the base comm room. It was twilight outside. A sprinkling of stars winked in the cloudless sky. Out on the main runway, Bolan saw one of the B-1 Lancers readying for takeoff. Moments later, he saw the other one come in for a landing.

"The Lancers will be rotating 24/7 until this is resolved," Air Force Colonel Tom O'Dell told Bolan when he arrived back at the same hangar where he and Kissinger had first rendezvoused with Nhajsib Wal and IB agent Hanji earlier in the day. Kissinger was there, too, as was Hanji, the base commander and another American, a Chinese American CIA field agent by the name of Charles Chengzhu. O'Dell, a beefy Irishman with rosy cheeks and a thick mustache, had arrived at the base earlier in the afternoon, Chengzhu less than an hour ago.

O'Dell continued the briefing.

"I've got some F-16s due at 2000 hours, and I'm trying pull a Nighthawk away from the Persian Gulf," he explained. "The Navy's kicking in a pair of EB-Prowlers. Add those to the half-dozen fighter jets our guests here have already sent out, and the Chinese'll know we're not screwing around."

Base Commander Munri Lapsoe, a lean, elegant-looking man in his late fifties, interjected, telling Bolan, "Our jets will do run-alongs just inside the border, starting fifty kilometers east of your insertion point. It will look like they're providing air support for men we're sending to a dummy staging area in the mountains near Rhanzhi Pass. Hopefully the

Chinese will go for it and shift away some of the forces where you'll be coming in.''

"A diversion will help, that's for sure," Kissinger said.

"That won't be their only distraction," Chengzhu added. He pointed to an area on a topographical map laid out on the table the men were gathered around. "We have well-placed contacts in the villages here to the south. They've instigated demonstrations to coincide with the Dalai Lama's speech. From the reports we've been getting, the turnout's even better than what they were hoping for. They estimate twenty thousand here in Xiang alone. And that's despite the weather.''

"What kind of weather?" Bolan asked. "I was just outside and there's not a cloud in the sky.''

"That's here," Chengzhu said. "Across the Himalayas it's a whole different story. There's drizzle now, and the forecast is for thunderstorms by late evening.''

"The rain will help you," Hanji told Bolan and Kissinger. "When it storms here in the mountains, visibility is cut to practically nothing. It will be difficult for them to see you coming.''

"That cuts both ways," Bolan reminded the Indian. "We could wander right into them.''

"You will have the Gurkhas with you," Hanji

responded. "The weather won't faze them. You watch, they are like bats in the dark."

"I believe you," Bolan said. "Now, supposing we get through. What kind of terrain are we talking about?"

Chengzhu said, "We've blocked out a hundred-square-mile search area from the point where we lost contact with the ES-1, as well as the Rangers." Again referred to the map. "Marco Polo supposedly came through this way on that big journey of his, but it's still about as far off the beaten track as you can get. The rest is pretty much of a no-man's-land. The desert ends here and gives way to slot canyons and a maze of gorges. You've got a river here, the Xiangshu, that wanders about depending on how much rain there is, and it usually winds up draining into this lake at the end of the canyons near Manakan. That's about it."

"What's this?" Bolan pointed to a dot located just north of the designated area.

"Uranium mine," Chengzhu told him. "They work it with forced labor. Falun Gong, student dissidents, anybody with a strong back who's stepped out of line with Beijing. As you'd expect, they don't bother with a lot of safety precaution, so the death toll's high, mostly from radiation poisoning."

"A little warm-weather Siberia," Bolan said.

"Pretty much," Chengzhu agreed. "I don't see it being a factor in the mission, though."

Bolan stared at the map silently, absorbing all the information and committing it to memory. As he did so, Kissinger interjected.

"Getting back to this aerial diversion," he said. "The Chinese won't be just watching all these planes with their hands in their pockets. What happens if somebody gets an itch in their trigger finger and tries to bring one down?"

Colonel O'Dell smirked. "If that happens, pardner, you'll have all the diversion you need. One swipe at my birds, and those Commies will have a war on their hands."

CHAPTER TWENTY

Xiangshu Province, China

Less than a hundred miles northeast of the Himalayas, the Xiangshu Mountain Range, while still imposing, on average reached only half the height of their glacier-tipped cousins to the south. There were more breaks, too, gaps between the mountains that made for easier passage between India and China. Roads, some paved, most crude strips pocked with boulders, traversed the narrower corridors and were the areas most heavily subjected to scrutiny by border guards from both countries. Normally traffic along these stretches was slight and sporadic, and after sundown it was rare for the guards on either side to encounter more than a handful of travelers.

This night was different.

Despite the late hour, there was heavy unexpected congestion at the Kashgur Pass border checkpoint forty miles north of Marjeelam. All of the traffic was from Chinese side, mostly in the form of Tibetan mountain villagers traveling by yak or camel. The most commonly voiced sentiment was that the Tibetans planned to reach Marjeelam by dawn in hopes they might, for the first time in their lives, glimpse their spiritual leader in the flesh before he flew back to Dharmasala. When told the Dalai Lama had already left Marjeelam, the villagers refused to believe it, and when they were further told that the border had been closed due to escalating tensions in the region, they likewise ignored orders to turn back and return to their homes. There were heated exchanges, and soon chants began to echo through the mountains.

"Freedom for Tibet!" some cried. Others shouted, "Long live his holiness!"

The border guards had their hands full, and controlling the crowd was just one of their problems. Most of the travelers' pack animals were weighed down with provisions, parcels wrapped in burlap or rolled up in rugs, all bound by crisscrossed, heavily knotted lengths of rope or twine. In nearly every case, the bundles were large enough to arouse suspicion that they might contain weapons or other contraband. Forced inspections only raised the ire of the villagers, and soon the guards gave up the task and retreated to their stations, hoping the demonstrators might be deterred by the sight of soldiers readying themselves behind mounted howitzers. The show of force only inflamed the villagers more, however. They begun to hurl stones as well as slogans.

For all its appearance of spontaneity, the altercation was, in fact, being carefully choreographed by the CIA. Collaborators amid the villagers were in constant contact with CIA Agent Charles Chengzhu, allowing him to monitor the demonstration from the nearby air base.

Further unnerving the checkpoint guards was an ominous thunder in the clouded night sky overhead, caused, not by the approaching storm, but by American and Indian warplanes that had been making aerial runs along the border for the past two hours. The demonstrators were equally aware of the overhead sorties and used them for leverage, taunting the guards.

''This is not Tiananmen Square!'' One of their ringleaders cried out, staring down the howitzers with angry defiance. ''You're being watched! Fire on us and the planes will come to our aid!''

When it became clear that the situation was getting out of hand, the guards put out a call for assistance of their own. Soon reinforcements were on the way, dispatched from the neighboring checkpoints and—more significantly—from the ranks of border troops patrolling the surrounding mountains.

After nearly two hours of growing unrest, the

demonstration began to subside. Seemingly intimidated by the arrival of reinforcements, the villagers ceased throwing stones and slowly began to disperse, heading back to their villages. Their retreat, however, had less to do with the increased show of force than the fact that the protestors had already achieved their objective, pulling troops away. At the same time Chinese were congratulating themselves on quelling the confrontation, Mack Bolan, John Kissinger and the Nepalese Gurkhas were quietly slipping across the border.

They were, as Kurtzman had put it, now in the lion's den.

BOLAN WAS in the clouds. They blanketed the mountains like a thick, dense fog, and even though it hadn't yet begun to rain, Bolan's fatigues were drenched as much from condensation as his own sweat. Like Kissinger, who stalked the rocky terrain twenty yards to his left, Bolan was carrying an Unger/Stinson Survivor Series crossbow, loaded and ready to fire. Bracketed to the stock for quick reloading were two additional jag-tipped bolts. His Desert Eagle was close at hand in a web holster, and slung across his back was an Indian-issue M-16 equipped with an undermounted Remington 870 pump shotgun. Rounding out his gear was a steel-bladed Kozar hunting knife strapped to his thigh, and a belt clip holding backup ammunition, as well as three AN-3 series frag grenades. Perched on his forehead was a pair of infrared night goggles. He'd used them briefly while coming up over the mountain but found them too disorienting and had taken them off.

For all the options they provided, Bolan's arsenal came at a price. The extra weight—added to that of his soaked outfit and a fanny pack stocked with a canteen and food rations—only increased the strain of trying to acclimate to the high altitude. Bolan's lungs were already beginning to pain him with their demands for more oxygen than the thin mountain air could provide.

But at least, he and Kissinger were finally heading downhill.

The Gurkhas, predictably, were nowhere to be seen. They'd taken the lead and vanished into the mist shortly after the border cross. Bolan took it on faith that they were close by.

The insertion point had been chosen not only because of its distance from the nearest checkpoint, but also because, had the diversionary ploy at Kashgur Pass failed to pull troops away from the mountains, it was the area least likely to be heavily patrolled due to the instability of the ground cover. The mountainside was layered with *choss,* a flimsy aggregate of small rocks that crumbled readily underfoot, making it at best, a nuisance to walk across. Every few steps, Bolan was forced to shift his weight to avoid slipping on the perilous terrain, in the process sending pebbles into a noisy roll down the path of least resistance. He and the others were relying on crossbows for the downhill journey for the simple reason that the mere echo of a lone gunshot would be enough to dislodge the *choss*, triggering a landslide.

Bolan wasn't the only one raising a clatter. All around him there was an almost constant patter of small slides, some caused by Kissinger and the Gurkhas, others by the drone of planes flying above the clouds overhead or the mere pull of gravity on clusters of stone weakened over time by the elements. The sound was unnerving, like the cracking of a thousand knuckles, but at least Bolan had been prepared for it. The Gurkhas had told him that the Chinese called the area Popcorn Pass.

After another thirty yards, Bolan and Kissinger converged near an outcropping and paused to catch their breath, sitting on a pair of smooth boulders that rose up through the earth's crust like large eggs. Kissinger, too, was making due without his goggles.

"Are we having fun yet?" he wisecracked.

"Walk in the park," Bolan deadpanned. He cupped a hand around his wrist and illuminated his watch, checking the time and getting a read off its embedded compass. The plan was to head downhill on a northwesterly course until they reached the Xiangshu River. The river coursed through a narrow canyon pocked with small caves situated a few yards above the waterline. By the time they reached the caves, it would be close to dawn. There the men would rest until the sun rose, then rendezvous at the first bend in the river and plan their next move.

At least that was the plan.

Soon after they'd resumed their trek, Bolan and Kissinger split off once again. Before long, he'd dropped below the cloud line. He was grateful for the increased visibility. Glancing down the side of the mountain, he saw that he was nearly halfway to the river. It shone faintly in the distance, snaking along the base of the mountain for several miles before heading inland.

As for the clouds, they formed an unbroken firmament across the entire night sky. Far off, Bolan heard the first rumblings of thunder. The sound was louder than that made by the planes, and it came in short bursts. As he stared northward, he saw a shaft of lightning reach out of the clouds and stab at the desert floor below. The storm was heading toward him. He continued on his way, fighting the urge to move faster.

Bolan had covered another few dozens yards when he heard a commotion behind him, roughly fifty yards to his right. He stopped and dropped to a crouch, listening intently. A few stones plinked their way past him. He stared past them, then resorted to the night goggles, hoping for a better look at whatever was moving overhead. He knew it wasn't Kissinger, and it seemed unlikely one of the Gurkhas had doubled back behind him. The mountain men had also told him that dumb as they were, even yaks knew better than to venture the loose ground. That left one disturbing possibility, and as he peered through the infrared lenses, Bolan's suspicions were confirmed.

Uphill, skulking down the same faint path Bolan had forged through the choss, was a uniformed member of the Chinese border patrol. Instead of a crossbow, he was armed with a conventional bow and arrow. The bow was arched, the drawstring pulled taut. The man was taking aim at Bolan.

The Executioner instinctively threw himself forward, landing hard on the slope. An arrow whispered past and caromed off the rocks to his left. He wasn't about to give the man a second shot. He lined the patrolman in the sights of his crossbow and let fly with a shaft of his own. The tip found flesh and the soldier groaned, losing his balance.

Bolan quickly yanked free a fresh bolt and was fitting it into the crossbow when a fresh hail of stone tumbled past him. There were more of them than before, and they were coming at him louder and in larger sizes. The next thing Bolan knew, the wounded border guard was crying out as an entire sheet of *choss* broke free beneath him. The other man was quickly swept up, along with the rocks and boulders around him. A growing roar filled the air, louder even than the next peal of thunder out over the desert.

Feeling the ground begin to quake beneath him, Bolan jerked off his goggles and struggled back on his feet. By then, however, the avalanche was already nearly upon him.

CHAPTER TWENTY-ONE

Bolan had a split second to react.

The swath was too wide for him to have any chance of sidestepping it, and trying to outrun it downhill was a fool's game. All that was left was for him to make sure he wasn't dragged under. He sprang from a crouch, meeting the slide head-on, leaping as high as possible while the rocks surged beneath him. He came down atop the slide and battled to stay there. Out of the corner of his eye he spotted Kissinger racing toward him.

There was nothing the armorer could do to help. He shouted Bolan's name once before being forced to back off.

Glancing around him, Bolan saw that a few of the larger boulders were apparently riding a cushion of smaller rock. Unlike the others, they weren't rolling end over end, but rather sliding in place. He threw himself at the nearest one and grabbed hold. His weight, however, sank the rock enough that it, too, began to roll, forcing him to let go to try his luck with another. Twice more he was thwarted by the same results, but finally he made it to a large slab—part of the outcropping he and Kissinger had rested next to—and it held under his weight. Although he was pelted mercilessly by other stones and rocks, he was safe, at least for the moment, coasting down the hill as if aboard some monolithic surfboard hung up on a slow-moving swell.

The avalanche continued to grow in size as it charged downhill, prying loose the *choss* in its path and adding it to its bulk. That worked to Bolan's advantage, as he found himself not only lifted up by the rising crest, but also drifting back from its edge. After more than a hundred yards, however, the slide came to strata made of firm bedrock that refused to feed it. At nearly the same time, the mountain began to level off.

Almost instantly the avalanche began to diminish and lose its momentum. Several times earlier, Bolan had seen thick trees snap like twigs under the slide's sheer force, but now trees of the same girth were holding their ground, forcing the slide to move around them. And each time the slide encountered another tree, it was sliced and forced to scatter in a wider swath. Soon the crest began to subside, and Bolan felt himself being drawn back toward the slide's leading edge. In time, he knew, the boulder he was perched upon would hit ground and pitch forward, throwing him as if he were a first-time buckaroo being tossed off the back of a rodeo Brahman.

He had other cause for concern, as well. The river was up ahead, and despite the swiftness with which it was breaking up, the avalanche still seemed likely to remain intact long enough to reach the water. One way or another, Bolan needed to find a way off the ride.

Seeing another stand of trees just up ahead, he decided to make his move. Most of the way down the hill, he'd lain flat atop his boulder, but now he rose to his knees and held his arms out at his sides, hoping he would pass under a tree whose lower branches were within reach.

At first, luck seemed on his side. Twenty yards directly ahead of him, an ancient poplar drooped slightly forward as if crouching to meet the slide head-on. Bolan braced himself, his eyes on a thick limb extending out ten feet up from the ground.

At the last second, however, the slide shifted beneath him. His boulder followed suit, veering directly into the trunk. There was a sickening crack as the huge rock slammed home. Its sheer weight and momentum was too much for the poplar. It gave way, even as Bolan was being thrown forward by the impact. Instead of grabbing the limb, Bolan crashed into it, shoulder first.

The blow stunned him, and the next thing he knew, he was once again being swept along, half-buried in the moving juggernaut. Within a matter of seconds, he found himself being carried over the edge of eroded canyon that led into the churning waters of the Xiangshu River. He felt the sensation of cold water rushing over him, then everything went black.

AS HE BEGAN to regain consciousness, Bolan's first vague sensation was that of water lapping against him. Bath, he thought to himself groggily. More thoughts drifted through his mind, as thin as clouds, a jumble of images and memories. He didn't know where he was. He was in darkness, surrounded by a tangle of loose brush and driftwood. Water was seeping through the debris. Nearby, he could hear the river. And rain. It was coming down hard, but it wasn't landing on him. Thunder crashed somewhere overhead. The sound reverberated around him, so loud it hurt his ears. Lightning was close behind. In the wake of illumination he saw that he was lying on a rock shelf in a cave situated just above the river. As the water roared past, more of it spilled up onto the ledge and trailed under him.

He thought back trying to fathom what had happened after he'd tumbled into the river. The current had to have dragged him along, he figured, then cast him aside as it rounded a bend. But how far had it taken him? Was this where he was supposed to meet the others? Where was Kissinger?

He tried to move but couldn't. A splintered tree trunk lay across his legs. Part of it was still half submerged in the river, jostling back and forth in the current so that it gnawed at his shins like a dull saw. Bolan rallied his strength and reached down, pushing the obstruction free. The trunk slid off his leg, and a branch whipped past his face as the current pulled the tree back into the river and carried it away.

Bolan wasn't sure, but it seemed to him the water level had risen in just the past minute. He stared out and waited for the next burst of lightning. When it flashed, he saw the river surging past and caught a glimpse of canyon wall on the other side of the water. He could see and hear the rain more clearly now. The storm wasn't letting up. If anything, the rain was coming down harder. If the river kept swelling, he realized it would soon overrun its banks and fill the cave. Rendezvous point or not, he couldn't stay here.

Slowly Bolan pulled himself to his feet. There wasn't a part of his body that didn't ache, but he was alive and in one piece which was more than he'd hoped for when the slide had carried him into the river. And as long as he was alive, there was a mission to be carried out.

The cave was small, so he had to crouch as he took inventory. He'd been stripped of his crossbow, as well as the M-16 and his grenade belt. That left the knife and his Desert Eagle. His cell phone was gone, too, no doubt transmitting from somewhere deep beneath the avalanche. Like Grimaldi, he'd lost contact with the outside world. For now at least, he was on his own.

Bolan unzipped his rations kit. Water had seeped in, sogging everything except for his canteen and some protein bars sealed in a waterproof pouch along with matches and a small penlight. Famished, Bolan tore off the wrapper to one of the bars and quickly devoured the snack, washing it down with a few sips from the canteen.

A wave crashed onto the ledge, adding to the pool of water collecting around his feet. Already it was up to his ankles. He didn't have much time.

Bolan groped through the darkness, making his way around the debris, feeling the cave walls for a way out. There was none. He moved to the mouth of the cave and reached out. The rain pelted his fingers as he ran his hands along the canyon wall above him. There was nothing to grab hold of, no way to pulling himself up to higher ground.

Thunder rumbled through the canyon, followed by yet another streak of lightning. Bolan gazed of the cave, trying to get a better idea of what he was up against. The river was more than forty yards wide, brown with silt, frothing from the current's pull. Another felled tree drifted past, and Bolan was forced to step back as it raked the mouth of the cave.

Bolan looked down at the debris strewed across the cave floor. It was mostly twigs and small branches, but there were a few larger limbs, two as thick as his leg, another the diameter of a bread loaf.

Working fast, he tossed aside the smaller branches, laying out those he could use in some semblance of a row. Next he tugged off his camou shirt, then unstrapped the knife from his thigh. In a few minutes he'd cut the shirt to ribbons, leaving him with a set of makeshift lashings. Once he'd strapped the branches together, he wedged twigs into the gaps. When he was finished, Bolan had himself a small raft. He had doubts it would support his weight, but it would have to.

Wading through the quickly rising water, he carried his creation back to the mouth of the cave. By now his eyes had adjusted to the dark. He stood before the opening and stared out at the river, waiting for the right moment. A few minutes later, he saw another tree drifting toward him. It was smaller than the last one, but denser and lying lower in the brackish water.

Bolan waited until the last possible second, then dived from the cave, raft clutched to his chest. He landed atop the tree and, as he'd hoped, it buttressed the raft, helping to displace his weight. He dipped briefly below the current, then bobbed back to the surface. The raft was pinned beneath his chest, allowing him to free his hands and secure a better grip on the tree. As with the avalanche, there was little more he could do but hold on and let nature play out its hand.

CHAPTER TWENTY-TWO

The river carved deeper into the canyons as it carried Bolan along. It was hard for him to hear thunder over the roar of the current, but when he could, the peals seemed fainter now and more spaced apart. When lightning flashed, it was behind his back. Soon the rain began to let up. The storm was moving into the mountains.

The river, however, continued to move swiftly. After a few miles, it came to another sharp bend and Bolan's ungainly craft was pushed up against a mound of flotsam jammed into a crevasse. The steep-pitched walls offered no escape, so Bolan stayed put, waiting for the tree beneath him to unsnag. The river was cold, and his legs were starting to go numb. There was nothing he could do about it.

After a few minutes, the tree finally broke free of the snag and he was back out in the current. A mile later, he felt the river dip. Whitecaps began to appear on the surface, and boulders began to appear above the waterline.

He was entering a stretch of rapids.

Beneath him, the tree began to come apart. Outer branches snapped against the large rocks, destabilizing Bolan's position. He began to drop lower in the water, twice wincing with pain as his knees bounded off unseen boulders. He shifted forward as best he could, trying to buy time as he scanned the way before him, looking for an opportunity to bail before the rapids dashed him against the rocks.

The gauntlet of boulders was unmerciful. Whenever he caromed off one, it felt as if he'd been broadsided by a small truck. His entire left side went numb after a particularly harsh blow, and when it was followed up by yet another, the wind was knocked from Bolan's lungs.

Stunned, he gave up the fight and was about to surrender to the rapids when they finally relented, flinging him down one last cascade and depositing him into a lake.

The water steadied around him. He dogpaddled with one arm until the feeling came back to the other, then slowly made his way toward the lake's edge, panting for breath.

Fatigued, he stopped halfway to the bank and turned onto his back, splaying his arms and legs so that he could float in place. He stared up at the sky.

The moon shone through a break in the clouds. He also saw a small plane flying high overhead. Observation craft, he thought. He doubted anyone could see him, but to be safe he flipped over so that only his head was above the water. With slow strokes, he made his way toward shore, taking care not to make waves.

The lake's shoreline was gravelly. Once out of the water, Bolan crawled across the rocks and quickly took cover beneath a stand of small trees. Soon the drone of the plane faded.

A breeze rustled the trees. Bare chested, bleeding from countless scrapes, Bolan shivered. A sneeze shot through him. He thought back to Li's remark after the Colwyss-8H had been shot out from under them, leaving them stranded in the jungle outside Marjeelam.

"This sucks," he muttered.

He sat at the base of one of the trees and drained his canteen, then finished off the last of his protein bars. He was contemplating his next move, battling his body's cry for sleep, when the breeze shifted, carrying with it a cloying, fetid stench. Bolan knew the smell all too well.

It was the smell of rotting flesh.

Unholstering his pistol, Bolan rose to his feet and sniffed. The odor was coming from behind him, back through the trees. The storm had apparently skirted the lake, because the ground was relatively dry and after he'd ventured twenty yards into the brush, Bolan saw boot prints. He placed his foot next to one of the prints. They were roughly the same size.

A thought flashed quickly through Bolan's mind, the memory of a mission ten years ago when he and Jack Grimaldi had wound up sharing the same room at a hotel outside Kosovo. One morning Grimaldi had put on one of Bolan's shoes by mistake. It fit and he didn't realize the mistake until he'd gone to put on his other shoe and saw it was for the same foot.

"No," Bolan muttered, the hairs on his raising. "It can't be."

He moved faster, following the prints past a cluster of wildflowers to a clearing. Thirty yards away, lying facedown in the moonlight, was a body.

Holding his breath, Bolan approached the corpse...or at least what was left of it. Vultures or crows had poked through the dead man's clothes and picked at his flesh. His entire backside had been eaten away to the bone, and there was little left of his right leg but a few shreds of mangled flesh. Decomposition had set in, accounting for the smell, and maggots squirmed amid the entrails.

Bolan found a stick and braced himself, then carefully turned the body over.

The man's face had been eaten away, leaving only cartilage and the gleaming bones of his skull.

It wasn't Grimaldi.

There were a few long strands of straight blond hair clinging to a small patch of scalp on one side of the skull. Grimaldi's hair was black and curly. And although the Stony Man pilot had served a tour of duty with the Air Force years ago, he'd long since hung up his dog tags. The man lying dead on the ground still had his tags, dangling by a chain from what was left of his neck.

Bolan flipped the tags over and flashed his penlight on them: Harmon Brown, U.S. Air Force.

One of the missing Rangers.

Bolan slowly stood and snapped off his light. Relying on the moon as he began to scour the clearing. He found more tracks—made by smaller boots—as well as dozens of spent shells, most of the same caliber. Bolan picked one up and inspected it. It was for an AK-47, the Chinese military's preferred assault rifle. Off near a cluster of rocks there were two blackened craters, as well, caused most likely by grenades or mortars.

Too much firepower expended for just one man, Bolan thought grimly. The others had to be close by, contributing to the odor of death that still choked the night air around him.

Bolan saw that the boot prints led in the direction

of the rocks. He followed them but stopped after a few steps. Something was moving behind the rocks.

He sidestepped, taking cover behind a nearby tree. He aimed his Desert Eagle at the rocks and waited.

The sounds continued.

Moments later an animal trotted into view. In the dark it was hard for Bolan to tell whether it was a wild dog or a jackal. He suspected the latter, because there was a severed arm clamped in its jaws, weighing down its head slightly. Bolan wasn't about to draw attention to himself by shooting at it. Instead, he grabbed some stones and began throwing them. The animal paused, looking around, hesitant to give up its hard-earned dinner. It was only after one of the stones glanced off its hindquarters that the beast dropped the arm, yelping as it scampered away.

Bolan moved from the tree and once more held his breath. As he'd feared, he found four more men lying sprawled behind the rocks. Except for the one missing an arm, they were more intact than the Ranger out in the clearing. They lay at odd angles, stripped of their boots and weapons. Behind them were traces of a makeshift camp: flattened grass, ration tins, discarded food wrappers.

Bolan tried to imagine what might have happened. The likeliest explanation was that the men had pitched camp, unaware the enemy was close by. Brown had to have ventured out, maybe to fetch water from the lake, maybe to go on patrol. He'd been followed back to the camp, unaware he was setting his men up for an ambush. Judging from the craters and spent shells, the Chinese had come in hard and fast, storming the camp before the Rangers had a chance to fully react. It had all the makings of a massacre. If the Chinese had lost soldiers, they'd been hauled away in the aftermath.

Bolan wondered how the Rangers had allowed themselves to be taken out so easily. It went against their training to camp so closely together, and they couldn't have picked a worse spot. True, they'd set up camp behind the rocks and no doubt there'd been a lookout posted for any sign of enemy approach by way of the lake. On the other hand, they'd literally backed themselves into a corner. Behind them, the canyon walls rose up almost perpendicular to the ground. It would have been far more difficult for them to go up than for the enemy to come down to them, capable of shooting them like fish in a barrel. Whatever the explanation, they'd taken it with them to their Maker. All Bolan could do for them was gather their dog tags. He knew from experience that, however macabre, they were a source of solace for loved ones back home.

He set about the task quickly, but was given pause when he noticed that all of the men's wounds hadn't been caused by gunfire or the bite of carnivores. The men's ears were missing, as were some of their fingers—pinkies mostly—all severed by the clean cuts from a sharp blade.

The Chinese had taken souvenirs.

A cold rage filled Bolan as he finished collecting the dog tags, sealing the tags inside his provision bag. He'd planned to change into one of the men's uniforms, but after seeing the mutilations, he couldn't bring himself to do it. The men had already been stripped of their boots. Dead or not, he wasn't about to rob any one of them of their dignity, as well, by leaving them naked to the elements. Instead, Bolan steeled himself against the reek of putrefaction and slowly dragged the bodies close together, setting each out in an angle of repose, then covering them with rocks and small boulders to shield them from predators.

Once the grim ritual was completed, Bolan stood exhausted before the burial mound. He wasn't a man of prayer, but believed there was a higher power, and he offered the fallen soldiers a moment of silence, wishing them peace and honor in whatever world might lie beyond the one from which they'd been so cruelly dispatched.

Afterward, he returned to the clearing, filled with resolve that they wouldn't have died in vain.

Shrugging off his fatigue, Bolan stared down at the footprints that had led him to the massacre site.

The same tracks led from the carnage in a westward direction, away from the lake and through the dense foliage at the base of the canyon. Tracking the prints, Bolan soon saw signs of a trail. He began to follow it, Desert Eagle in hand, filled with savage determination.

Bolan was hoping for a chance to show the ambushers just why he'd come to be known as the Executioner.

CHAPTER TWENTY-THREE

Once it cleared the foliage, the path rose upward, leading to a series of switchbacks that took Bolan up the side of the canyon. The ground was solid beneath his feet, a welcome change from the brittle *choss* that had detoured him from his original mission. He wondered how Kissinger and the Gurkhas were faring. Perhaps once he'd reached higher ground he could find his bearings and find a way to hook back up with them.

Bolan paused just shy of the canyon's rim and glanced out, trying to commit the terrain to memory so that, if all went well, he could arrange for the retrieval of the slain Rangers insuring a proper burial back in the States. From where he was, he couldn't see their temporary grave; trees concealed it from view. He could see the lake, however, as well as the rapids that spilled into it. Across the gorge, he thought he detected a faint dome of light. Once again recalling the topographical map back at the air base, he was puzzled. The only possible source of such light would have to be Manakan, but as CIA Agent Chengzhu had described it, the town was as small as it was remote. Even if they had electricity, he doubted there were enough homes to give off that much illumination.

That left the uranium mine, but on the map he remembered it being miles north of the search zone. Had Bolan been carried that far after losing consciousness in the river? It seemed impossible to him. There had to be another explanation.

He put the matter out of his mind and turned his focus back to the moment. His legs were cramped from the climb. He massaged his calves briefly, then moved on, clearing the rise and finding himself on a vast, barren plain dotted by several small mountains and hillocks. The footprints led directly across the open plain toward the nearest rise.

Not good, he thought. Without cover, there was no way he could advance without being spotted by sentries, which he assumed were likely posted up in the hills.

Bolan was trying to figure his way through his quandary when he was startled by the sudden barking of a dog. Glancing to his right, he saw the animal some forty yards away, standing its ground in front of a herd of several dozen larger beasts. They were similar in appearance to goats, but the size of oxen.

Yaks.

As Bolan watched, a herdsman appeared out of the flock, riding a dark horse. He called out something to the dog, then slapped the reins and urged his horse in Bolan's direction. The dog followed suit, bounding loudly across the flatland.

Bolan slowly backtracked, easing himself down the trail he'd just climbed. He held his pistol level. If the dog tried to attack, he would have no choice but to shoot it and, if need be, the herdsman, as well.

The dog, a long-haired breed Bolan was unfamiliar with, continued to race forward, then stopped and continued to bark, apparently trained only to corner any threat to the herd rather than attack it. Bolan kept his gun trained on the animal, then shifted it as the herdsman drew near, armed with an ancient flintlock rifle. Bolan kept his finger on the trigger but held his fire.

The herdsman was a boy, no more than ten.

The youth seemed every bit as taken by surprise as Bolan and made no effort to aim the rifle at him. Instead, he stared at him quizzically. Bolan, bare chested, his dark hair matted with sweat, stared back.

For a moment neither of them spoke. Then the boy broke the silence, speaking in faltering English.

"Are you Rambo?"

"Yeah, and I'm on a mission," Bolan said simply, thinking it might be to his advantage to pretend to be fictitious warrior.

"Against the soldiers?" the boy asked. There was hope in his voice.

Bolan went with it, nodding. "They killed some people," he stated. "Good people."

"They killed my father," the boy said. "In the labor camp."

"Over there?" Bolan asked, indicating the dome of light across the canyon.

The boy nodded. Apparently Manakan had not only electricity, but also a sufficient enough supply of pirated Hollywood movies for the boy to have taught himself English. He chose his words carefully, eager to impress his favorite movie hero, miraculously brought to life before his very eyes.

"The soldiers came to my village looking for Falun Gong," the youth explained. "My father said for them to leave them alone, that they were hurting no one."

"And for that they sent him to a labor camp?"

The boy nodded again. "They say he died working, but my father was strong. My mother says they are lying. She says they killed him. I believe her."

"Did your father belong to the Falun Gong?" Bolan asked.

The boy shook his head. "No, but he thought it was right to leave them alone."

"And that's why you're in charge of the herd now?" Bolan asked. "Because your father died?"

"I take turns with my brother," the boy said. "He is eight."

"The men who did this should be punished," Bolan told the boy. "Do you know where they are?"

The boy, who was riding, not on a saddle but rather a folded blanket, turned and pointed to one of the hillocks. "There," he said. He hefted his rifle, which dwarfed him. "I would shoot them but I am afraid. And if they killed me, my mother would be sad again."

"I think there is a way you can help," Bolan told the boy. "You can make your mother proud."

"She is already proud of me," the boy said. "But I can still help."

"Good. Tell me, do the soldiers do anything when you herd your yaks past them?"

"Sometimes they laugh," the boy said. "They point to my rifle, then pretend that I shot them. They fall down, then they get up and laugh some more."

Bolan pitied the boy and had qualms about drawing him into collusion, but he felt it might be possible to make use of him without putting him in danger. "How close are you to them when they do this laughing?" he asked.

"There is grass on the hills," the boy responded. "They let me bring the yaks over for grazing. That way they know I can see them pretending to be shot."

"I will see that they stop laughing at you," Bolan promised. "Here is my plan...."

Bolan told the boy what he had in mind, then followed him back toward the herd, making sure to stay alongside the horse so that anyone looking down would be able to see him. The dog stayed close to him, as if guiding back a stray that had wandered from the herd. Once they reached the yaks, the boy nudged his horse through their ranks, looking them over. Bolan had no doubt that the boy could tell the beasts apart. Finally he pointed to one of the larger yaks.

"Yaru will let you ride him," he said.

Bolan eyed the creature; it was the one he would have picked, too. Yaru's coat was thicker than the others, and he felt he could ride flat on the beast's back without anyone being able to see him. As an added precaution, however, he asked to borrow the blanket the boy was using in place of a saddle. The boy shifted on the horse's back and pulled it out from under him.

"My mother was making it as a present for my father before the soldiers took him away," he explained. "It is special."

"I'll take good care of it," Bolan promised, draping the blanket like a cape over his bare shoulders. The blanket was dark, nearly the same color as the yak's coat. It would further camouflage Bolan as he rode on the animal's back.

It took them a while to reach the hills. Bolan had instructed the boy to take a meandering course so as to not draw suspicion. The beast's coat stank, but not nearly as bad as the smells Bolan had had to contend with while burying the Rangers. It was a small price to pay, and he put up with it.

As they drew closer, Bolan peered over the yak's shoulder and saw that, along with tall grass, the hill was mottled with brush. Perfect, he thought to himself.

Once the beasts came to the hill, they spread out and began to chew at the grass. Bolan stayed put atop Yaru, looking for some sign of activity atop the hill. There wasn't any. Apparently the sentries were unfazed, both by the dog's earlier barking and the appearance of the yaks. The boy had said the soldiers only teased him during the daytime, again because they wanted to be sure he could see them mocking him.

When he felt certain the coast was clear, Bolan slipped off Yaru's back and paused long enough to return the blanket to the boy. He put a finger to his lips, cautioning the youth not to speak, then offered him a salute. Sitting tall astride his horse, the boy beamed and saluted back.

Gun in hand, Bolan crept into the brush, moving from thicket to thicket as he made his way up the gentle slope. He was nearly all the way to the top when he spotted a brief flicker of light twenty yards to his right. One of the sentries was lighting a cigarette. His face was illuminated briefly, the he waved the match out and tossed it aside, blowing smoke as he stared out at the flatlands.

Bolan carefully slipped his Desert Eagle back into his holster, then reached down and unsheathed his hunting knife. He held it behind his back to conceal the faint gleam of its nine-inch serrated steel blade, then moved away from the brush and crept stealthily the rest of the way up the hill.

Bolan was less than five feet away before the sentry heard him coming up from behind. He was about to turn when the Executioner sprang forward, clamping his left hand over the man's mouth. In the same motion, he leaned into the man, supporting him so that he would not fall, then dragged the knife's blade across his throat, slicing into his esophagus and vocal cords, then drawing blood from a severed artery. He pulled the man down to the ground, then crouched over him, watching the life fade from his disbelieving eyes.

CHAPTER TWENTY-FOUR

Three more soldiers were camped halfway down the other side of the hill. One was asleep, half burrowed beneath a cheap army-issue bedroll. The other two were crouched before a gas lantern turned down to its lowest setting, providing just enough light to play cards by. As he inched toward his prey in the tall grass, Bolan heard them talking, laughing among themselves. They were speaking Chinese, but now and then Bolan picked up a word of English.

"Ambush!" one of them called out at one point, obviously mimicking a cry they'd heard while assaulting the cornered Rangers.

The other chuckled.

Bolan had taken the sentry's bayonet-tipped AK-47, as well as his binoculars. Quietly he parted the grass and peered through the glasses. His blood began to churn as he focused on the flat rock the men were using as a card table. Instead of chips, the men were gambling with their battle trophies. Lying in small piles before each man were wristwatches, pocketknives and signet rings taken off the bodies of the slain Rangers. As one of the soldiers began to deal another hand, they each set out an ante and Bolan realized they were also wagering the severed ears and fingers of their victims.

Holding his rage in check, Bolan continued to draw nearer, moving from the grass to a hedgerow of wild brush that brought him to within ten yards of the encampment. The two card players had their assault rifles close at hand, propped against either side of the rock. Bolan wasn't about to let them bring their guns into play. Once the soldiers had picked up their cards, he made his move.

Rising to a crouch, he drew his arm back, then let fly with his knife. End over end, the steel-edged blade, already red with blood, somersaulted through the air before embedding itself in the chest of the man facing Bolan.

Stunned, the man staggered backward, toppling off the log he'd been sitting on. The other soldier turned, reaching for his AK-47. Bolan was already on top of him, however and, with brutal force, he stabbed forward with his assault rifle, driving the bayonet between the soldier's ribs and twisted it, killing the sentry instantly.

With no wasted motion, Bolan jerked the bayonet

free and finished off the other man, stabbing him through the heart.

The skirmish, however brief, had roused the third man. He was struggling to crawl out from under his bedroll when Bolan turned on him, cracking him across the skull with the butt of the AK-47. The man went down, unconscious.

Wanting him alive, Bolan left the man where he lay and returned to the rock where the others had been playing cards. The lantern allowed him a better look at the grisly plunder the men had been betting with. He tossed aside his canteen, leaving room in his kit bag for the rest of the slain Rangers' belongings.

One of the watches in particular drew Bolan's attention. It was a moderately expensive Seiko, gold trimmed with a worn leather band. Bolan recognized the timepiece. He picked it up and turned it over. The watch was engraved: To Johnny U. With love/ Mom & Pop.

Jack Grimaldi had been christened John Udolf. Bolan knew the watch had been a high-school graduation present, back then Grimaldi'd been nicknamed after legendary football quarterback Johnny Unitas.

Bolan was pondering the implications when he heard a rustling in the brush behind him. Instinctively he dived right, throwing himself to the ground. Two gunshots rang out in the night air. One sent a slug dancing off the flat rock, clanging off the lantern's fuel reservoir. The other produced a loud, startled grunt.

Glancing over his shoulder, Bolan saw a Chinese soldier twist to one side, dropping his handgun as he crumpled into the grass. The man had apparently been out on the patrol and stalked back at the sound of Bolan's confrontation with the two card players.

But who had shot him?

Bolan turned his gaze uphill. There, silhouetted against the moon, the young herdsman stood holding his flintlock rifle.

Bolan scrambled to his feet and rushed through the grass to where the fourth soldier had dropped from view. The man lay still on the ground. Blood seeped from a bullet hole in his right cheek. His days of pretending the boy had shot him were over.

WHEN THE SURVIVING Chinese soldier regained consciousness, he found himself spread-eagled on the ground, his ankles and wrists pinned to the earth by crisscrossed bayonets. Any movement and the honed blades would cut into him. He wasn't going anywhere. Bolan crouched over him, his Desert Eagle pointed at the man's forehead. The boy, who'd told Bolan his name was Avil, stood a few paces back, trembling. Bolan hated himself for forcing the boy to be present for the interrogation, but he needed a translator.

The prisoner looked past Bolan and saw his comrades lying dead nearby. He turned his gaze on Bolan, his eyes filled with hatred.

Bolan held Grimaldi's watch out where the man could see it, then asked the boy, "Tell him I want to know what happened to the pilot."

His voice quavering, Avil relayed the question. The soldier stared at the watch and said nothing.

"Ask him again," Bolan said patiently.

Avil complied. Still the man refused to talk.

"Turn around," Bolan told the boy.

When Avil did as he was told, Bolan reached out, shoving one of the bayonets deeper into the earth. Its blade cut into the prisoner's wrist and the man let out a pained cry, then muttered something.

"He says he will talk," Avil said without turning.

Bolan eased up on the bayonet, then repeated his question, this time in Chinese, parroting Avil's translation. For emphasis, he held Grimaldi's watch closer to the prisoner's face.

The man answered quickly. Avil translated.

"He says the watch is black market. He knows nothing about a pilot."

"Liar!" Bolan accused.

The man shouted back angrily.

"He says he is telling the truth," Avil told Bolan.

Bolan told the boy to keep his back turned. He set aside the watch and grabbed the knife he'd already used on two of the other sentries. Grabbing hold of the prisoner's left hand, he spread the man's fingers and, with one fierce stroke, sliced off the right pinky. The prisoner screamed and writhed, inadvertently cutting himself on the crisscrossed bayonets pinning him to the ground. Bolan ignored the cries and held the man's severed finger out before him.

"Tell him I got this off the black market, too," he told Avil.

The boy turned his head slightly and spoke to the prisoner. The man stopped his screaming long enough to shout back at the boy.

"He says they found some bodies of American soldiers and took their belongings."

"I already know about the soldiers!" Bolan retorted. "I want to know about the pilot! The pilot of the spy plane!"

Avil translated again. Despite his pain, the prisoner refused to cooperate. He muttered something.

"He says he only knows about the soldiers. Not any plane or pilot."

"Liar!"

Bolan glanced over his shoulder and saw that Avil was trying to sneak a look at the proceedings.

"Look the other way!" Bolan commanded.

The boy meekly complied. Bolan turned back and leaned over the prisoner, pressing his palm hard against the bridge of the man's nose to keep his head still. With his other hand, he placed the edge of his knife against the man's ear, letting the blade cut into the lobe. He glared at the man and once again mimicked Avil, repeating the question foremost in his mind.

"What happened to the pilot!"

The prisoner cursed, then spit a few angry words. He'd finally decided to tell the truth.

Avil told Bolan, "He says they took him to the labor camp."

THE SOLDIER CLAIMED no knowledge as the specifics behind the downing of Grimaldi's plane. All he knew was that the plane had come down a mile to the north, landing in a narrow valley between two other small hills. He, along with the men Bolan had just killed, had been among the first on the scene. They'd held the pilot prisoner until their superiors arrived, bringing with them a truck to load the plane onto. Both Grimaldi and the plane had then been whisked off to the labor camp.

Bolan told Avil, "Ask him if the pilot was injured."

Avil passed along the question. The soldier shook his head and murmured a few words.

"He says no," Avil told Bolan. "He was fine when they took him away."

"Where in the labor camp were they taking him to?"

When Avil translated the question, the soldier shook his head again. He responded, through Avil, that he'd divulged all he knew.

Bolan chose not to press the matter. And much as he wanted to ask about the killing of the Rangers, he had the information most vital to him. It was time to move on. First, however, he wanted to see to it that the military wouldn't connect Avil or anyone in the village with what had just happened.

"Go back to your herd and wait for me," he told Avil. "It will be a few minutes."

"What are you going to do?" the boy wondered.

"Go," Bolan told him firmly. "Now."

The boy obeyed.

Once they were alone, Bolan turned back to the soldier, who was still stretched out on the ground, pinned by the bayonets. The man stared at him and began to talk as fast as he could. From the look of desperation in his eyes, Bolan guessed he was pleading for his life.

Even though he knew the man couldn't understand, Bolan told him, "Even if there were a way for me to turn you in, you would never stand trial for what you did to those men back there." He gestured toward the canyon where the massacre of the Rangers had taken place. "Your superiors would let you off the hook and probably even give you a medal. That leaves only what we call back home frontier justice."

Bolan grabbed one of the bayonet-fixed AK-47s and raised it in the air, butt first, as if he were about to plunge a stake into the ground.

Ignoring the man's cries, Bolan brought the rifle down, driving the bayonet through the soldier's chest, killing him. Then, with cold efficiency, he pulled away the other bayonets and stripped the man to his skivvies. One by one, he quickly did the same with the others, leaving them where they had fallen.

Once he was finished, he piled the uniforms in a heap near the rock where the lantern rested. He doused the lamp and poured its fuel over the clothes. There was more fuel in a two-gallon container stored a few yards away in a crate filled with provisions. Bolan unscrewed the cap and walked about the encampment, spilling kerosene over the bodies and onto the ground and surrounding brush. When the canister was empty, Bolan tossed it aside, then turned to the sentries' radio transceiver he'd seen mounted on the provisions crate. He lacked Aaron Kurtzman's knack for electronics and wasn't about to even try putting a call out to Kissinger or the

Gurkhas. Instead, he grabbed the radio and smashed it against the rocks.

There was one last task.

Taking a few dozen small rocks bordering a firepit near the provisions crate, Bolan rearranged them in a tight ring several yards away, then used his knife to scrawl a message in the dirt. The rocks would insure that the message wasn't obliterated by fire.

Stepping back from his handiwork, Bolan raided his kit bag for matches. He struck one and tossed it atop the pile of uniforms. Flames immediately leaped into the air, sending of a foul black cloud. Within seconds the fire was already spreading across the trail of poured kerosene.

Bolan fled the growing inferno, confident that by the time the military came to investigate, there would be nothing left by charred bodies and the un- touched message, which would leave no doubt but that the countermassacre had been the work, not of the villagers, but American soldier seeking retribu- tion for the earlier killing of the Rangers. Bolan whispered the message to himself as he headed downhill to where Avil had gathered his herd of yaks.

"Payback is a bitch."

Avil was watching the blaze with awe when Bo- lan caught up with him.

"I'm sorry you had to see what you did," he told the boy.

"It was like a movie," the boy replied. "I was thinking maybe I was wrong. But you really *are* Rambo."

Bolan changed the subject. "You saved my life, Avil. Thank you."

He swore the boy to secrecy, stressing that his life, as well as that of his mother and brother, depended on his telling no one about what had happened.

"No one," he repeated.

"I understand," the boy said.

"You need to go now," Bolan told him. "But I have one last favor to ask."

"What?"

"Can you ride Yaru back to town?"

The boy frowned, puzzled. "Yes. But I have my horse."

Bolan held out a fistful of currency he'd taken off the bodies of the slain soldiers. He told the boy, "I need to buy the horse from you."

CHAPTER TWENTY-FIVE

The ride took Bolan longer than he'd expected. Avil had told him of a route to the labor camp that steered clear of other military outposts situated near the canyon's perimeter. Understandably the way was circuitous and often led over treacherous ground: steep-pitched ravines, streams choked with boulders, stretches of loose, shifting sand. The boy's roan was old and unaccustomed to such rigors, and Bolan had to stop often to let the horse rest. Avil's directions had been convoluted, too, and several times Bolan found himself lost, unable to spot landmarks the boy had told him to follow.

In all, the forty-mile trek took more than four hours. By then Bolan's legs were chafed with saddle sores. The horse was suffering, too, and had begun to hobble after snorting its way up a particularly difficult incline. Dismounting, Bolan had inspected the roan's hooves. It had thrown a shoe. Bolan had coaxed the horse to softer ground, then turned it loose at the edge of a pasture where cattle were grazing. Hopefully someone would spot the roan and attend to it.

He covered the last few miles on foot, following a narrow uphill path choked with bramble. Morning had crept up on him, arriving without the fanfare of a sunrise. The sky was leaden and overcast, filled with the promise of rain.

Soon he spotted the final landmark, a top-heavy pinnacle rising up through the brush like a large mallet. Spurred on by the sighting, Bolan, who'd feared he'd lost his way again, broke into a sprint. The path soon leveled off and once he reached the base of the pinnacle, he caught his first glimpse of both the labor camp and uranium mine.

The two sites were adjacent to each other, both cordoned off by a tall cyclone fence topped with barbed wire. The light Bolan had seen from afar the night before had come from halogen lamps mounted high on poles fixed to the rooftops of watchtowers spaced evenly about the fence's perimeter. Bolan assumed the lights were more than merely a security measure. If this was like most labor camps he knew of, the prisoners were no doubt forced to work in shifts around the clock.

Peering through the binoculars he'd taken from the slain sentries, Bolan saw a crew near the entrance to the mines, using shovels to transfer loads of gritty, mineral-enriched soil from small rail carts into the hold of a large flatbed truck. Bolan couldn't see a refining plant, but he knew there was probably one close by where hauls from the mine would be sifted, then converted by centrifuge to uranium hexaflouride, the first step toward producing yellowcake, the uranium oxide used in power reactors and, if enriched to ninety percent, nuclear warheads.

The CIA had mentioned any link between the mine and China's supposedly secret race to stockpile its nuclear arsenal, but Bolan knew there had to be a connection. He also knew that even though processing was required to boost the volatility of soil scooped out of the mines, the dirt still contained dangerous levels of radioactivity. The guards apparently knew it, too, and watched the unloading from a distance. As Bolan expected, the workers were forced to brave the hazards of their job without the benefit of protective clothing or masks to filter out the toxic dust that rose in faint clouds each time a shovel was stabbed into the mounds of soil.

Bolan thought again about Kissinger and the Gurkhas. He'd been on the lookout for them while riding around the canyon, but there'd been no sign of them. He couldn't see the point in waiting for them. He'd reached his destination. It was time to carry out the mission.

Along with the binoculars, Bolan had taken several grenades and rearmed himself with one of the sentry's assault rifles. Still, he wasn't about to take on the entire security detail single-handedly in hopes of liberating those held prisoner in the labor camp. That would have to wait for another time, and it would require more men. As it was, he knew the odds were against his being able to get to Grimaldi, much less be able to spirit him away from the facility.

Avil had known the way to the camp because he'd come once, along with his mother and two cousins, to visit his father. Official visits were banned, but the villagers of Manakan, many of whom had loved ones imprisoned at the facility, had found a way around the restriction. Avil had told Bolan that on the far side of the camp there was an area where the brush grew right up to the fence and then continued on the other side, running downhill to the large canvas tents that served as the laborers' barracks. At certain hours of the day, usually during lulls between a changing of the guards, there would be an opportunity for prisoners to steal up through the brush for a brief rendezvous with family members.

To Bolan, it sounded like the best way to enter the camp unnoticed.

TWO SEPARATE RIVERS—one an offshoot of the Xiangshu, the other a smaller tributary—ran along either side of the mining compound, making for a lush oasis in the otherwise arid desert. As Bolan circled the perimeter of the labor camp, he found concealment in the shade of tall acacias and was further helped by rampant clusters of rose wort and fang thistle. Twigless, the ground cover silenced the sounds of his advance, springing back into place, leaving no sign of a trail. The thistle was actually a variety of creeping vine, and there were places where its prong-ended leaves had grabbed hold of the trees and pulled itself all the way up to the higher branches. It tended to fall back on itself, forming large, misshapen clumps. Whenever the breeze picked up, the clumps seemed to take on life, and several times Bolan froze in midstep and drew aim with his AK-47, thinking he'd spotted snipers in the trees. There were also a few false alarms involving wild monkeys and large birds, mostly crows and vultures.

As Avil had explained, the fang thistle also reached up to the perimeter fence, that encircled the labor camp, weaving a screen through the gaps before tumbling back to the ground on the other side. The growth was thickest at a spot roughly equidistant from the two nearest watchtowers. It was there, Bolan had been told, that the villagers of Manakan would go for their clandestine rendezvous. They'd trimmed out a cavelike enclosure within the billowing growth, allowing them to linger near the fence without being seen by sentries posted in the towers. Bolan knew a set of bolt cutters would have been a godsend, but once he reached the fence he hoped the serrated edge of his hunting knife would serve the same function, snipping enough of the chain lengths to let him squeeze through.

Bolan was within thirty yards of the fence when he saw the hollowing. To his surprise, villagers were huddled inside the enclosure, a woman and two young children. Bolan found cover behind a grouping of rhododendrons and waited. He would give them a few minutes in hopes they would leave without his having to approach them. He was concerned they might let out a cry at the sight of him, tipping the guards off to their presence.

As it turned out, the villagers had already been discovered. Less than a minute after he'd settling in behind the rhododendrons, Bolan saw soldiers converging on the hollow from separate directions. There were four of them, two in each party, and all were carrying AK-47s. Bolan doubted the villagers could see the men through the fang thistle.

The first two soldiers stopped once they were within a few yards of the enclosure. They waited for others to catch up, then all four men slowly raised their assault rifles and prepared to fire into the brush.

Bolan wasn't about to stand by and witness the

slaughter. Betraying his position, he rose into view, AK-47 blazing. He strafed the two men closest to him, aiming chest high, then quickly turned the rifle on the others. The return fire was brief and wild, striking nothing save for a few leaves of rhododendron. In a matter of seconds, all four men were down.

But Bolan knew it wasn't over. He was certain that others, drawn by the sound of gunfire, would soon be on the way. He saw the woman and children staring out from the enclosure, fear stricken. He waved to get their attention, then pointed over his shoulder, back toward the path that would eventually lead them back to Manakan.

"Go!" he shouted. "Run for it!"

If they didn't understand his words, they made sense of his gestures. Grabbing each child by the wrist, the woman dashed out of the hollow and ran toward Bolan. As they did so, gunshots sounded from one of the watchtowers. Bolan whirled and returned fire. The tower was barely within range of the assault rifle, but the Fates compensated for having thwarted his plan, and at least one of his rounds caught the sentry.

As the man slumped from view, Bolan pivoted, anticipating shots from the other tower. He didn't bother firing; it was too far away. Instead, he sprinted from the fence in the opposite direction of that taken by the woman and her children. As he hoped, he drew fire his way, giving the villagers more time to make their getaway. Bullets slapped through the foliage around him, and even though he veered from side to side to make himself a harder target, the rounds were closing in.

Bolan's diversionary ploy may have saved the villagers, but he couldn't have picked a worse direction to run in. He'd covered less than fifty yards when a military jeep rose into view, plowing through the fang thistle. Another was directly behind it, with yet a third bringing up the rear. There were gunners aboard all three vehicles, the two in front positioned behind rear-mounted 7.62 mm Gatling guns, the other clutching what looked to be a pump-action riot gun.

Bolan knew there was no way he could outmaneuver the jeeps; he was trapped in an open field. He wasn't about to surrender, though, so he decided to go down firing. As the second two jeeps fanned out from the column, Bolan emptied his AK-47, dropping the tail gunner in one vehicle and killing the driver of another. By then the lead jeep was almost upon him.

Bolan was clawing for his Desert Eagle when the soldier with the riot gun took aim and unleashed a glorified leather beanbag filled with buckshot. Back in the States SWAT teams called them numb-nuts after the most frequent part of the anatomy they aimed for when trying to subdue unruly suspects. Bolan took the bag higher up; it smacked off his forehead with a dull crack.

For the second time in the past few hours, Bolan found himself flung into the black void of unconsciousness.

CHAPTER TWENTY-SIX

When he came to, Bolan found himself lying on the dirt floor of an empty cell. The Chinese had taken his boots, watch and kit bag, leaving him his tattered pants. Sitting up, he rubbed the egg-sized welt poking up through his hairline. His skull was throbbing. He looked around him.

The walls were made of slump stone and there were no windows. A thin shaft of light shone through a small ventilation grate high up near the ceiling. There was a narrow gap, roughly the same size, at the base of the heavy wooden door to his right. A thin plastic tray had been shoved through the opening. On it was the usual Geneva buffet: a crust of bread and a shallow bowl half filled with rusty, tepid water.

He assumed he'd been taken alive for the same reason he'd initially spared the last sentry back near the canyon. The Chinese wanted to question him. By now he was sure word of the sentry killings had reached the camp. They would be looking for answers and viewed him, no doubt, as the one most likely to have them.

Fine, Bolan thought. He'd dished it out; he could take it, as well.

Bolan's stomach rumbled, but the cell's rank smell of stale sweat, urine and feces curbed his appetite. He ignored his ration, stood slowly and went to the far wall, aching with every step. The ventilation shaft was too high up for him to see out, and because it was set flush against the wall with grating too small for his fingers to fit through, there was no way for him to pull himself up. He assumed he was somewhere inside the labor camp.

He paced the cell briefly, then sat again, back to the wall. The ball was in their court. All he could do was wait. He sat staring at the opposite wall, nodding off every few minutes, only to awaken with a start each time his head drooped forward.

An hour passed, then two.

Then he heard someone outside the cell. A hand reached under the door and pulled away his tray. Moments later, there was a rattling of keys, followed by the sound of the door's lock springing back. The door opened. In walked an armed soldier, followed by an older man dressed in full uniform. He spoke English fluently.

"You're awake," he said. "Good."

"Colonel Rance Pollock," Bolan said tiredly, offering up a well-used alias. He threw in a serial number as well.

"Hello, Colonel Pollock," the officer said pleasantly. He motioned for the soldier behind him to close the door, then told Bolan, "We have something in common. I am a colonel, as well. Colonel Mishu at your service. I think you know why I'm here."

Bolan said nothing.

"Would you be so kind as to hold your hands out before you?" the colonel asked.

When Bolan failed to respond, the soldier stepped forward and lashed out with the butt of his assault rifle. Bolan saw it coming and leaned to his left. Still, the butt grazed his skull just above his right ear, knocking him to his side. The soldier was a big man, the same height as Bolan but twenty pounds heavier, much of it toned muscle. He was agile, too. He shoved Bolan to the floor and twisted one arm behind his back. Bolan didn't bother fighting back. He was conserving his strength for a battle he knew he could win.

Colonel Mishu knelt before Bolan, sniffing his fingers. Satisfied, he stood.

"Kerosene," he said, gesturing for the soldier to let Bolan go. The soldier released Bolan and retreated to the doorway. He was smiling, self-satisfied. Bolan ignored him. He returned to the same position he'd been in before the attack, ready for whatever the soldier might dish out next.

"Do the words 'Payback is a bitch' mean anything to you?" Mishu asked.

Bolan met the officer's stare. "Colonel Rance Pollock." He repeated the same serial number.

Mishu sighed. "You Americans are so predictable."

"Colonel Rance Pollock," Bolan replied.

"What, no serial number this time?"

"Colonel Rance Pollock."

Mishu seemed unperturbed by Bolan's intractability. The soldier, however, stopped smiling and began to move forward, anticipating approval to have another go at the prisoner. The colonel, however, held his arm out, motioning for the soldier to stay put.

"This is getting us nowhere," he said. "Excuse us a moment. We'll be back shortly."

Mishu turned to the door. The soldier opened it for him, then glowered back at Bolan as he followed Mishu out of the cell.

The door slammed shut on Bolan. He now had dueling headaches. Closing his eyes, he breathed in slowly, held it for a count of ten, then let the air escape just as slowly from his lungs. It didn't help much, but at least it gave him something else to focus on besides the pain. He continued to repeat the exercise for another few minutes. Then he heard the key go in the lock again.

The door swung open. The first man to walk in was neither Colonel Mishu nor his armed goon.

It was Jack Grimaldi.

"...AND EVERYTHING'S going hunky-dory when these two MiGs come up on me," Grimaldi whispered. The pilot seemed none the worse for wear from his ordeal. He looked as tanned and healthy as always.

The Stony Man pilot was relating the events that led up to his forced landing of the ES-1 spy plane. Left alone in the cell, Bolan and Grimaldi had quickly searched for bugs. They hadn't found any, but to be safe they'd huddled close near the wall farthest from both the door and the ventilation grate. As they spoke, each took turns scraping the slump stone with their fingernails, figuring the noise would be sufficient to drown out their conversation to anyone eavesdropping.

"I smelled trouble, so I start locking them in on my air-to-airs Cowboy helped rig up," Grimaldi went on. "Next thing I know, the cockpit goes dead on me. Nothing. The instruments are down and the missiles won't fire. I'm up shit creek without a paddle, only I'm twenty thousand feet up."

"It wasn't the weapons system," Bolan assured Grimaldi. He explained how the plane had been sabotaged back at the air base in Marjeelam, then briefly sketched out the web of intrigue he'd become embroiled in back at Collier Springs.

"Whew!" Grimaldi said afterward. "And here I'm thinking I must've tripped the extension cord or something."

"It was out of your hands," Bolan said. "Except for bringing it down in one piece."

"That part was a breeze," Grimaldi said. "That baby was so light I could play it as a glider. Rode the currents and had enough steering control over the steering to ease her down. Of course, the whole time I'm sweating bullets waiting for MiGs to start venting me with 30 mms."

"They wanted the plane intact," Bolan said. "For obvious reasons."

"Well, on that front I helped them out the best I could," Grimaldi said. "I had to set her down in the sand without landing gear, which roughed the hell out of my pod, I'm telling you. Any rocks down there I'd have had me a free prostate exam."

"I know the rest."

Bolan told Grimaldi about his encounter with the sentries who'd met up with the plane after it landed.

"That's what they want to grill me about," he

added. "They want to make sure I'm their guy so they can have last laugh. Where's the plane now?"

Grimaldi shrugged. "Last I saw, it was in the truck. I'm sure they've got it squirreled away somewhere around here along with a crew of retroengineers."

Bolan nodded. "Who knows, by now they might have the plans to go along with it."

"ES-1 knockoffs, here we come," Grimaldi muttered. "Chinese eyes in the skies."

"Where are we now?" Bolan wanted to know. "The labor camp?"

Grimaldi nodded. "VIP suites for troublemakers," he said. "You probably didn't see them because they're part of a bunker built into the hill near the barracks. They've been keeping me down the hall. Room's nearly as nice as this one. I'm not sure why they're doubling us up here, though. Must be somebody else had reservations for my place."

"I don't think that's it," Bolan said.

Colonel Mishu showed up five minutes later. This time he'd brought along a second soldier. Bolan didn't think the came any bigger than the guard he'd already tangled with, but the new guard proved him wrong. He stood six-six and was easily three hundred pounds. Like his partner, he was no stranger to the weight room. Biceps as large as cantaloupes threatened to burst through the fabric of his shirt.

The first guard whispered something to the other soldier and pointed to Bolan. The other man nodded and sized Bolan up as if the Executioner were going to be served up for his evening meal.

"I was glad to see you two knew each other," the colonel told Bolan and Grimaldi. "It will hopefully make things a lot easier for everyone."

"Colonel Rance Pollock," Bolan responded tauntingly.

"Airman First Class Orville Wright," Grimaldi joined in.

"You are like two peas in a pod, as they say." Mishu chuckled. "Almost like brothers."

Calmly the colonel reached to his side, pulling out a service revolver. It was an old Colt .45 with a pearl-inlaid grip. "Nice, yes?" he told the prisoners. "I got it in Korea, during the war. A present from one of your forefathers."

Neither Bolan nor Grimaldi rose to the bait. They stayed put, waiting for the colonel's next move. Mishu stared admiringly at the gun, then slowly turned it on Grimaldi. He held his other hand out, showing Grimaldi the graduation watch that had passed hands several times since being taken from him after his forced landing. The colonel wasn't about to give the watch back, however.

Instead, he turned to Bolan and told him, "This is how it is going to be. You have thirty seconds to start talking before I pull the trigger on your friend."

CHAPTER TWENTY-SEVEN

"Thirty seconds," Colonel Mishu said, beginning the countdown.

Bolan stared impassively at the officer and said nothing. Behind Mishu, the two heavyweights smirked.

"Twenty-five seconds."

Bolan's gaze held fast, as did his silence.

"Twenty seconds," the colonel announced.

This time it was Grimaldi who spoke up. Calmly he told Mishu, "I guess they don't play chess here in China, eh, Colonel?"

Mishu shifted his gaze to the pilot. "What is your point?"

"I'm your bartering collateral," Grimaldi said evenly. "Shoot me and you've sacrificed your queen. For what?"

Mishu thought it over briefly, then responded, "For the satisfaction of seeing the look on your friend's face once he realizes his silence has cost your life." Almost as an afterthought, he added, "Ten seconds."

Bolan, who'd been standing straight, slowly unlocked his knees and began to tense the muscles in his legs, imperceptibly shifting weight off his heels and onto the balls of his feet. His jaw remained set. His gaze remained locked on Mishu. His lips remained sealed.

Mishu pulled back the hammer on the old Colt .45. "Five seconds."

"All right, all right, he did it!" Grimaldi interjected. He spoke fast, pretending fear. "He told me everything! I'll give you all the details! Please, just quit pointing that gun at me!"

Mishu quickly thought it over. At the last second, he stopped the countdown. He turned the gun from Grimaldi, shifting his aim to Bolan's groin. The Colt's hammer was still pulled back.

"I'm waiting," he told Grimaldi.

"You want to know about last night, right?" the Stony Man pilot said. "Well, he's the one, all right."

"I want the details," Mishu said coldly.

"Fair enough," Grimaldi replied. "He slipped in and did the deed. Took his time about it, too. You know, milking it for all it was worth. Of course, the way he tells it, she didn't mind a bit."

Mishu frowned. "She?"

"Your mother," Grimaldi told him. "Matter of fact, he says she was moaning so much she woke the neighbors."

The colonel's face reddened. A tremble coursed through him. Realizing he'd been had, he began to turn the gun back on Grimaldi.

Bolan made his move. He torqued his body and his right leg shot out from under him. The karate kick caught Mishu's wrist squarely. The Colt fired as it flew from his hand, scarring the wall behind Grimaldi's head.

The pilot's reflexes were every bit as fast as Bolan's. He lunged forward, dropping one shoulder. At 150 pounds, he was barely half the weight of the guard he tackled, but he had momentum and the element of surprise on his side. He caught the man flat-footed, slamming into his chest with enough force to knock him off balance.

The other guard lurched backward to keep from being knocked down. He raised his AK-47, but before he could fire Bolan had already grabbed the fallen Colt. The .45 barked a second time, biting a hole in the shorter guard's midsection. He let out a cry that was quickly drowned out by a third gunshot, this one ripping through the larger guard's skull, spattering his brains on the walls and ceiling.

Bolan finished off the shorter guard with a killshot to the chest, then turned the gun on Mishu. The colonel, who'd staggered back into a corner, stared at his fallen guards, then looked down the bore of his .45. It was Bolan's turn to cock the hammer.

"Next one has your name on it, Colonel," he stated.

Mishu was clearly bewildered. It'd taken Bolan and Grimaldi less than ten seconds to turn the tables.

"My apologies to your mother," Grimaldi called out as he quickly gathered up the assault rifles. "I'm sure she's a fine person."

The colonel was silent a moment. "What do you want from me?" he finally asked.

Bolan picked up Grimaldi's watch and traded it to Grimaldi for one of the AK-47s. Tucking the Colt .45 inside the waistband of his pants, he told Mishu, "I want my kit bag and gun back, then I want you to get us out of this hellhole in one piece."

GUN TO HIS BACK, hands placed on his head, Colonel Mishu was the first to leave the cell. A trio of guards responding to the clamor stood at the end of the hall. Mishu shouted for them to hold their fire as he started down the hall toward them. Bolan was directly behind, with Grimaldi bringing up the rear, checking up and down the hall for signs of other soldiers. The corridor was long, lined with more than a dozen cells on each side. The doors were all closed. Cries and moans issued from inside the cells.

Bolan and Grimaldi guessed the other prisoners had jumped to the conclusion that one of their fellow inmates had just been executed and were fearful they might be next.

Bolan extended his arm in front of Mishu, jangling the ring of keys he'd taken off one of the guards they'd left behind in the cell.

"Which one's the master for the cell doors?" he demanded.

"The large brass one," Mishu said. There was weariness in his voice. He sounded defeated, already resigned to the humiliation he would face during the court-martial that would be sure to follow the sorry debacle his interrogation of the prisoners had turned into.

Bolan tossed the keys to Grimaldi, who then began to go from door to door, springing the other inmates. Bolan, meanwhile, ordered Mishu to have the guards lay down their assault rifles and step back. Mishu had to repeat the order twice, the second time screaming, before the guards complied.

Halfway down the hall a call box was mounted on the wall. Bolan indicated the receiver and asked Mishu, "Is that hooked up to a public-address system?"

Mishu nodded. "There are speakers throughout the camp and at the main entrance to the mine."

Bolan handed Mishu the receiver and laid out his

terms. "I want all the sentries out of the watchtowers, and the rest of the guards are to hold their fire when we come out. Wherever you've stashed away the plane, I want it put back on the truck and I want the truck filled with enough gas to get us back across the border to India. You'll come along for the ride. If all goes well, we'll turn you loose at the border."

It took Mishu a moment to weigh the demands, then he nodded bleakly and punched the phone's keypad. Before he could speak, Bolan put a finger to the colonel's lips and glanced at the prisoners who'd stumbled out into the corridor. Most of them were middle-aged men, although there were also a few in their twenties. One boy looked to be in his teens. They were all gaunt faced and emaciated, their bodies covered with sores incurred from poor conditions inside the cells. They were all in various states of disbelief.

"Do any of you speak English?" Bolan asked them.

To his surprise, half the inmates raised their hands. He told them, "I need it quiet so you can listen and tell me what the colonel is saying when he speaks over the intercom."

There were brief murmurings among the men, then they feel silent. One of the older men stepped forward. He was stooped and frail, and his face was bruised from beatings he'd received for failing to keep up with the other workers.

"I will translate for you," he told Bolan.

He thanked the man, then pulled his hand from Mishu's face and motioned for him to make the call.

There were no speakers in the cell block, but the colonel's voice resounded clearly over the outside PA system. Every few seconds, the old man interjected, whispering confirmations as to what was being said. Mishu was holding up his end of the bargain.

Once he'd finished, Mishu slowly hung up the phone and told Bolan, "I'm sure it will take them awhile to load the plane."

"Where have you been keeping it?" Bolan wanted to know.

"Near the mines we have a small refining plant," Mishu said. "The plane is being kept in a warehouse there."

"Does the refining plant have a centrifuge?" Bolan asked.

"I don't know what that is," Mishu said.

"I think you do," Bolan replied.

Grimaldi, who'd just finished releasing the prisoners, helped the colonel. "It's what you use to goose yellow-cake till it's bomb grade."

"I just run the labor camp," Mishu said. "I have no say in what goes on at the mines."

"You're dodging the question, Colonel," Bolan said. "You don't have to be in charge of the mines to know what goes on there. Now, out with it. How much of the uranium turned out here goes into weapon programs?"

Mishu sighed and gave it up.

"Two shipments a week are sent to a reactor plant in Jaingsing, four hours north of here," he said. "I don't know percentages, but a small portion of the load is ninety percent U-235."

"It doesn't take much," Grimaldi said. "Mix a little with the plutonium they yank out of their fuel rods and you've got Nukes-R-Us."

Bolan and Grimaldi exchanged an ominous glance, then the pilot went to retrieve the assault rifles dropped by the hall guards. Bolan turned to the prisoners and said, "I need three men who can fire an AK-47 accurately and without hesitation."

There was renewed murmuring among the inmates, then three men stepped out of their ranks. Two were older; the third volunteer was the teenager.

"Are you sure you know how to use one of these?" Grimaldi asked as he returned with the rifles.

The youth took one of the AK-47s and, before Grimaldi could intervene, he leveled it and felled the three unarmed guards at the end of the hall. He turned back to Grimaldi, stony-faced.

"I'll take that for a yes," Grimaldi told him.

Once the other two men had their rifles, Bolan explained, "There has to be a back way out of here. I want the three of you to take the rest of the prisoners with you and go to the barracks. I'm sure you know about the meeting place by the upper fence."

When the three men nodded, he resumed, "You'll need to find some sort of bolt cutter you can use on the fence. Once you've made an opening, stand watch and see that as many prisoners as possible can escape. You can join them afterward and head back to Manakan."

"If we try to escape, they will hunt us down like dogs," the oldest of the three men said. "They will burn the village to cinders if they have to."

"That's all I can offer you," Bolan said. "A chance."

"I will help you to escape," the oldest man said. "After I will stay and take my chances here. I have caused my family enough suffering without bringing more to their doorstep."

The other man concurred, but the youth told Bolan, "I will see to it that the fence is cut open so that everyone can make their own choices."

The older men conferred and reached a compromise—they would help the prisoners make it as far

as the barracks. After that, they would double back
and guard the rear as best they could until Bolan
and Grimaldi had been allowed to leave the compound with their hostage and the ES-1.

Bolan asked Grimaldi for the time.

"Let me just check this lost heirloom a friend of
mine tracked down for me." Grimaldi winked his
thanks to Bolan for the return of the watch, then told
him the time.

"I know the truck's probably not ready, but I
think it's time we got out of here," Bolan said.
"Let's wait outside where we can keep a better eye
on things."

While the prisoners headed the other way, Bolan
and Grimaldi led Mishu to the end of the hallway,
where an unused cell had been converted into an all-
purpose room for the guards.

"My things," Bolan reminded the colonel, gesturing inside the cell. "Are they in there?"

Mishu nodded and the men followed him into the
room. There was a row of cheap lockers along one
wall. Mishu had the keys to one of the locks. Inside,
amid other stashed belongings, were Bolan's boots,
kit bag and Desert Eagle.

As he watched Bolan put on the boots, Mishu
asked a favor. "I need you to beat me."

Bolan didn't understand. "I think we've already
done that."

"No, *beat* me," the colonel repeated. "Strike me. If I go out there with nothing to show but a sore wrist, I will be disgraced. It would help if it looked like I had put up more of a fight."

When Bolan hesitated, Grimaldi stepped forward and said, "Allow me."

Grimaldi laid a roundhouse right punch on Mishu's cheek, high up enough to insure that the colonel would soon have a black eye. For good measure, he followed up with a left cross to the officer's midsection, doubling him over. When he tried to stand, Grimaldi came back with a final right, this time drawing blood from the colonel's nose.

"Was it as good for you as it was for me?" Grimaldi asked, rubbing his sore fists.

Mishu was in no mood for wisecracks. He glared at Grimaldi, his eye already beginning to swell. "I didn't ask you to enjoy it," he wheezed, still trying to catch his breath.

"You're welcome." Grimaldi turned to Bolan. "Let's go, big guy."

"Right there."

Bolan knotted his last shoelace, then strapped on both his kit bag and the .44 Desert Eagle. Fortified, he helped Grimaldi escort Colonel Mishu out of the cell block and into the open air of the labor camp.

Bolan immediately knew something was wrong. There was a watchtower in clear view from the front entrance. Not only had the sentry failed to leave his station as ordered, but he'd also been joined by another two snipers. All three men had their rifles aimed toward the entryway. If Bolan and Grimaldi had taken two more steps out into daylight, the snipers might well have had a crack at them.

And the snipers weren't alone in having ignored Mishu's command. Bolan and Grimaldi saw more than two dozen soldiers positioned in the hills around the cell block, all of them ready to open fire. For the coup de grâce, an aerial droning soon announced the arrival of a Black Dragon HD-11A gunship, the Chinese answer to the PaveHawk. The war chopper rose into view from beyond the acacias and hovered over the proceedings, its armor-plated skin as black as the grim reaper's cowl.

"I thought we were doing without the send-off party," Grimaldi said.

Jerking Mishu by the collar, Bolan yanked him back into the shadows and threw him against the wall.

"You tossed out some code word while you were on the PA," he accused. "Something that countermanded the orders."

Mishu rubbed blood from his nose with the back of his hand, then smiled at Bolan. "Do you think you are the only man here who is not afraid to die?"

Before Bolan could respond, Mishu shouted out to his men, giving the order to fire.

CHAPTER TWENTY-EIGHT

The Black Dragon fired first, even before colonel had a chance to finish shouting for his men to open fire.

Instead of the cell-block entryway where Bolan and Grimaldi were holding the colonel hostage, however, the war chopper turned its pod-mounted cannons on the nearest watchtower. A chatter of 30 mm high-artillery rounds splintered through the wood shell, killing the snipers. Then with deadly ease, the Dragon began to circle the perimeter of the compound, wreaking the same destruction on other towers.

The soldiers on the ground were dumbfounded. Most of them held their fire, glancing up with disbelief, wondering why one of their choppers had turned on them. Their hesitation gave Bolan and Grimaldi the break they needed. Mishu had already earned his martyrdom, dying in the first volley of gunfire intended for the Americans. Shoving the officer's corpse out of their way, Bolan and Grimaldi quickly bolted from the entryway.

The Stony Man pilot dodged right and rolled to cover behind a brick well ten yards from the cell block, Bolan went the other way, finding protection between two old mining carts that had long been taken off the rails and converted to water basins. This, no doubt, was what the prisoners were offered by way of bathing accommodations. Rounds skimmed through the water and clanged off the thick wrought iron. It was only once he'd reached the carts that Bolan saw one of the watchtowers being turned into kindling and realized he and Grimaldi weren't being targeted by the Black Dragon gunship. If anything, the copter was drawing fire away from the Americans. Like the enemy forces around him, Bolan found himself wondering just what the hell was going on.

The answer came soon enough, as the Chinese ground forces found themselves not only having to worry about the renegade chopper, but also increased gunfire from within the compound. The three prisoners who'd been given AK-47s back in the cell block had forsaken any attempt at escape, at least for the moment, and joined in the fray. And they weren't the only ones gunning for the Chinese. At various strategic points throughout the camp and the commons linking it with the mines, Gurkhas appeared, almost magically, like so many heavily armed jack-in-the-boxes.

Once he spotted the Nepalese warriors, Bolan paused between blasts of his assault rifle and glanced skyward at the Black Dragon. The gunship, its thick armored plating deflecting the shots being fired its way, continued to fire on other watchtowers, to the point where sentries began to flee their posts. Besides the 30 mm cannons, the Dragon had a smaller pair of 7.62 mm guns that raised dust in dotted patterns across the terrain below, more frequently than not turning the ground red with the blood of slain camp guards.

"Cowboy," Bolan muttered aloud.

He wasn't sure how Kissinger had pulled it off, but given the presence of the Gurkhas, the only possible explanation for the Dragon's tactics was that the Stony Man weaponsmith not only had discovered Bolan and Grimaldi's whereabouts, but had also somehow gotten his hands on one of the enemy's prized gunships.

Once it became clear that their longtime oppressors were being crushed, laborers and prisoners alike saw an opportunity for escape and made the best of it. Some slipped up through the slit in the fence that the teenager managed to make after helping fend off the enemy during the first stages of the assault. Others, more brazen, went the other way and charged through the main gates, which the Black Dragon had blasted open between one of its forays against the sentries in the watchtowers. Unlike the older prisoner who'd expressed concerns about retribution by the military, most of those fleeing the camp had only one thought on their mind—to be rid of this living hell once and for all.

The battle, such as it was, ended quickly. As with the two guards Bolan and Grimaldi had slain while taking Colonel Mishu hostage, an initial mismatch favoring the Chinese had turned quickly into a rout. More than half of the security detail had gone down before the remainder surrendered, throwing down their weapons and putting their hands in the air. Bolan, who'd seen enough bloodshed the past few days, quickly shouted out for the Gurkhas to hold their fire.

Giving up the offensive, the Nepalese mercenaries began to round up the soldiers with help from the older prisoner and a few others who'd elected to remain behind—if only temporarily. Meanwhile Grimaldi, who'd advanced halfway up the hill chasing down enemy shooters, returned with two he'd taken alive.

"I say we lock 'em in the cells and throw away the keys," Grimaldi said. "Give the bastards a taste of their own medicine."

"Not a bad idea," Bolan agreed. He passed along

the suggestion to the Gurkhas, and soon a column of downcast soldiers was filing past the body of their fallen leader, Colonel Mishu, into the cell block.

Once it had finished decimating the last of the watchtowers, the Black Dragon made a quick pass over the entire compound, then drifted down out the dull gray sky, landing outside the compound in a field of fang thistle.

"I guess they didn't want to risk stirring up any uranium dust," Grimaldi said as he and Bolan broke into a slow jog, taking the road through the main entrance to where the chopper had landed. On the way, both men made a point to offer the Gurkhas a nod of appreciation for their timely arrival.

"Who the hell needs a cavalry when you've got Gurkhas," Grimaldi wisecracked.

Not to mention Cowboy, Bolan added. "I'm sure he had a hand in this."

Sure enough, the first man out of the Black Dragon was John Kissinger. He beamed at the sight of his two comrades. "Hot damn!" he cried out. "I knew we went to all the trouble of hijacking this whirlybird for a reason."

BOLAN HAD BEEN RIGHT about Kissinger being misled at first into thinking he'd perished in the landslide back near the border.

"Longest damn two hours of my life," Kissinger

said, explaining how he and the Gurkhas had clawed through the rubble of the avalanche after the Farm has passed along a GPS reading on Bolan's cell phone. "But once we found that sucker by its lonesome with you nowhere in sight, I figured there was still hope."

Kissinger, Bolan and Grimaldi were inside the Black Dragon gunship, sharing the rear compartment with the Gurkhas. The Nepalese soldiers were subdued; they'd lost two men during the siege of the labor camp.

Stacked beside the Gurkhas along one wall was a small cache of armament: two HN-5 surface-to-air missile launchers, a half-dozen AK-47s and a five-pound packet of C-5 plastique.

Flying full throttle back toward the Himalayas, the hijacked chopper was expected to reach the Indian border in less than twenty minutes. Like the others, Bolan was understandably anxious to get back as quickly as possible. Their brief stay in China, after all, had to have raised the hackles of the Chinese military, as well as the government politicos back in Beijing. It wasn't just the matter of the killings at the sentry outpost or the liberation of the labor camp, either. After a quick raid on the uranium mine's refining operations had confirmed Bolan's suspicions that the facility was a supply source for China's nuclear arms program, the commandeered Black Dragon had emptied its missile load into the plant, leveling it along its concealed centrifuge plant, as well as the missing ES-1 spy plane. Airlifting the plane back to India hadn't been an option, and it had been decided that destroying the aircraft would be preferable to leaving it in the hands of the Beijing's retroengineers.

Kissinger had yet to explain how he'd wound up riding shotgun in the helicopter during the assault on the labor camp. As they continued their flight across the barren, rain-soaked desert, he continued to lay things out chronologically, picking up from the point where he and the Gurkhas determined that Bolan hadn't been claimed by the avalanche.

"We kept following the river hoping to find you," Kissinger explained. "We were on foot, though, remember, and we'd just spent a couple hours combing the rubble, so you were way ahead of us. And every time we came on a snag in the water, we'd have to send some guys down to sift through things."

"In case I'd been pulled under," Bolan said.

Kissinger nodded. "Needless to say, we were glad to come up empty-handed on that front."

As Kissinger went on to explain, it was past dawn by the time they'd reached the lake at the northernmost edge of the canyon. There, they'd discovered the site where the Rangers had been ambushed.

"And when we saw the burial mound, I figured it had to be your doing," Kissinger told Bolan. "Of course, we had your boot prints to go by, too. We started following them up the trail. That's when we first heard the chopper."

As it turned out, the Black Dragon's crew had apparently just finished searching the desert plain in connection with the killings at the sentry outpost.

"By the time we reached the canyon's rim," Kissinger said, "they were already on their way to Manakan.

"Once we got a look at that charred hill, we thought maybe they'd caught you and taken you to some base in town. We decided to sneak in and check things out."

On the way, Kissinger explained, they'd encountered none other than Avil, who'd brought his yaks back to his family's farm, located just on the outskirts of the remote village.

"He saw that I was American and started babbling about some strange encounter with Rambo," Kissinger told Bolan with a smirk.

"I *knew* he wouldn't be able to keep quiet," Bolan said.

"Well, you can count your lucky stars he didn't," Kissinger went on. "Once he tells us what happened and where you were headed, we figured we better haul ass to the labor camp, but quick. I was thinking maybe we could score a truck or something when one of the Gurkhas says we should take a stab at the chopper instead. Turns out one of them—Dan Savan up there in the cockpit—has pilot's training and figured he could fly the bird if we could just get our hands on it.

"So we slipped into Manakan. The kid'd already told us there was no base there, so we figured the chopper crew'd come looking for witnesses or at least somebody they can pin the sentry massacre on.

"We were right. They had troops going door-to-door, which worked in our favor, because that left only a couple guys watching the bird. Took us all of two minutes to grab it out from under them. Some of the soldiers doubled back when they heard the ruckus, but by then we were airborne. I got a quick read on the gun controls and covered our getaway."

"And at some point you dropped the Gurkhas off near the camp," Bolan guessed.

Kissinger nodded. "The kid had already told us about the rendezvous point near the barracks, so we stayed low and took a roundabout way so nobody'd spot us from the watchtowers. We got as close as we could, then dropped off the Gurkhas and let them foot it the rest of the way. We looped back around, then came in straight so it'd look like we were the legit crew, just on our way back from Manakan. Worked like a charm."

"Sure did," Grimaldi interjected. "Trojan horse all over again."

Bolan started to tell Kissinger his side of the story. Grimaldi, who'd already heard it, excused himself and went up front to check on the situation in the cockpit. Less than two minutes later, he poked his head out of the cockpit and stared back at Bolan.

"Remember those two MiGs that were on my tail when the ES-1 conked out on me?"

Bolan nodded.

"Well, they're back for an encore," Grimaldi said. "I've got them fixed on radar and there's no way we can outrace them to the border."

"Damn," Kissinger muttered. "We've about shot our wad ordnance-wise, too."

"We still have more rounds in the cannons, though, right?" Bolan said.

Grimaldi nodded. "Yeah, but cannons won't do us much good if they hang back and use their air-to-airs."

"What do you suggest, then?" Bolan asked.

Grimaldi had a quick answer. "I suggest you talk the Gurkhas into letting me take the cockpit. I think I can wrangle us out of this mess."

CHAPTER TWENTY-NINE

Less than a minute later, Grimaldi set the Black Dragon near the edge of the slot canyons that flanked the Xiangshu River. Kissinger was the first one out, followed closely by Bolan. Each man carried one of the HN-5 shoulder launchers. The moment both men were on the ground, the chopper lifted back up and drifted out over the narrow fifty-yard gap leading straight down to the still churning current of the river.

"Clock's ticking," Kissinger told Bolan as he dropped to a crouch and propped the HN-5 against his shoulder. "Follow my lead."

Bolan readied his launcher and put one eye to the scope. Kissinger had already briefed him on how to acquisition a target. He raked the skyline until he had a bead on the approaching MiGs, then told Kissinger, "I'll take the one on the right."

"Fair enough." The armorer barked a few last-second instructions, then told Bolan, "Let 'er rip, then hit the deck!"

The HN-5 bucked against Bolan's shoulder as he fired. He lowered the weapon and watched his missile's fly through the air on a course parallel to Kissinger's. The MiGs, meanwhile, had fired their warheads, as well. Two surface-to-surface missiles streaked toward the two men, their heat-seeking guidance systems no doubt locked on the Black Dragon chopper directly behind them.

"Down!" Kissinger repeated, diving to the ground.

Bolan turned his back to the MiGs and lunged earthward, his eyes on the Black Dragon. The gunship tilted slightly, then began to drop from view into the canyon. An ominous whoosh drowned out the sound of the Dragon's rotors, then gave way to a deafening series of back-to-back explosions. The ground beneath Bolan quaked, and he buried his face in his arms as a hail of flying rock rained on him and Kissinger. Most of the rocks were small, stinging him much as the flying cinders had back in California when he'd hopped the PACRIM train to Collier Springs. A couple larger stones packed a harsher punch, bounding off his thigh and shoulder more like blows from a cudgel.

Bolan stayed put, waiting out the rain of shrapnel. Behind him in the distance, he heard yet another explosion. Glancing back over his shoulder, he saw a black cloud where one of the HN-5 warheads had connected with one of the MiGs. The second missile missed its mark but achieved its objective when the other fighter jet spun out of control trying to get out of its way. Before the pilot could right his course, the MiG slammed into the ground and disintegrated into a fireball. Once again, the earth beneath Bolan trembled.

Struggling to their feet, the two men made their way toward the canyon's rim. There was still thundering in the gap, and a billowing cloud of dust made it impossible to see into the gorge. Grimaldi's plan had been to drop into a narrow crevasse once it had drawn fire from the MiGs, figuring the warhead's guidance systems wouldn't be able to compensate for the tight downward turn. From the sounds of it, Bolan guessed the ploy had worked.

"I think both air-to-airs hit the canyon," he told Kissinger, staring across the abyss.

"Yeah," Kissinger said, "but unless Jack pulled away before all that debris starting raining down..." He didn't bother spelling out the likely consequences of the chopper having its rotors fouled by a downpour of flying rocks.

Both men stared into the chasm. As the dust cloud began to settle, they saw huge scallops where the missiles had collided with the far canyon wall. A shower of loose stone continued to tumble downhill from the gouges, and as Bolan followed their course, soon he could see that all the fallen rocks had begun to choke off the river, creating yet another seething rapids as the water struggled to funnel past the obstruction. There was no sign of the Black Dragon, however.

Then, through the fading din of the landslide, Bolan and Kissinger heard the gunship's engines. They shifted their gaze to their right. Eighty yards away, the Black Dragon soon rose up through the thinning cloud of dust, intact and flying steady.

"He pulled it off," Bolan murmured.

"He sure did," Kissinger replied. A grin spread across his face as he waved to get the chopper's attention. "He sure as hell did."

The Black Dragon rose out of the canyon and set down once again, only a few yards from where it had dropped off Bolan and Kissinger. The two men quickly clambered on board. The Gurkha who'd relinquished the pilot controls to Grimaldi shook his head with disbelief as he helped the Americans board.

"Your friend," he said, "he flies like a madman."

"Sometimes that's what it takes," Bolan replied.

Kissinger eased his way past the other commandos and poked his head in the cockpit, telling Grimaldi, "If you're through showing off in there, hotshot, how about getting us back to Marjeelam."

EPILOGUE

Marjeelam, India

The debriefing back in Marjeelam was relatively quick and painless. During separate interviews, Bolan, Kissinger and Grimaldi offered straightforward accounts of their various intrigues across the border, leaving little out and prompting only a handful of questions, most of them dealing with the layout of the uranium mine facilities and the location of the temporary grave where Bolan had laid the slain Rangers to rest. Bolan, the last to be questioned, was assured that diplomatic pressure would be brought to bear on the Chinese to insure their return to the states for proper burial.

Unfortunately the relocation of the bodies was—and would likely remain for some time—but one small bone of contention between Washington and Beijing governments. Both the U.S. and China had cranked up the rhetoric as they haggled over everything from the spy plane incident to the rumored military takeover of Tibet. For once, however, there was a sense that, rather than escalating the possibility of armed conflict, all the bluster was actually reducing tensions between the rival powers.

"Yes, we're both looking for leverage," CIA agent Chengzhu told Bolan as he walked the Stony Man commando out to the airfield's runway, "but at the same time I think we're both looking for a way to bow out of a confrontation gracefully."

"I guess that happens when both sides get caught with their fingers in the cookie jar," Bolan ventured.

"You may be right," Chengzhu said. "In any event, the Chinese are already pulling troops back from Tibet in exchange for our promise to admit the ES-1 had strayed into Chinese airspace before it went down."

"I'll take that tradeoff any day," Bolan said.

Grimaldi and Kissinger were already out on the airstrip, standing alongside the Starlifter transport that would be taking them back to the States. A dust-covered Hummer had just pulled up next to the men, and as Bolan drew closer, he saw Jen Li and Nhajsib Wal step out of the vehicle. Both seemed weak but in good spirits. The woman was on crutches, her wounded foot covered with a plaster cast.

"We just wanted to see you off," Nhajsib Wal

told Bolan when he joined them. "I'm catching a later flight back to New Delhi."

"He's taking me with him," Li gestured at her foot. "Apparently there are some specialists there who can see to it I get out of this without a limp."

"You look like you could use another couple days off, anyway," Bolan told her.

"Look who's talking," Li said. "You look like you just went ten rounds with a blender."

Bolan grinned. "Close to it," he said. "At least we're flying something slower than a B-1 back to the States, so I'm guaranteed at least a good twenty hours of downtime."

Li looked intently into Bolan's eyes. He returned the gaze.

"I enjoyed working alongside you," she told him.

"Same here. The Bureau's lucky to have you."

"And that lady friend of yours is lucky to have you," Li countered. "Send her my regards, would you?"

"I think I can manage that."

She turned to Wal. "Well, I suppose we'd best let these gentlemen be on their way." With a nod toward Chengzhu, she added, "The intelligentsia awaits."

"Yes, of course," Wal said. He finished shaking hands with Kissinger and Grimaldi, then stepped back, letting the Americans board the cargo plane.

Grimaldi had wanted to fly the plane back to the States but had been overruled. He joined Bolan and Kissinger in a crude passenger compartment fashioned out of the cargo bay. The seats were hand-me-downs from an old 747. The upholstery was worn and so was the padding, but they tilted nearly all the way back.

"Sandman, here I come," Kissinger said, putting his feet up and kicking off his shoes.

"I'll race you to dreamland." Grimaldi yawned.

"No deal." Kissinger yawned back. "I've done my share of racing for the time being."

As the transport aircraft began to roll toward the nearest runway, Bolan peered out the window. The late-morning sun had just pried its way through the cloud cover, igniting a rainbow that slowly stretched across the horizon. He traced the rainbow and found it settling on a row of prayer flags snapping in the mountain breeze. A procession of monks was threading its way up the nearby mountainside, returning from their trip to Marjeelam. Bolan hoped their prayers were closer now to being answered.

DEATH LANDS®

Damnation Road Show

*Available in June 2003
at your favorite retail outlet.*

Eerie remnants of preDark times linger a century after the nuclear blowout. But a traveling road show gives new meaning to the word *chilling*. Ryan and his warrior group have witnessed this carny's handiwork in the ruins and victims of unsuspecting villes. Even facing tremendous odds does nothing to deter the companions from challenging this wandering death merchant and an army of circus freaks. And no one is aware that a steel-eyed monster from the past is preparing a private act that would give Ryan star billing....

James Axler
Outlanders®

TALON AND FANG

Kane finds himself thrown twenty-five years into a parallel future, a world where the mysterious Imperator has seemingly restored civilization to America. In this alternate reality, only Kane and Grant have survived, and the spilled blood has left them estranged. Yet Kane is certain that somewhere in time lies a different path to tomorrow's reality—and his obsession may give humanity their last chance to battle past and future as a sinister madman controls the secret heart of the world.

In the Outlands, the shocking truth is humanity's last hope.

GOUT25

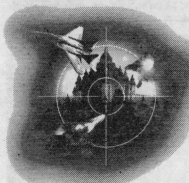